Squeezed

By the same author

Love Byte

Squeezed

David Atkinson

buried
river
press

ISBN 978-1-910208-38-0

Buried River Press
Clerkenwell House
Clerkenwell Green
London EC1R 0HT

www.halebooks.com

Buried River Press is an imprint of Robert Hale Ltd

2 4 6 8 10 9 7 5 3 1

Printed and bound in Great Britain by
CPI Antony Rowe, Chippenham and Eastbourne

Chapter One

HANNAH WAS ACTING strange. This was our first day of total freedom from our two gorgeous children, Tessa and Lois, in almost three years, and she'd gone all weird on me. Maybe having some proper 'alone time' on our honeymoon was freaking her out. I hoped it was as simple as that.

I stood alone on our hotel balcony, sipping champagne. The view over Cape Panwa was breathtaking. The sun had started to dip its toes into the ocean, bathing the water with a wonderful rich crimson light. The last few rays from the sinking sun projected long shadows, silhouetting the palm trees along the beach. As this was our honeymoon, it would have been even nicer had my wife been standing beside me enjoying the view, but I suppose you can't have everything.

Then suddenly she *was* there, leaning on my shoulder, peering over the balcony at the sandy beach three storeys below. 'What are you looking at?'

'The sunset.'

'Oh, yeah, pretty.' She was distracted and distant.

'Hannah, what's wrong?'

'Nothing.'

'You're acting weird.'

'Am I?'

'Uh-huh.'

Her phone started ringing; well, that was probably the old-fashioned word for it, it began to blast out a Rihanna song and she hurried inside to answer it.

The sun was almost gone now and Hannah had missed it, but there would be another one along tomorrow – that was the good thing about sunsets.

I went back inside our room and closed the balcony door, which kick-started the air conditioning. Hannah hung up as soon as she saw me, and smiled nervously.

'What's going on, Hannah? If we weren't in Thailand a million miles from home, I'd almost accuse you of having an affair.'

'An affair? When would I have time for that?' she said, a half-smile softening her voice. She patted the bed and I sat beside her. She kissed me quickly, and said, 'I've got a wee surprise for you.'

'A surprise? I like surprises.' I was intrigued and quickly flicked my eyes around the room. I didn't notice anything new or different. My gaze lingered on the flat-screen TV. 'Did you order up the Man U game?'

'That wouldn't be very romantic, would it?'

'Ahh ... so it's a romantic surprise? Is it red roses? Chocolates? Or maybe you're dressed in some new red underwear?'

She shook her head. 'Nope, no flowers or chocolates, but the underwear isn't a million miles away.'

I was flummoxed. 'Err, me in red underwear?'

I could tell she was about to make some sarcastic comment when her phone beeped, signifying a text. She read it quickly and said, 'That's your surprise on its way; well, our surprise really.' She paused and stared at me intently for a moment, then revealed, 'I've ordered us a Thai hooker called Marilyn.'

I was shocked, in fact I was beyond shocked. I didn't know how to respond so I just sat there staring at my wife. My thoughts were scrambled. 'Ordered us a Thai hooker', just like that, as if she was some kind of takeaway meal.

'How did you do that?'

'I found her on the Internet.'

'What, on eBay?'

Hannah shrugged. 'Something like that.'

'I don't believe this.'

'You're very ungrateful. I was trying to do something nice.'

'What are we going to do with her?'

'I thought you had more imagination than that.'

'Hannah, this is the first time in five years we've had some adult time together and on the first night you invite a stranger into our bed.'

'Don't you want to even see what she looks like?'

I sighed. 'Why, Hannah? Why have you done this?'

'I thought you'd be pleased, we sometimes fantasize about it when we make love ...'

'Yeah, the operative word being fantasy ... and only occasionally when you're not really up for it and it helps to get ...'

'Yeah, OK, Scott, I'm getting the message – loud and clear – BAD IDEA – but it's too late now, she's on her way and we have to pay her, even if she just sits and watches us argue for an hour or two.'

'How much is she costing?'

'About three thousand bahts.'

'That sounds a lot.'

'It's about sixty quid.'

'Oh, that's not a lot really, is it? She must be ugly.'

I perched on the edge of the bed and tried to organize my thoughts. Bizarrely, the first thing that I considered was the cost. We'd used every penny we'd had, and many more pennies that we didn't, to pay for the wedding and get out here. Still, sixty quid sounded really cheap; then again, nearly everything here was cheap compared to back home, and then it struck me that Marilyn was a weird name for a Thai girl.

Hannah was sitting on the other side of the bed with her head in her hands. I moved over to her and pulled her close. She had tears running down her face, and when I touched her she started to sob. I held her close, and felt guilty.

We'd been married all of five days, seven hours and twenty or so minutes but my wife had been my lover, confidante and best friend for over seven years, so she really should know me better by now. She had genuinely thought this was something I would like, when all I really wanted was a few days alone with the woman I'd fallen in love with all those years ago. Hannah had been a wonderful lover and friend. When we first met we spent most waking and (sleeping) minutes together. Weekends would see us out in Edinburgh's bars and clubs, or if we were feeling more adventurous we'd take an occasional city break to Amsterdam, Paris or Prague.

Once the children came along our focus changed, like most couples, I suppose, and Hannah became a natural mother. I can't put my finger on the exact moment our relationship shifted from close couple to 'old married parents' – as I tended to think of us now. Maybe it was a gradual shift or maybe a gradual 'grind' would be a better description.

I was mature enough to understand that this was mainly down to the fact that looking after two young girls, working part-time, and running a household on a very tight budget was tough. Despite the long hours I put in, it still felt like we never had enough money to enjoy the kind of life our efforts deserved. I remember having a conversation about this the year after Tessa was born.

'Hannah, we never get out any more. I'm not saying I want to spend every weekend in a nightclub until four in the morning these days, but we need to get some alone time, even if it's just like a "date night" once or twice a month where we go for dinner or something.'

'Date night?' she queried, raising an eyebrow. 'You've been on Facebook again.'

'How'd you work that out?'

'They talk about "date nights" all the time on Facebook; you shouldn't go on there, it's just full of people bull-shitting about how great their lives are. Most of it's made up.'

I nodded. 'I realize that, Hannah, but we *should* go out so we can have time to talk.'

'We're talking now.'

I laughed. 'Yeah, I know, but it would be nice to spend some time with you without worrying about what Tessa is doing, or even just to feel like a couple again and not just parents.'

'Tessa's only a year old and you're fed up of being a parent already?'

'That wasn't what I meant and you know it.'

Hannah sighed and smiled weakly at me. 'I'm sorry, Scott. I didn't mean to snap. I'm tired. Being back at work and juggling the new mother thing takes a bit of getting used to. You're probably right, going out as a couple would be a good thing. We should save a little money every week so we can go somewhere nice. But on one condition.'

'Yeah, what?'

'You never refer to it as a "date night".'

'Deal.'

*

For a little while we'd managed to do it. We'd get Hannah's mum to babysit when we went out for a meal or sometimes we'd just head to a bar and share a bottle of wine, and talk. Then we started to miss a month and gradually our 'date nights', though I never called them that, drifted and then stopped altogether when Hannah became pregnant with Lois. Money was too tight then. One thing I was sure of, though – we definitely didn't talk enough these days.

Maybe that was why she had thought a threesome was a good idea, but in reality all it did was compound my insecurities. It filled my head with all sorts of bad thoughts. 'Didn't she want to make love with me any more? Was this her very weird way of telling me that? Did she want to have a lesbian experience?' If so, she'd kept those thoughts well hidden.

Instead of vocalizing my concerns, I remembered this was our honeymoon and tried to push all the negatives away and changed the subject; well, almost.

'Why does she call herself Marilyn?'

Hannah dried her eyes. 'It's probably not her real name – it'll be a stage name.'

'Is she an actress as well?'

'How would I know? Look, if you screwed people for a living, would you want them to know your real name?'

'Probably not,' I admitted.

Hannah was angry, but she sighed and I could tell she didn't want to fight on our honeymoon, either.

She took a deep breath and when she spoke, she was much calmer. 'Maybe she's just a big movie fan.' Encouraged by my questions she opened up Marilyn's webpage (proof that you can get just about anything on the Internet). 'It says she calls herself Marilyn because she has a beauty spot on her cheek in the same place that Marilyn Monroe had one.'

Sensing we were back on more of an even keel I leaned over and kissed her.

'I'm sorry, babe, I was just surprised, that's all. We never talked about this and I was just looking forward to some alone time with you.'

'Yeah, I'm sorry, too. We should have discussed it, but I wanted to surprise you.'

'You did that, all right.' I leaned over and stared at the attractive young girl staring out from the webpage. 'Yeah, she's definitely got a beauty spot. Weird that, isn't it? If you've got a mark on your face, you call it a beauty spot; if it's on your arse, you'd just say it's a mole.'

Hannah laughed. 'How would you know if you had a mole on it or not? You can't see your own arse.'

I tried to put on my serious thinking face but failed miserably. 'Well, I think mine is OK, I've seen it in the mirror in the bathroom.'

Hannah punched me on the arm. 'Yours is all right, Scott, but it's not like Mel Gibson's or anything.'

'Mel Gibson's an old man now,' I said indignantly. 'You can't compare my arse to his, he must be what, pushing sixty now? Mine *has* to be in better shape than his.'

Hannah pushed me onto my front, lifted up my bathrobe and examined my bum closely.

'Well?' I asked.

'Mmm, I don't know, it's a bit scrawny. I think I'd still rather have Mel Gibson's.'

I laughed. 'So what you are saying is that if I have a mark on my arse, it's a mole and if Mel Gibson has one, it's a beauty spot?'

Hannah giggled again. 'I don't know, I'll think about it and let you know.'

Before I had a chance to respond there was a gentle knock on our door. Hannah smiled nervously at me and announced, 'Show time.'

She got up from the bed, pulled her bathrobe tightly around her waist, and opened the door. Standing there, wearing a vivid red dress and short black heels, was Marilyn. Her web pictures didn't do her justice. She was exquisitely beautiful and reminded me of a delicate china doll. She stepped into the room and smiled, but I couldn't help noticing it didn't reach her eyes. Over her shoulder she had a large canvas bag, which she removed and dropped onto the bed.

She introduced herself and accepted the glass of champagne that Hannah offered. She sipped it demurely and gazed up at us from under her long false eyelashes.

It was obvious she was sizing us up. I glanced over at Hannah and couldn't help comparing her with this little doll. Hannah was slightly taller than Marilyn, her blonde hair a complete contrast to the jet-black curls that danced along Marilyn's shoulders, especially when she moved. Hannah's eyes were cornflower blue, her nose slightly turned up and her lips full and sensuous. Marilyn's eyes were so dark they appeared black, her nose was like a tiny button and her mouth was shaped like a little cherry.

Hannah was not fat but she definitely carried a few more pounds these days, a result of spitting out two kids, too many sweets and the lack of exercise time available.

Marilyn was dainty, her tight little body undulated under her dress and I realized that Marilyn was much younger than Hannah. We were both over thirty now – Marilyn was maybe twenty-two or twenty-three. At that point I stopped comparing – it wasn't fair.

I noticed the Thai woman doing the same thing, and she casually checked out the apartment, noting all the exits. I suspected she did this with all her 'jobs' and it was simply a survival instinct. I was sure many of her clients were not as benign as we were. I couldn't comprehend anyone who endured such an existence.

Marilyn smiled at Hannah, and appeared to relax as she probably realized we were relatively harmless. Then she spoke, her voice low and smooth as she got into her role. 'You like Thailand?'

Hannah nodded. 'Yes, it's very beautiful, and so much warmer than back home.'

'You from England, yes?'

I decided to break my silence. 'No, Scotland, very much like England – but colder.'

Marilyn smiled at me and held my gaze until I had to look away.

Hannah decided a compliment might be a useful way of breaking the ice with this apparently shy Thai call girl. 'Your English is very good.'

'I attend class for the English. One day I be actress and my teacher say I want to say English good.'

She sat down on the chair near to the bed and removed her shoes. She let her eyes wander around the room again before fixing her gaze back on Hannah. 'You find Marilyn on web, yes?'

Hannah nodded. 'Yes, it seemed easier and less—'

Marilyn interrupted. 'Is OK. It good – Marilyn get money, no matter …' She paused, nodded and smiled at both of us again before continuing. 'You pay Marilyn tip if you like what she does, yes?'

It was a little weird listening to someone talk in the third person about themselves, but I smiled and waited for Hannah to speak.

'Yes, Marilyn, I understand how it works, but we've … well, we've never done anything like this before.'

Marilyn put her champagne flute down on the little bamboo table beside the bed, opened her canvas bag and removed a few small bottles. I couldn't read the labels as they were in Thai. Well, I think it was Thai, it could have been anything really; Egyptian hieroglyphics would have made more sense to me. She twisted open the lid of one of the bottles and tipped a little of the contents into her hand. She walked over to Hannah and gently rubbed the oil onto the skin on her arm.

'You like, yes?'

Hannah nodded. The oil smelled like orange blossom.

Marilyn then stared at us expectantly. When we didn't move or say anything, she mumbled something we didn't understand, then unhooked her dress. It slipped silently to the ground. Underneath she was completely naked.

Marilyn left with a large tip but it obviously wasn't enough to make up for what had happened. I closed the door and stared at Hannah.

'What?' she asked.

'I can't believe you just did that.'

'Did what?'

'Make love to a woman.'

'You did it too.'

'I do it all the time.'

'What do you want me to say, Scott?'

I laughed. 'I don't know actually, I'm just shocked, I suppose.'

'It wasn't just your fantasy, you know, I've kind of always wondered what it would be like. Anyway, did you think I was just going to sit there and watch you two?'

'Maybe, I'm not sure – I just didn't expect you to be so *into* it.'

Hannah shrugged and laughed. 'If I'm being honest, I wasn't. I just pretended that it was you down there.'

'Well, I *could* have done it and saved us a few quid.'

14

'What about you, when she was on top of you, did you pretend it was me?'

I knew I should probably do the whole white lie thing and say yes. But I didn't. 'Sorry, Hannah, I couldn't because she kept making me look at her face.'

'That's only because you couldn't take your eyes off her tits.'

'They were nice tits.'

'Yeah, OK, but let's see what hers look like after two kids have sucked the life out of them.'

Hannah came over to my chair and sat on my lap. She draped her arm around my neck and nuzzled into my neck. The scent of her arousal and the orange blossom filled my nostrils in a heady mixture.

After enjoying my wife's embrace for a few moments, I asked, 'What do we do about the "problem"?'

When I had climaxed inside Marilyn, she had climbed off me and discovered the condom had ripped. The prostitute had babbled incoherently for about thirty seconds before realizing we hadn't understood a word. We got the gist though, she was deeply unhappy. I wasn't exactly chuffed, either.

I already knew the answer to my question but I wanted to talk about it so it didn't hang over the rest of our honeymoon.

'It's simple,' said my wife pragmatically. 'You get tested when we get home, for the rest of the time we use condoms, starting now.' Hannah pulled me down onto the bed, ground her body hard against me and kissed like she used to seven years ago.

I thought to myself, maybe we should hire a hooker more often.

Chapter Two

WE'D ARRIVED IN Thailand with our two children – Tessa, a smart five-year-old with a determined streak, and Lois, who'd just turned two. We'd also brought along Hannah's mum, Carol, and Jane, who was Hannah's chief bridesmaid and best friend. Part of the reason for them tagging along was so that we could escape for our few days of freedom. We'd travelled south to Phuket for our alone time and the encounter with Marilyn that Hannah had been organizing for weeks before the wedding.

We were definitely getting on better now, but I didn't think it had much to do with Marilyn. The simple fact we were in a beautiful country away from the mundane day-to-day existence we had at home was enough to bring about the change. The few days we'd spent alone being lovers instead of parents had reminded us why we'd got together in the first place.

However, by the end of the week, we were both missing our girls – whom we'd seldom been apart from since their births – and as we headed north by train to Pattaya, where the rest of our party was staying, we felt like we needed to be a family again.

Sitting by the pool the day after our return, we really started to relax. Sipping a cocktail before noon was a first for me on holiday. By mid-afternoon I was starting to feel the effects, as was Carol.

'I'm glad your dad's not here, Hannah, he'd be away googling all those bar girls, and some aren't even girls.'

'Googling?' Hannah asked, slipping further down her sunbed.

'Yeah, staring at them.'

'Oh, you mean ogling?'

'Yeah, same thing.'

'Not exactly, Mum, but I know what you mean. Don't worry about him, he'll be having a great time – two weeks of nag-free footy on the telly.'

'I've left him a list of jobs to do whilst I'm away.'

'Don't get your hopes up.'

Jane was on child-watching duty, which was why we were able to chill out. Normally one, or more than likely, both of us, would be on high alert to make sure our darling daughters weren't doing anything destructive to themselves or each other, like falling or pushing each other into the pool. Tessa was learning to swim and would probably have managed to scramble to the side. Lois, without her armbands on, would sink without a trace. Jane had eliminated that risk by taking them away to the 'kiddies klub'. This was run by the local Thai reps in an air-conditioned block behind the hotel near the kitchens. It was pretty basic by UK standards but the girls seemed to like it. The previous day they had made puppets from faces cut from magazines, sticking them onto sticks. Tessa had spent ages making Rita Ora fight with Hugh Grant and Eddie Izzard. An unlikely, but no doubt fun, threesome should they ever get together in real life. In Tessa's world, Rita won. In the real world I suspected it might have been much the same.

I was due to take over from her around three to allow her and Hannah to go shopping at the local market. I would need to sober up by then, and decided that my next piña colada would be my last.

By 2.30 I had a sore head, probably my earliest hangover ever. My squealing daughters gave me no mercy and I spent the remainder of the day keeping them amused. Later in the evening Carol took over, and Hannah, Jane and I headed out for dinner. This set the tone for the remainder of the holiday, and we spent most of the time playing by the pool and on the beaches with the girls. Twice we visited the nearby water park that Tessa loved, and on our last day we took a boat trip out to some reefs and snorkelled among coloured fish, and ate some freshly grilled snapper, washing it down with ice-cold white wine.

Far too soon it was time to return home and on the 6th June, we boarded our plane and left Thailand with mixed feelings. The country was breathtakingly beautiful, but the obvious poverty and huge disparity between the rich and the poor made us both uncomfortable, especially me. In my more reflective moments, I pondered the wisdom of our decision to indulge in the fantasy with the Thai woman, not so much due to the broken condom, which definitely spoiled the moment, but more because I felt guilty at potentially adding to the exploitative nature of the relationship that existed between the rich and poor countries of the world.

Had Marilyn been born in the UK she could have hoped, or even expected, to go to university, build a meaningful career and meet someone who was captivated by her beauty and would ultimately marry and have children. In Thailand, Marilyn was unlikely to achieve any such lofty ambitions, and even though I was completely ignorant about Thai prostitutes and their life expectations or expectancy, I assumed neither would be very high.

As with many who return from far-flung places however, the minute the plane touched down on the tarmac at Gatwick Airport, my guilt began to fade, and after a few days back in our normal Edinburgh lives, where we spent more on a cup of coffee in Starbucks than many people in the Third World earned in a day, any lingering remorse faded away like the steam from my skinny latte.

Hannah returned to work a few days after we got back and learned that her company was planning a strategic takeover of a rival firm. I didn't really understand what that meant, but Hannah, who worked as an administrator, was happy as it made her job more secure. She was employed within the finance function of Douglas, Roberts & Cusack, which to me always sounded like a bunch of Hollywood actors that had got together to form a company. In fact, DRC, as they were very sensibly abbreviated to, were an Edinburgh property management company that dated back to 1971. Founded by the aforementioned trio, they initially bought a few flats to rent out, then expanded into offering property management and eventually specialized in commercial property – office blocks and the like. Douglas and Roberts had died a few years ago and following the death of his partners, Phil Cusack sold out and at the ripe old age of eighty-nine, moved to New York.

Hannah had told me the history ages ago and for some reason, boring as it was, it had stuck. The firm was now a publically quoted company (I didn't know what that meant) and employed four hundred people in twelve offices across the UK.

To my eternal credit, however, I always tried to be interested.

'So who are you taking over, then?'

19

As usual when I asked questions about her work, Hannah frowned and searched for an explanation that wouldn't over tax my brain. 'It's not a takeover – it's more of a merger.'

'Why'd you call it a "takeover", then?'

'Well … because when it's all finalized we will be the lead firm.'

'What's the other firm called?'

'You wouldn't have heard of them.'

'Try me.'

Hannah sighed. 'They are a young firm, Portman, Michaels and Thomson.'

I hadn't heard of them, but no surprise there. I smiled and asked, 'I take it young means not as old as your company rather than populated by children, and I assume they don't do what you do and abbreviate the names?'

Hannah nodded thoughtfully, and then smiled. 'Yeah, they were formed sometime in the eighties, and you're right, they don't abbreviate – no wonder.'

'So by lead firm, you mean that when all the dust has settled all that will remain is DRC, and PMT will be confined to the great corporate dustbin?'

'Pretty much.'

I laughed. 'And you don't think I understand anything about your high-flying business? That's a takeover – "Greed is good".'

Hannah didn't give me enough credit, I was a little more switched on than she thought – even though my own career had been stop/start for years.

Neither of us had managed to get to university. I was probably too thick, I certainly didn't do well enough at school, which bored me to tears, and Hannah had wanted to get a job and earn some money. We had both listened to Hannah's friend Jane many times when she'd talked about her uni days. She had completed a degree with honours, which sounded to me like four years of drinking and shagging, interrupted by the occasional lecture and the odd pesky exam.

I'd left school at sixteen (on reflection, I might have been asked to leave) and became an apprentice mechanic. Over the years, helped by lots of day release and night school courses, I'd progressed to running the parts and service department of a car dealership on the outskirts of the city. They were called PXW, which as far as I know wasn't short for anything and had only been around for a paltry fifteen years.

Hannah and I met at the day release college. I can remember the day like it was yesterday. She was sitting across the aisle from me in the raised seating of the lecture theatre. I'd noticed her the week before and thought she was the most beautiful thing I'd ever seen.

Some dullard in a cardigan and ripped jeans was standing at a lectern, wading through some of the most tedious slides I'd ever seen about profit and loss accounts. Hannah was scribbling away like crazy, writing down every word he said. I just sat and stared at her, not hearing a word the lecturer was saying.

Eventually she looked up from her notes, noticed me staring, and smiled. That was the only encouragement I needed and once the class eventually ended, I slipped alongside her on the way out. I was much cockier back then; I couldn't imagine doing something like that now.

'That was boring.'

Not the best opening line, especially when she frowned and responded with: 'I thought it was fascinating – how a company like that can go from huge profits to massive losses within two years simply down to one throwaway comment made by the CEO to a newspaper reporter on a night out.'

I blinked. 'I don't remember hearing any of that amongst all the spreadsheet guff he was spouting.'

Hannah stopped and turned to face me. 'That was probably because you spent most of the lecture staring at me.'

'You were much more interesting to look at than slides about spreadsheets.'

'I'm not sure that's much of compliment, to be honest.'

I laughed. 'No, I don't suppose it is. Look, I've got to get back to work now, but would you like to meet up for a drink or something sometime?'

She laughed. 'How do you know I haven't got a boyfriend already?'

'I reckon that if you had you'd have said so by now.'

Hannah nodded. 'Very good, I would have.' She held out her hand. 'Hannah Harris.'

'Great name.' I took her hand and a thrill shot through me as I touched her skin. It was like electricity but I managed to retain my composure. 'Scott McEwan.'

'Pleased to meet you, Scott McEwan.'

That was how the bright and beautiful girl with the cool name ended up with the grease monkey. I reckoned initially there might have been an element of 'beauty and the beast' about our relationship, although I always thought (and still do) that my dark, tousled hair, brown eyes and sharp features were the perfect foil for Hannah's softer, more rounded face. Her slightly upturned pointy nose was the one thing that stopped her being so lovely that she would never have looked twice at me. (She had a thing about her nose and had talked about surgery a few times, which to me was silly but to her had been a real issue.) Thankfully, the birth of our daughters had stopped her obsessing about her nose, at least for the time being.

I ran my hand through my thinning hair, which was not so tousled these days, and I still mourned the loss of my last passport photo, which I'd had to update for our honeymoon.

When Hannah and I first got together, we may have seemed like an unlikely couple to outsiders. Hannah's dad, initially, didn't appear very keen with the arrangement. That changed the day I managed to spot a few issues with his Land Rover Discovery – issues that if left unattended would have cost him upwards of three grand to fix.

After that, I became his technical guru and he'd phone me whenever anything stopped working, even though I only really knew about cars and engines. Over the years he'd expected me to fix three laptops, two washing machines, one tumble dryer, a fifty-two-inch plasma TV, his automatic garage door, a leaking Velux window and his wife's (Hannah's mum) iPad.

From that list I'd only had some success with the garage door, but even that seized up permanently two days after I sprayed all the moving parts with WD40. After that, he stopped phoning me to fix things, which was a relief all round.

A week after we returned from our honeymoon, we needed to deal with the elephant in the room and decided that the issue of whether I was harbouring any venereal disease needed to be sorted.

Hannah's solution was typically pragmatic. 'I've made the appointment for you tomorrow; you can go first thing and that means you will only miss the first hour or so at work.'

'You could have told me you were booking it.'

'Then you would only have found an excuse to put it off for longer.'

'I am a bit scared.'

'Don't be a baby.'

'I'm not being a baby – I don't like having strange people

poke my cock.'

'I poke it.'

'You're not strange, and actually I don't think you've ever poked it; you've done all sorts of things with it and to it, but I don't think you've ever specifically poked it.'

'Don't be pedantic, and anyway ... how do you know they poke it?'

'I've looked it up on their website, they take some blood ...'

'From your cock?'

That got me worried. 'I hope not. From my arm, I think, to test for HIV and syphilis, and I think they take a swab – which is where the poking comes in – for other stuff.'

Hannah nodded. 'OK, do they get you to spunk into a cup or something as well?'

I laughed. 'No, that's for the sperm donor thing – I'm not doing that.'

'Oh, yeah, that's right. I think they do it in the same place, though, and you get paid for it – might make the trip worthwhile,' she said mischievously.

'Now you want me to become a sperm donor?'

'Just a thought,' she said brightly. 'It might give some needy ladies the chance to have some beautiful daughters like ours.'

'I think the fact our girls are so gorgeous might be down to you, sweetie.'

'Thank you for the compliment, my lovely husband, but Tessa's hair is starting to go dark so I think there might be more of your genes in there than you think.'

I shook my head and smiled. 'Hannah, you're not blonde. Well, you are, courtesy of the hairdresser, but your natural hair is almost as dark as mine.'

Hannah giggled. 'Oh yeah, I forgot.'

In the end it only took about twenty minutes and I

passed up the opportunity to father children with numerous unknown women. Later that evening, I handed Hannah the piece of paper the nurse had given me. It confirmed I was negative for gonorrhoea and chlamydia but it would take another week for the results of the blood tests to come back.

Hannah read the results. 'Well, that's a little bit of encouragement at least, but you still might have syphilis or AIDS or something.'

I nodded, then corrected her. 'HIV, not AIDS. AIDS is what HIV turns into.'

Hannah thought for a second. 'Like a caterpillar into a butterfly?'

'More like a maggot into a fly, but the nurse said it was unlikely.'

'What, you mean you told a stranger all about our threesome in Thailand?' Hannah asked, her eyes widening.

I frowned at her. 'Of course not, I just said I'd had an accident with a condom splitting.'

'With a Thai prostitute?'

'Well, no … I left that bit out as well.'

Hannah smiled. 'No wonder she thought there was little risk, then; the good doctor probably thought you were bonking some nice clean Scots girl.'

I agreed with her, then reluctantly revealed, 'She did find something, though – she said I had a low-intensity candidiasis.'

Hannah bit her lip thoughtfully. 'That doesn't sound good, but probably better than a high-intensity candidiasis – what the hell is that?'

'A yeast infection – a bit like athlete's foot …'

'Athlete's foot on your cock?'

'Kind of.'

'How did you get that, have you been shagging old

25

socks or something?'

'The nurse said I'd probably got it from you.'

Hannah's eyes widened in shock. 'From me? I've not had old socks anywhere near me. You must have caught it from Marilyn.'

I hadn't considered that. 'Maybe, but they said that women from this country tend to get it if they've been somewhere really hot.'

'Like Thailand?'

'Like Thailand.'

'I'm starting to hate that place.'

'She gave me some cream for it, and just in case, this is for you.' I handed her the small packet I had been given. Hannah peeled back the packaging and took out the large white pessary tablet.

'I can't swallow this.'

I laughed out loud. 'You don't swallow it, you insert it.'

'Oh.'

Chapter Three

FRIDAY THE SEVENTH of July was an important date. I got the results through from the VD clinic confirming that all was well with my world, and it was the morning that Hannah spent puking her breakfast down the toilet.

She pottered back through to the kitchen and slumped down onto the small couch we kept in the corner. 'How come you've not been sick? You had the same as me for dinner last night.'

I tried to recall what I'd eaten and remembered we'd had a Chinese delivered. 'You had the soup, though, and I only had a wee bit.'

Hannah nodded. 'I'm never eating Chinese again.'

She looked so miserable. I sat beside her and put my arm around her shoulders but the faint smell of vomit wafting over onto me made me hurry up and get ready for work. I needed to be at the dealership before eight, so I was nearly always out of the flat before Hannah if she was working. Sometimes Hannah got to work from home, depending upon what project she was assigned to. I reckoned today would be a 'vomiting-from-home day'.

Lois was still sleeping, but Tessa was up and about. She sat at her pink table near the window, drawing a rainbow on a large piece of paper and eating Rice Krispies.

'Mummy's not well,' she said. I marvelled at her insight.

After I'd showered and pulled on my corporate uniform, which consisted of a blue company sweatshirt and matching trousers, I was nearly knocked over by Hannah running down the hall to the bathroom again. The door slammed shut and the sound of Hannah retching filled the small space.

I waited for her to emerge, pale and shaking, and asked, 'Do you want me to get you anything?'

She smiled weakly at me. 'A new stomach?'

'Can your mum come over early?'

Hannah shook her head. 'I'll be fine until she gets here, but can you wait a bit, though, and drop Tess at school?'

I phoned my department to make sure there was someone to deal with the customers who had booked their cars in early. I then poured myself another coffee and watched *BBC News 24* until our childcare arrived.

Hannah's mum, Carol, came to our cramped flat to look after Lois the two or three days that Hannah worked and to be there in case Tessa came back from school before Hannah made it home. I was rarely home before seven in the evening.

It was soon time to pack Tessa in the car and take her to school. One of the perks I did get from work was taking home the odd car here and there. I currently had a Honda CRV, which was like a big jeep – the visibility was great as you sat above most of the traffic, but it wasn't particularly quick, not that this mattered much on the daily commute into work, which rarely saw me get above twenty miles per hour.

We had our own car, a small ageing Vauxhall Corsa that

we'd managed with for six years. Hannah used it mainly to ferry the girls around to their various activities. It was a rust-bucket, but mechanically sound. Being in charge of a servicing department helped keep the thing roadworthy, and if I didn't do that for a living it would be unlikely that we could have afforded to run a car at all. I was aware that we would probably need to change it as soon as something broke or dropped off that I couldn't get repaired for nothing.

After I'd taken Tessa to school, I used the hands-free connection to phone Hannah.

'What's up?' she asked, sounding tired.

'I've dropped Tess off; are you feeling any better?'

'Scott, you've only been gone ten minutes, why would I be feeling any better in that time?'

Good point, I really only wanted to use my hands-free kit and didn't have a good answer ready.

'Oh OK, sorry, is Lois up?'

'Yeah, just this second, she's in a moany mood. I hope she's not feeling sick, too.'

I thought for a moment. 'Do you want me to take a day off and come home?'

'No, don't be silly, Scott, you don't get paid if you're off and anyway, I'd prefer to be alone – I'm not good company when I'm sick…. Maybe I'll phone Jane and get her over to help, I think she's off this week.'

I wasn't sure how preferring to be alone fitted in with having her mother about and getting Jane over, but I let it pass; I really didn't want to take the day off and spend it listening to Hannah vomiting. I hung up and concentrated on driving.

My day passed relatively quickly. I'd tried a few times throughout the day to phone Hannah, but it had just gone to voicemail so I assumed she'd gone back to bed and was sleeping.

When I pulled up to our designated parking space after work, I discovered that Jane's Audi A3 was in it. (Hannah always parked our Corsa in the next street, unless it was raining, as she was ashamed of it.) I sighed and parked across the road in an empty space. It belonged to Mr Spencer two doors down, who didn't need it any more as he was dead – having passed away just after Easter. His flat was still up for sale. I scanned along the road and noticed the large number of sale boards. The property market was supposed to be picking up, but obviously it hadn't reached our street yet. Our small, red, sandstone apartment block was over a hundred years old now. The roof, which had been replaced in the eighties, was starting to show signs of wear and tear, unsurprising for something exposed to the wind and rain that battered it on a regular basis. Being so close to the sea had its disadvantages.

We knew any necessary repairs would be shared between the tenants but it was likely to be a bill too far for us when it eventually happened.

When I opened my front door and walked in, I heard some excited voices coming from the living room. It sounded like some kind of party was going on. This really didn't fit with the vision I had in my mind of the queasy Hannah I'd left hanging over the toilet bowl.

I flipped off my shoes, walked into the living room, and was greeted with the shiny-eyed, grinning face of Jane Sweeney, my wife's best friend. Her luxurious red hair was tied back in a loose ponytail and she was nursing a glass of something bubbly.

Behind her were my parents, Jean and Paul, Hannah's parents, Carol and John, and lingering near the window, Jane's mother, Paula, and stepfather Graham. Also, there was my best mate Dave Hughes, who came in behind me from the kitchen. Everybody had champagne in their hands.

I was staggered; I could count on the fingers of one hand the number of times all our respective parents had been together in one room. I couldn't imagine what had happened to get them all together. Only Dave had a habit of turning up unannounced but I suspected even he had been invited on this occasion.

I turned to Hannah. 'What's going on? When I left this morning you were puking for Scotland.'

Hannah handed me a glass of bubbly. 'I feel much better now.' She moved and sat down on the couch.

'Is that what we're all celebrating?'

Hannah giggled. 'In a way.'

Jane laughed. 'Hannah's got some news for you.'

I walked over and sat on the floor at Hannah's feet. I noted she was the only one not drinking champagne, which didn't surprise me that much given her state this morning.

Lois bounded over and bounced onto my knee. Tessa approached more slowly, and looked at me strangely.

I glanced at Hannah, then back to Tessa. 'What's going on?'

'Tell Daddy,' instructed Hannah to our elder daughter.

'Well?' I asked expectantly.

Tessa opened her hand, and held out a small white stick.

I didn't understand. 'What?'

Tessa sighed. 'Mummy's got a baby in her tummy and she says it's your fault.'

The whole room erupted into laughter, including Lois, who just giggled because everybody else was laughing.

I looked more closely at the stick and noticed the little screen on the other side which read: *Pregnant 7 weeks*. I was stunned. I drained my glass in one go, laughed and gave Hannah an enormous hug. Seven weeks ago: that must have been on or around our wedding night. I was sure Hannah had told me she was due her period and shouldn't have been fertile; so much for that idea. We probably wouldn't get to restart our date nights any time soon, but that didn't matter now given this great news.

Jane laughed at my happy face and topped up my glass, and her own. She won't be driving home tonight, that's for sure, I thought.

'Did you buy the champagne?' I asked Jane.

She nodded her head. 'Yep, special offer in Morrisons.'

After we'd calmed down, Hannah had explained what happened.

'I phoned Jane and told her I had a vomiting bug, and that if she wasn't busy, I wouldn't mind some company.'

Jane picked up the story. 'As soon as she said that, I thought, I bet she's pregnant again. So I picked up a testing kit and headed over. It took some persuading to get her to use it but when she did – BINGO! Then I got on the phone and rounded everyone up for a wee party.'

I smiled at everyone in the room. I wasn't sure what Jane's parents had to do with anything, but I was glad to see them here anyway.

I realized that I needed to pee and was glad to escape to the bathroom for a few minutes. When I came out, Dave was waiting to go in.

'Busy place,' he commented.

'Yeah, it usually is anyway, but it's bursting at the seams tonight. Did Jane phone you too?'

Dave nodded. 'About three, I think. Good news for you, eh, another mouth to feed.'

'Hopefully, one day, yeah. Listen, don't say anything to Hannah for God's sake, but all this celebrating, it feels … well … a little premature. I mean, the baby's only been in there a few weeks and anything could happen, you know? I know Hannah's first two pregnancies went like clockwork so I'm probably worrying about nothing….'

'You *do* worry too much. Have a few drinks and chill out.'

Dave knew little about pregnancies, despite having been married twice and engaged three times. He'd even managed to be engaged to two of the girls at the same time until they found out about each other. One dumped him, the other married him. Now recently divorced for the second time, he was enjoying his freedom. Sometimes I envied his easy life.

I left Dave to pee and returned to the noisy living room to discover Jane taking orders for pizza.

I perched on the chair arm beside Hannah. 'What are you having?'

'Nothing, even the thought of pizza makes my stomach churn. I'll maybe just have a few breadsticks or something.'

After the pizzas had been devoured, everyone started to drift home. I saw mine and Hannah's parents out, and as I turned back into the hall, I encountered Jane again.

She blocked my path as I tried to squeeze past and handed me another glass of champagne. I took it, though I was starting to feel like I'd had enough.

'It's nice to have something to celebrate for once.'

Jane shrugged and fixed me with her big green eyes. 'Well, I suppose *you* can celebrate, that's Hannah's career put on hold for another five years of domestic drudgery.'

I laughed. 'Hannah seems very happy with the news to me. I don't think she sees it that way, Jane, and neither do I. Children are wonderfully rewarding and—'

'Bollocks,' Jane spat. 'I like Tessa, she's now at the stage where you can have a sensible conversation with her. Until then, kids are just little poop machines, sucking the life out of you and then pumping it out the other end. It's a pity you can't shove them into a cupboard for five years and then bring them out.'

I laughed. 'Feeling broody are you, Jane?'

To her credit, she laughed. 'Not particularly, no. Maybe one day I'll get with the programme, but hopefully by then I'll have enough money to pay someone to do the dirty stuff and I'll just dress them up and take them out.'

'Nice idea, Jane, sometimes I wish I could do that.'

She smiled cynically then turned away, saying over her shoulder, 'Not on your salary, Scott, not on your salary.'

Jane's initial assessment of me seven years ago had been that I wasn't good enough for her friend. She'd mellowed over the years and we now had a decent relationship, though occasionally, like now, after a few drinks she would revert back to type. There was, I'm sure, an element of jealousy in there, especially as Jane couldn't seem to keep a boyfriend for more than six months.

Later, when we were snuggled up in bed, Hannah said, 'Thanks, Scott.'

'What for?'

'For giving me another baby.'

'That was the easy bit, you've got to do all the hard work.'

'I know. You looked worried tonight, is it the money?'

I smiled, though in the darkness Hannah couldn't see me. 'No, I've not even started to worry about that yet.' I paused, reluctant to worry Hannah. 'I think it was just because everybody was celebrating and it just ... well, felt a little premature.'

'I did think that as well but you know what Jane's like when she gets a bee in her bonnet. She just kind of took over and I was in no state to object.'

'Jane's funny. One minute she's all happiness and light with me, the next she's all resentful, saying that your career's on hold again because you're pregnant and it's all my fault.'

Hannah laughed. 'Yeah, she gets like that when she's drunk. She loves kids really. One day she might have some and she'll realize what life's all about.'

I was quiet for a moment before saying, 'Dave said I worry too much and I should just chill out; he's probably right. Your last two pregnancies went off like clockwork, so I'm sure everything will be fine.'

Hannah leaned over and kissed me on the mouth. 'As long as you're with me, it will be. Night, Scott, I love you.'

'Night, Hannah, I love you, too.'

As usual, within minutes, my wife's breathing deepened as she drifted into sleep. It took me a little longer as some niggling doubt was hanging around the back of my mind, keeping me awake, but when it didn't reveal itself, I soon slipped away, too.

Chapter Four

OVER THE NEXT few weeks, Hannah's nausea started to reduce and vomiting was only triggered by certain smells, the most troublesome of which was my aftershave, which got binned, and the curry shop across the road from our flat, which was harder to resolve.

One issue Hannah complained about more than the vomiting (eventually) was her baby-brain. I'd been reading up again (it's amazing how quickly you forget – well, as a bloke, anyway) on what to expect as her pregnancy progressed. I hadn't found much on the phenomenon of baby-brain so I wondered if Hannah had made it up but her explanations of what had happened always made me laugh.

'Scott, it's like my whole brain chemistry is out of kilter; there I was today in the middle of a presentation to the board of directors and suddenly instead of concentrating on the graph and figures on the screen, I'm thinking about whether we would be better with a Bugaboo Chameleon or a MacLaren All-Terrain.'

Now, despite sounding like some kind of military transporter, I'd read enough to know that it was actually a pram or buggy. I also knew they cost more than what we'd paid for our last car, which meant Hannah had better be searching on Gumtree if she wanted one. I didn't want to spoil her story, though, so I nodded sagely as if I knew exactly what she was on about. My wife, however, knew I was bluffing so after a withering glance at my nodding head she said, 'I'll show you them both later. Anyway, there I am on my fifty-third slide and my mind, after conjuring up images of buggies and car seats, goes completely blank.'

I wasn't surprised if most of the directors probably had blank minds by then. Fifty-three slides about office reorganization was way over the top. In my mind office reorganization meant moving a few desks and the water cooler. The death by PowerPoint reminded me of the day I met Hannah at college and made me smile.

My wife was still speaking. '... then an hour later Mr Trenchard invites me into his office ... you remember I've told you about him before, the sleazy old executive director who hardly ever comes in but has a huge office on the top floor...?'

I nodded, trying to confirm that I did in fact remember the sleazy Mr Trenchard but I had no recall at all about said gentleman. It might have been that Hannah had told me once and I simply did not remember, but it was more than likely she had told Jane rather than me – this happened a lot. Jane and I had compared notes once, and the same happened to her. In Hannah's brain, Jane and I were interchangeable and she expected us to be connected like some kind of Apple device, whereby if you load something onto one device, it is duplicated across all the other ones you own. Maybe that would be possible one day via some chip you can get implanted into your head, and for me (and probably Jane) the sooner the better.

Hannah went on talking. 'Anyway, he asked me in,

closed the door behind me, and then he brushed himself against me, if you know what I mean?'

I didn't really, I wasn't sure how you brush up against people; given my work was populated mainly by smelly oily men, I went out of my way to avoid brushing up against anything.

I nodded again and Hannah shuddered. 'Yeah, he pushed his hips at me when I walked past. Then he got me to sit beside him on his sordid little couch.' She shuddered again. 'God knows what he's been up to on that thing over the years. Yeah, so he's got me sitting there and he starts to tell me how much he enjoyed my presentation, but all the time he doesn't take his eyes off my tummy; what do you think of that?'

I didn't know what to think; my wife was sitting beside me on the couch in her work clothes, and to be honest, given the relatively low-cut nature of her blouse, I would have been staring at her tits, not her tummy. I said as much.

Hannah sighed with exasperation. 'He's got maiesio-philia.'

I gave her a blank look. 'Poor chap, is it terminal?'

Hannah cracked a smile. 'That's the name for people who find pregnant women sexy. He's thinking about me being pregnant, which means I've had sex, and that turns him on.'

'Now, I'm not the most worldly-wise man ever, but surely most people by the time they get to our age have had sex, usually more than once, so how does that work?'

'I read up on it today, do you want me to show you?'

I didn't think I would be able to handle a fifty-three-slide presentation so instead I said, 'Maybe he just fancies you.'

Hannah shook her head vigorously. 'No way, he had Gillian and Elaine in earlier this year when they were pregnant too – he's just an old perv....'

'So what happens now? It doesn't sound like he's really done anything you can complain about … yet?'

My wife sighed, and held her tummy in that unconscious way that pregnant women seem to do, even though she was hardly showing yet.

'I don't know, he wants me to meet with him every second Friday for a progress report where I'll talk and he'll stare at my bump.'

I was pretty sure the business arena was full of characters like Trenchard, who trod a very fine line. I didn't inhabit Hannah's world; I'd never had to, so I didn't quite know how to advise her. 'Isn't there anyone you can talk to?'

'I'm talking to you.'

'Yeah, I know, but to be honest I'm not much help. I meant somebody at work.'

Hannah sighed in exasperation, probably at me, but more than likely at the world in general. 'I can't be seen to cause trouble, it was hard enough to go back part-time after Lois was born. They don't really want part-timers, which means the glass ceiling for me is even thicker, so I guess I'll just have to avoid him or become a hard-assed bitch.'

She said the last three words in an American accent, which brought a smile to both our faces. She knew that I knew she wasn't 'hard-assed' in any way, and to break through a glass ceiling she'd be better off having a hard head.

I smiled. 'You need bigger balls than the men?'

Hannah laughed, then she leaned into me and sighed. 'I'm glad you don't work in an office, Scott, our life would be so boring.'

I smiled; my work had its moments, and they were usually centred around Sandra.

Sandra was technically my boss, though she normally

left me to get on with running the service department with little interference. She was more interested in the sales operation. It was much more profitable.

I've always thought it was unusual to have a female boss in the car sales world. Sandra was one of a rare species. She'd come to the franchise as a naïve petrol-head who'd done a bit of amateur motor racing. Initially she worked in the back office, but proved to be a quick learner. Blessed with good looks, guile and a posh-sounding English accent, she soon became the most successful salesperson in the network and progressed to become sales manager. I reckoned she would soon move on and take up a higher-profile role in the group. My initial thoughts of her were that she was completely ruthless and ran her team with a rod of iron.

Last week I had to reassess that appraisal after I spoke to her about a problem. I'd knocked on the door of the glass cube at the back of the forecourt that passed for her office.

'Sandra, have you got a minute?'

She glanced up from a spreadsheet and smiled, revealing her even white teeth. Sandra always looked fabulous. She usually wore dark skirts and tailored jackets during the winter and lighter clothes in the summer. I preferred the summer outfits as they tended to reveal more of her legs. With short-cropped dark hair, sultry eyes and pouty lips, she was the perfect salesperson. Women instinctively trusted her because she shared the same sex organs and men subconsciously thought they might get a piece of her if they bought a car. The combined effects of those two aspects made her the perfect choice for couples thinking of buying a car too.

'Hi, Scott. Yeah, sure, what's wrong?'

'Does there have to be something wrong for me to come over and say hi?'

She smiled. 'We've worked together for what, five years now, and I don't think you've ever come over here to just say hi once.'

'Maybe today's the day I start.'

'OK, hi, then.'

I laughed. 'No, OK, you're right. I've got a problem.'

'Stevie?'

'How'd you guess?'

Sandra shook her head. 'I don't have to guess he's struggling just now. What's he done?'

'He's given an F trade-in for an old Fiesta that, frankly, we'd be lucky to get scrap money for.'

When negotiating deals with customers, the sales team had two trade prices. An F trade was where we thought we could sell on the forecourt as a used car and an A trade was where we would have to send it to auction. The F trade-in was better for the salesman as it allowed him to quote a better trade price with the customer.

'How bad is it really?'

'Even I wouldn't take it home.' Sandra laughed. She knew about our old Corsa.

'OK, leave it with me, I'll sort him out.'

I nodded, feeling a little guilty for landing him in it, but the alternative was that Sandra would chew my balls off if she found out later. I was about to leave when she said, 'I've got a customer appointment if you want to hang around for a bit. I might be able to undo a bit of the damage.'

'Yeah, OK, I get to see the master in action.'

'Mistress, you mean?'

'Do I?'

She smiled. 'Oh yes.'

A few minutes later, a young couple – Chloe and Darren – were seated in her little cube. I was introduced as the Head of Servicing which was a grand new title for me, but I just nodded and didn't argue.

Eventually, it all came down to how much Sandra was going to offer them as a trade-in on their old Saab.

'Now the list price on the new Corsa is £7,695, with electric everything and three years' free servicing. Looking at the state of your old Saab, the best we can do is ...' Sandra paused and calculated a long series of numbers onto a bit of scrap paper. '... £1,200.'

The couple looked disappointed. 'That's not as much as we were hoping for ...'

Sandra nodded sympathetically. 'I know, but the thing is they've gone bust and used prices have tanked. There are no Saab dealerships any more, so nowhere to take them when something goes catastrophically wrong.'

Sandra chewed her thumbnail thoughtfully and said, 'I'll tell you what, can you step out of the office for a minute while I phone my boss and see what I can do? I don't want you to hear him swearing at me.'

Chloe looked alarmed. 'Why would he swear at you?'

'Because I'm going to get you a better deal and that's what he'll do.'

'Do you do that often?'

'Hardly ever.'

'Why do it for us, then?'

Sandra shrugged. 'Because you're a nice couple who deserve a new car.' She smiled and looked to me. 'Scott, can you take Chloe and Darren, and get them something to drink?'

'Of course.'

Twenty minutes later, we were back in the cube and Sandra was beaming. 'I've managed to get the trade-in up to £1,600 but that's the best I can do.'

Chloe was beaming. 'Thank you, hope your boss didn't swear too much.'

'He had a good rant but then he does that a lot. If we can get the paperwork sorted, you should be able to pick the car up tomorrow if that suits you?'

The couple were more than happy.

Later, after they'd gone, I asked, 'Given that you're the boss, Sandra, who the hell did you spend twenty minutes on the phone to?'

'Sam, of course.'

Sam Dawson, her boyfriend, was a professional footballer, a goalkeeper to be specific, with Partick Thistle, the 'third' Glasgow club, which lived in the proverbial shadow of Rangers and Celtic. They were once mentioned by Billy Connolly in one of his live shows that I went to see, and he said when he was growing up he thought they were called 'Partick Thistle Nil'.

'Did he approve the extra four hundred quid?'

Sandra laughed. 'He knows nothing about cars, but the Saab is in good nick, isn't it?'

I nodded. 'Yeah, it's been well looked after, full service history as well.'

'Can you get it tidied up and out for sale by the weekend?'

'Yeah, should manage that. How much do you want to advertise it for?'

'Stick a screen price on it of £2,995. If we get anything over £2,500, we'll be more than covering our costs and it'll help wipe out Stevie's cock-up.'

'So you've covered for him?'

She shrugged. 'He's a good bloke and a good salesman. He's got a few issues at the moment; his mum's ill in hospital so I'm making some allowances for him.'

'That's a nice thing to do, Sandra.'

She laughed. 'He'll still get a good bollocking.'

'Glad I'm not Stevie.'

'No chance of that, Scott.'

'Why?'

'You'd never make a salesman, Scott, you don't have the stomach for it.'

I pretended to be hurt. 'That's not very nice.'

Sandra laughed at my pouty face. 'It's not an insult, Scott, you're just too nice, that's your problem. You care about people.'

'You looked like you were very caring with that couple: what was your line, something like "because you're a nice couple who deserve a new car"?'

Sandra's smile vanished. 'Chloe was nice, too nice for him. They won't last.'

'How'd you work that out?'

'He kept staring at my tits. When you're in love with someone, you don't stare at another woman's tits all the time.'

'I didn't notice.'

Sandra laughed. 'No, you wouldn't. One, you don't have tits. And two, you can't read people like me. That's why I'm so good, I'm a great people person.'

'Can I ask you a question, a personal question?'

Sandra smiled. 'About my tits?'

I laughed. 'Err, no, I don't think so. Why are you with a footballer? You don't come over like … well, like … the type.'

Sandra laughed. 'Good question, Scott. How long have you been thinking about that?'

I was taken aback. 'Well, probably since you started going out with him, I suppose.'

'Two years, Scott, I've been going out with him for two years, and it's taken you this long to ask?'

'Well, it's really none of my business.'

'That's why you'd never make a salesman, Scott. All my

team knew about Sam within a month of me meeting him.' Sandra shook her head. 'Anyway, to answer your question, he's a little different from your average footballer: he started out studying law at Glasgow Uni but then his football career took off and he had to choose between the sport he loved and the law, so he dropped out after the second year.'

That was impressive, as the closest most Scottish footballers ever got to Glasgow Uni was driving past it on the way to the pubs in Glasgow's trendy West End.

Sandra's display of sympathy for her salesman surprised me. I'd always considered her to be hard and ambitious and I was slightly in awe of her ability to thrive in such a hostile environment. I also knew her pretty well by now because we were often the only two people left at night as we shuttered up and set the alarms on our own respective little empires. Occasionally we would linger a little longer than necessary and talk.

Sandra's work world was undoubtedly harsh and stressful, which probably made it hard for her to talk about with anyone who didn't understand the motor trade. I think it served as an outlet and a safety valve for both of us. Hannah had about as much interest in cars as I had in spreadsheets.

There was a time when I used to talk about Sandra a lot but Hannah understandably got fed up with it and suggested that if Sandra was 'so bloody great, maybe you should go and live with her instead'.

I learned a valuable lesson that day – at least I think I did. Women like you to talk about people, your work and what makes you happy and what worries you. But they don't want to hear about women who are doing better than they are.

Between us, Hannah and I barely made enough to cover

our bills. Christmas was always a struggle and inevitably we could never buy all the things we would have liked for our daughters. Both of us were overdrawn at the bank and our joint budget account that we paid all the bills from never had much left at the end of the month.

As well as being good-looking, Sandra had earned nearly £95,000 last year, which wouldn't help Hannah like her.

Chapter Five

ONE NIGHT IN mid-September, after a few days of freakily warm weather, described as an Indian summer by weather experts and newspaper headlines alike, we were so hot and sticky we found it impossible to sleep, and tossed and turned in bed.

Eventually Hannah said, 'It's no use, Scott, I can't sleep in this room, I'm roasting. It's a shame we can't turn on the air con like we did on honeymoon.'

I sat up and pushed the sweat-soaked sheet off me. 'I wonder how Marilyn's getting along.'

Hannah frowned. 'Where did that come from?'

I wiped the sweat from my forehead with the back of my hand. 'I don't know, she just popped into my head when you mentioned the honeymoon. I still feel guilty about that night.'

Hannah put her hand on my arm. 'I know, I do as well, but there's not much we can do about it without changing the world's economic system.'

'I wonder if she'll ever get married and have kids?'

Hannah plumped up her pillow. 'I'm not sure. It must

be really difficult to meet any normal people when you do what she does for a living.' Hannah paused and peered at me before smiling slyly. 'It was very erotic though, wasn't it?'

I smiled. 'Yeah, it was, especially when she was between your legs.'

'That was your favourite bit? Not when she was on top of you?'

I had to think about that for a minute. 'No. I definitely think watching my prudish wife with another woman was the highlight.'

'I'm not prudish.'

'You are a little, especially now that you're a MILF.'

'I'm a MILF, now, am I? Have I got that old?'

I screwed up my eyes and smiled at Hannah. 'You're no spring chicken any more, but then neither am I.' I was silent for a minute, thinking about Marilyn and Thailand, then I added, 'On the subject of eating Thai, do you remember our first date?'

'Yeah, the Thai restaurant in York Place when you ordered that really hot red curry. I think you were trying to impress me.'

'I wasn't actually, that was the first time I'd ever had Thai food.'

'Really? You've never told me that before.'

'I know. I'm not sure why, but I hadn't a clue what I was ordering and it was so bloody hot. I mean, I'd had Indian food before then, even a few vindaloos, but nothing came close to that red curry.'

'It made you almost as sweaty as you are tonight, I think it was coming out of your pores the rest of the evening, even later on in the pub next door.'

'I'm surprised you agreed to another date after that.'

'I probably wouldn't have if you hadn't kissed me

goodnight.'

'Why's that?'

'Well, to be honest, I don't think I really fancied you all that much. I mean, I thought you were a nice guy and all that, but there wasn't that … I don't know what'd you call it … the oomph factor?'

'Oomph?'

'I can't think of a better description.'

'But that changed when you kissed me?'

'Uh-huh, it was amazing, like being shot through with electricity.'

'You've never told me that before, and you know the weird thing? That was exactly what happened to me when you touched my hand in the lecture theatre.'

'You've never told me that either.'

'It must be confession night.'

We were both silent for a few moments. It was amazing that even after seven years together, we still didn't know everything.

Hannah stared at me for a moment, then said, 'The combination of thinking about our honeymoon, our first date, and especially the heat, has made me horny. Will you do what Marilyn did, please?'

I leaned over and kissed my wife hard on the lips, she responded by slipping her tongue gently between my teeth. After a moment or two, she pulled her head away and gripped my face in her hands and started to pull my head down towards her thighs.

'I love kissing you, Scott, but right now I need you down there where it's warm, wet and welcoming.'

'Yes, miss.'

'Don't you mean "Yes, MILF"?'

The mini heatwave fizzled out over the next few days

and as summer gradually faded into autumn, it was soon time to put hats on Tessa and Lois every time we left the flat. In mid-October we had our first real argument since our honeymoon, and typically it was started by something trivial.

Hannah wanted the box room cleaned out and decorated. One of the problems we had with our impending new arrival was space. Our two-bedroomed Leith flat was barely adequate for the four of us, let alone with a new baby on the way. In my opinion, this tiny windowless space was little more than a glorified cupboard. My fears were that our new sprog would grow up thinking it was in a prison cell.

'Why can't the new baby sleep in with Tessa and Lois?' I suggested.

'Its crying will wake them up and Tessa needs her sleep now that she's at school.'

'We could keep her in our room until she's bigger.'

'Then we would both be awake all night – then you'd be knackered for work and I'll be knackered all day trying to look after a new baby and Lois.'

'Your mum will be here most of the time.'

'My mum's sixty-three and not a bloody slave, we'd be royally buggered if she wasn't here....'

'My mum can help more....'

'Your mum's hopeless with kids....'

'She brought me up all right.'

Hannah did that annoying eyebrow-raising thing that she utilized when she knew she could make her point by saying nothing.

I reacted as I always did to the silent treatment by shouting. 'What's wrong with me? You bloody married me and had kids with me, so I can't be that bad.'

In reality, I knew that the main problem was that my mum and Hannah's mum couldn't occupy the same space for more than an hour at a time or it drove Hannah bonkers. I also hated how she managed to manipulate things to subtly switch an attack on my mother to an implied one on me. I couldn't do that kind of thing, I wasn't clever enough and I guess I wasn't female enough.

Another issue I had with the box room was that it was still full of boxes from when we'd moved from my even smaller flat in Meadowbank.

Most of them had never been opened since that day. As we'd now been living in our new space for nearly five years and I hadn't missed anything, there was probably a good argument for binning it or sending it all to a charity shop unopened.

However, I knew that if I suggested that, Hannah would start rooting through all the boxes and suddenly discover her life would be impossible without electric nail clippers – more likely to clip off the tips of your fingers than anything else – a face steamer (whatever that was) or the electric fluff remover. What it actually removed fluff from remained a mystery, even after reading the box.

I usually broke the silence that settled onto us like a cloud after a fight, but this time Tessa intervened. She'd obviously been listening and encouraged by the quiet that now occupied the little box room, she stuck her head in the door and shouted, 'Stop arguing.' She then pulled her head back out and we heard her walking down the hall, muttering.

I looked at Hannah and we both burst out laughing, then rolled among the boxes, kissing like teenagers.

Eventually we lay still, Hannah's head lying on my chest with my hand on her small bump. I started to slide my hand lower. Hannah grabbed it and put it firmly back on her tummy.

'Oh no, you're not getting me all hot and bothered just now.'

I pouted, then had an idea. 'You know what?'

'What?'

'We've never made love in this room.'

'No wonder, there's no space with all this stuff in here.'

'I'll make a deal with you, then.'

'What do you have in mind?'

'I'll help turn this into a nursery if we have a shag in here once it's all cleared out and before it's all baby-fied.'

'Sounds like an interesting proposal.'

'More like an indecent proposal.'

'Mmm, the best kind. OK, I'll go with that. I'll get my mum to stay later on Friday and help clean it out if you can take the girls out for the afternoon.'

'I'm at work.'

'No, you're not, you've taken a day off.'

'Have I?'

'Yeah, for my scan – the fourteen-week scan that I missed, remember?'

'Oh, yeah.' I'd completely forgotten. 'Maybe I've got baby-brain too.'

'I hope not. If that happens, we'll end up depending on Tessa to remind us about things and that won't end well.'

I was still reluctant to let Hannah get among the boxes and clutter our life up further. 'I could take some of the boxes to charity shops while on my way to work tomorrow.'

Hannah smiled. 'You multi-tasking, Mr McEwan? I think not.'

'I can do multi-tasking,' I protested weakly.

Hannah kissed me and laughed. 'Scott, to you multi-tasking is reading a car magazine while sitting on the toilet.'

I couldn't win that argument, so I let it drop.

On the Friday morning, we came out of the health centre, gripping the little grainy black and white picture of our latest family member. The ultrasound technician wasn't supposed to reveal the sex of the baby, but Hannah pleaded with her until she'd relented and now she was ecstatic.

'I can't believe it's another girl, Scott. Do you know what that means?'

'My world is about to turn even more pink.'

'Yeah, probably, but more than that, we don't have to buy loads and loads of new stuff now. She can wear Lois's baby clothes and use all her old toys.'

I gazed at Hannah. 'You've kept them from when she was a baby?'

'Yep,' Hannah announced triumphantly.

I tried to think where they were. I'd not seen them. 'Where are they all?'

Hannah laughed. 'In a big box in the …'

'… box room,' I finished the sentence for her.

Up until that point I hadn't given much thought to the sex of the baby. I'd taken the view that as long as it was born healthy I'd be delighted, but at least I knew what to expect now. I took Hannah in my arms and said, 'We've got some boxes to unpack so let's go and sort out our new nursery.'

Hannah beamed at me, and leaned up to kiss me. We stood snogging, oblivious to the rain that soaked our hair and ran down our faces.

Chapter Six

HANNAH GREW BIGGER as the days grew shorter, until one Wednesday evening in late November, autumn turned into winter almost overnight – as it is apt to do in Scotland. A sleety rain lashed against the windows of our flat, and the icy wind whistled as it whipped around our solid, old tenement building. When the weather turned really cold, like this, it was the only time having a small home had advantages. It was easy to heat and felt cosy – cluttered and crowded but cosy.

I'd arrived home from work to find Jane sitting at the kitchen table, munching on something. I nodded a hello, and noted that she was being entertained by Tessa, who was churning out some badly drawn trees and cats. Well, for a five-year-old, I suppose her pictures were OK and, if I'm being honest, mine as a 32-year-old man would be no better (and probably worse). I leaned over Tessa's shoulder to have a closer look.

'Daddy, you're annoying me.'

'I haven't done anything.'

'You're looking over my shoulder, I'll make a mistake.'

'Not one of your best, Tessa. I don't think it's worthy of the fridge.' All her best drawings got stuck onto the fridge.

Tessa stopped drawing and put her crayon down. 'Mummy put one of Lois's scribbles on the fridge yesterday and it was rubbish.'

I peered over at the fridge door, and noticed near the bottom a blue and yellow smudge.

I smiled. 'Yeah, I know, sweetie, but we need to encourage her. Otherwise she'll never get better. Anyway, it's near the bottom so it won't last long.'

We had a hierarchical fridge arrangement where the best drawings were stuck near the top and the poorer ones at the bottom. It was a self-limiting arrangement for Tessa, because as she got older, her drawings got better so more went to the top and the older ones dropped down and eventually were taken off. Hannah told me she binned them but I knew she actually kept them in a secret folder under our bed. Well, not so secret now.

Jane sat listening with a straight face. I was pretty sure she knew of the fridge art league from Hannah. Tessa had been excused a bath and had undergone a thorough hand and face wash. Lois was in the tub, having coloured her fingers and toes in with a black 'magic' marker. I think it might be named 'magic' due to the fact it was practically impossible to wash off in one go. As a result, when Lois appeared seconds later, she had slightly grey fingers and toes and appeared to be remarkably pleased with herself, whereas my tired, pregnant wife was red-faced and annoyed.

She noticed me sitting expectantly at the kitchen table beside her friend. She smiled malevolently. 'If you're looking for your dinner it's in Jane.'

I pouted across the table at the red-haired minx who smiled smugly.

'Aren't we supposed to get a dog for that sort of thing?' I asked Hannah, never taking my eyes from Jane's face.

'You calling me a dog, Mr McEwan?' Jane asked, with more than a little bite in her voice.

'If the cap fits,' I replied, smiling.

Jane relaxed in the chair. 'Dogs don't wear caps.'

Hannah intervened before the conversation got even sillier. 'There's some lasagne in the oven and some salad in the fridge.'

I noticed Jane was drinking white wine, virtually an unknown luxury during the week in our flat. Jane followed my eyes to her glass. 'You can have some if you want. The bottle's in the fridge beside the salad.'

'Thanks, babe.'

'Oh, so I'm a babe now, am I? What happened to the dog?'

I smiled. 'The dog didn't have any wine.'

Later, once Tessa and Lois were asleep for the night, the three of us seated ourselves in the living room. Jane and Hannah were sharing the couch and I had the comfy chair, my big, padded, black leather 'monster' that Hannah hated because it didn't match the brown leather couch and reclining chair we'd bought three years ago. Her idea had been to replace my monster with the recliner but it just wasn't comfortable. I'd lost most battles over the years with Hannah. The monster had the dubious honour of being my only visible victory and I was holding onto it for dear life, it being one of the few remaining reminders of my masculinity.

The TV muttered away quietly to itself in the background with nobody paying any attention to it. Jane was on her third glass of wine and would now require a taxi to get home. There was no way we would let her drive.

'What's up, Jane?' I asked. 'Drinking on a school night; don't you have work tomorrow?'

Jane swirled some wine around her mouth like mouthwash and swallowed noisily. 'Yeah, I'm working. It's all I ever seem to do. Work hard, work hard, work hard – no play, no fun.'

She sounded sad, so I asked flippantly, 'You're here with us tonight, doesn't that count as fun?'

Jane frowned at me. 'Scott, I like you, OK, and I LUUUURVE my friend Hannah here, but even then I'm really sitting with … well … with an old married couple. I'm young … well, youngish. I'm free and single, and I've spent the last three Wednesday evenings with you two.'

I wasn't sure how to take that. 'You didn't have to come, nobody forced you.'

She waved her glass at me. 'But then you wouldn't have had any wine to drink.' She made it sound like she was supplying us with some kind of social service. Maybe she was.

In reality though, I'd had one glass with dinner, Hannah wasn't drinking for obvious reasons, and Jane had polished off the rest on her own. I didn't say anything because I knew her well enough by now to know that she was building up to something.

She sighed and noisily plonked her empty glass down onto the wooden coffee table. She picked up the bottle and upended what was left into her tumbler, which filled about a quarter of it. She stared at the amber liquid in disappointment and announced, 'I hate you two, do you know that?'

A moment ago she'd liked me and *luurved* Hannah, so I wondered what had changed.

'I hate you both because you're … well, you're happy. You shouldn't be happy, you should be bloody miserable.'

I let Hannah handle it. 'Why shouldn't we be happy?'

Jane leaned over and gave Hannah a hug. She clung to Hannah and looked up at me.

'Because you never go out as a couple any more, you haven't got money – you practically sold your souls to get married. You live in a tiny flat, never get any real time to yourselves, and … well … that's enough to be going on with....'

Hannah replied, 'There are more important things than money. We get by. Why are you so sad, Jane? You've got a great job.'

'Great job? Yeah, right, I'm an arse-licking PA to an idiot director. You know what? In the last five years, three of the directors I've worked for have lost their jobs; what do you think of that?'

I answered, 'You're either a bad PA or a jinx.'

Jane managed a weak smile. 'Well … yeah, maybe … but they've gone and I've kept my job, which means I'm a world-class arse kisser.'

I wondered if being an arse kisser was worse than being an arse licker. Probably not in my book, but I supposed it depended on the arse and the circumstances.

'Anyway …' Jane sighed heavily and picked up her wine and drained it. 'I've had enough, I want to have a baby.'

The last statement caught us both completely off guard. Jane was a little drunk, but not pissed. I didn't say anything (I was getting good at that), simply played spectator for the next few minutes.

'Jane,' exclaimed my wife. 'Where did that come from?'

'I'm fed up of being alone.'

'Don't you think you should maybe find a boyfriend first and work up from there?'

'Men are all rubbish. Besides, you don't need a man any more. You can go to a clinic and get a designer baby – you know, pick from a catalogue what eye colour, skin tone and intelligence etc, based upon the guy who wanked into a cup.'

'I'm not sure if that's exactly how it works, sweetie,' Hannah advised. 'Scott nearly did that a few months ago.'

'Really? Would I want one of yours? I'm not sure ... maybe ... but it might be a tad weird.'

'Just as well I didn't donate, then.'

'My husband's sperm is fantastic, Jane,' Hannah said, smiling. 'Look at my gorgeous daughters.'

As pleased as I was that Hannah was defending my semen, I wasn't sure it was a conversation I wanted to develop, but I was spared further embarrassment when Jane asked, 'What were you doing down there anyway?'

Hannah jumped in before I could answer, just as well as I would probably have told her the truth. 'Look, Jane, you've had loads of boyfriends, and will no doubt meet someone nice one day.'

'I doubt it. All my men were arses, every last one of them. That's why I dumped them, I can only attract arses. I'm an arse magnet.'

'The last one, Tim – the guy that worked on the ferries; wasn't he about to get made up to ship's captain?'

'Yeah, ship's arse. I dumped him for being an arse.'

I stifled a laugh. Hannah noticed and frowned at me. Jane was oblivious to my sniggering and leaned onto Hannah again who pushed her away,. 'Sorry, Jane, you're leaning on my bump. What happened to the other guy – you know, the one that you thought would always be there for you, no matter what? What was his name? Colin something?'

Jane shook her head. 'Colin Brown, yeah, we were ... well, I don't know exactly what we were. He recently moved to London and shacked up with a transvestite, or at least that's what he says on his Facebook page. So he's an arse as well.'

Having revealed her secret longing, Jane seemed in

a better mood or maybe it was just the last of the wine kicking in.

'Anyway, I only seem to be able to attract arses, including ones who don't know if they like men or women, and in Colin's case he obviously still isn't sure.' She got up, walked over and sat down on the arm of the monster. 'Do you find me attractive, Scott?'

I glanced over at Hannah, who was smiling. I was in a quandary; if I answered in the affirmative to the slim, red-haired honey with the bewitching green eyes and lovely pale skin, I would immediately be classed as an arse. So instead I laughed, pulled her onto my lap, held her face in my hands and said, 'I wouldn't shag you if you were the last woman on earth.'

Jane laughed out loud, and rubbed herself against me like a cat. I enjoyed that; she smelled nice and her slim, lithe body was sexy.

'See, you two, that's why I hate you both. I want someone like your husband, Hannah, but all I attract are fuckwits.'

I wondered what was worse, a fuckwit or an arse. It would probably be a close call.

Chapter Seven

HANNAH HAD MANAGED to get Jane to drink some coffee and nibble on a chocolate digestive, which she kept perched over her mug to catch any crumbs.

'Right, m'dear,' said Hannah, sounding like an elderly aunt. 'If you really want to have a baby, there are a few things you need to know.'

Jane feigned shock. 'Oh no, not the birds and the bees chat. I had that with my mum years ago, and at school when I was about twelve.'

The birds and the bees thing never made any sense to me. As far as I know in the history of nature, no bird and bee had ever got it on, and barring some grotesque muta-tions caused by a nuclear war or by man pouring too much gunk into the environment, they never would. I thought about making some smart comment but Hannah jumped in before me.

'Yeah, right, Jane, you could probably teach me a few things given the way you go through men, and in fact, that's one of your problems – you never give anyone a chance – or at least long enough of a chance.'

'Rubbish, you either know or you don't. It's a chemistry thing, isn't it? You just know when you've found the right person, don't you? Wasn't it like that with you and Scott?'

Hannah paused before answering. 'No, not at first. He was funny and kept staring at my face and hanging on my every word, which was flattering, but until I kissed him I really wasn't sure. After that kiss, well, everything changed. Up until that point I thought he was ... well ... a bit of an arse.'

Hannah and Jane fell about laughing. I didn't find it funny at all, she hadn't said that in bed to me the other night. Hannah noticed my grumpy face and leaned forward, kissing me slowly on the lips. 'Only teasing, Scott.'

'Yuck', said Jane, screwing up her face. 'Get a room already.'

Hannah dug her friend in the ribs. 'You're just jealous.'

'Damn right I am. What about other men, both before and after meeting Scott, have you never met anyone who rocked your boat?'

'Since the night I kissed Scott, that's never happened.'

Jane narrowed her eyes and stared at Hannah. 'I don't believe you, there must've been times you've seen someone or met someone when it's been like fireworks, and you know you're instantly wet.'

Hannah smiled. 'Maybe, but I'm not telling you with Scott sitting here.'

'You didn't do anything, though, did you? So it doesn't matter if he's here or not. Besides, he's probably had those moments too, especially with that Sandra woman.'

'I've never fancied Sandra, she's too ... too ...' I had to think for a moment and while I paused, I was aware of Jane and Hannah watching me closely as I tried to come up with an adequate ending to a sentence I wish I'd never started. '... she's too good.'

Jane cackled. 'Too good? Too good at what? Riding you in the back office with the blinds drawn?'

I was shocked and it must have shown in my face because Hannah laughed at my expression, and I relaxed, realizing Jane was teasing.

'No, she's too good at selling cars. She's much better than the blokes and I find that hard to understand.'

'You think that women can't be better than men at doing stuff?' Hannah asked gently.

'No, no, of course they can, it's just ... well, oh I don't know, it's like cars are one of the things men have always been interested in and good at. Henry Ford wasn't a woman ...'

'If he had been, cars would have got comfier a damn sight sooner and they'd have less knob things in them,' Jane said firmly.

'Knob things?' asked Hannah.

'Yeah, gearsticks, they look like cocks, so do the indicator stalks.'

'I think you've got a bit of knob fixation, sweetie,' Hannah teased.

Jane sighed. 'Yeah, maybe it's been a while since I had a good shag, or even a bad shag. On that subject, Hannah, one thing I meant to ask, did you ever tell Scott about your first time?'

Hannah shrugged. 'Of course I did. We did all that after we first met.' Jane nodded and fixed her green eyes on me and narrowed them; she looked like a cat ready to pounce on a mouse.

'What about you, Scott?'

'I'm not telling you. Hannah knows who it was and that's all that matters.'

'Aww, come on, Scott, it'll be a laugh. I'll give you some wine.'

I pointed at the empty bottle. 'There's none left.'

Jane pouted huffily. 'Right then, you two sit here a minute while I go to my car.'

'You're not fit to drive, sweetie,' Hannah warned.

'I'm not driving anywhere, I just need to get into the boot. I've got six bottles of wine in there.'

'We don't need six bottles of wine,' Hannah observed.

'You're not getting six bottles of wine, I might bring up two. Technically you shouldn't have anything at all in your state.'

Hannah pouted. 'A little drop won't do me any harm.'

A few minutes later, Jane and I had wine glasses filled to the brim; Hannah's was only half full. This was only her second or third drink in five months and the first few sips hit their mark.

'OK then, who's going first? Scott, I think you should kick us off – I know who your first shag was anyway, it was Martin, wasn't it?' Hannah sat back and looked expectantly at me.

'Martin? Your first shag was with a bloke?' asked Jane incredulously.

Hannah looked smug. She knew it wasn't Martin but now I'd have to explain and extricate myself from the hint of homosexuality.

'It wasn't Martin, it was *Martine*, as you well know, Hannah.'

Hannah giggled. I noted she'd drunk half her glass already. 'Yeah, I know, but honestly, Jane, it's not worth hearing – just a quick shag in the back of a car, no big deal.'

'It was quite a big deal to me,' I said huffily.

Hannah smiled slyly at me. 'I think it would be much, much better if you were to tell Jane all about Sabrina.'

I couldn't believe she'd dragged that up out of her memory banks. I'd told her about Sabrina years ago when we'd both been completely pissed at some music festival in London's Hyde Park. I must learn never to underestimate a woman's ability to remember stuff.

'Nah, I don't think so, Hannah, she'll just think it's stupid … it *was* kind of stupid.'

'Aww, c'mon, Scott,' encouraged Jane. 'It honestly can't be any worse than my experience, can it, Hannah?'

'Probably not. On you go, Scott, or no more wine.'

The threat of having my glass taken away made me reluctantly tell Jane my story.

'Well, it was a long time ago. Do you remember how every August the fair came to the Meadows?'

Jane took a slug of wine. 'Yeah, we used to go, usually on the Saturday, we never called it the fair, though, it was always the shows.'

'OK, yeah, we did too. I used to go with my mates from school. For me it kind of epitomized summer. The scent of freshly mown grass mixed with the heady mixture of popcorn and diesel created the smell of summer for me, and still does a little bit.

'We used to go along in a squad; there'd be about ten of us, all hoping to meet girls and stuff – not that it ever happened. It's probably nostalgia, but I love the memories of those lazy, carefree summer days of laughter and joy, especially the particular summer when I was fourteen – it coincided with a really hot spell of weather and we hung around the shows for days. We loved watching the exotic travelling girls who worked the waltzers, dodgems and other rides. The power they had over us teenage boys was immense.'

I stopped my story for a minute whilst I remembered. They seemed impossibly glamorous and unobtainable in their skinny jeans and tight tops that accentuated every curve from every angle. With their dark eyes, dark hair and adult make-up – they were completely different from the girls at school. So much more grown up and worldly wise.

'You'd probably get arrested if you did that now,' Jane interrupted. 'And anyway, I bet their lives were pretty shit really.'

I nodded. I knew now of course that their existence was far from perfect, always moving, always unsettled, but for a few days every summer it seemed like they owned the world. They knew it too, and they would tease and flirt with us, leaving us grasping for more coins for one more ride, one more opportunity to get close enough to smell their perfume and maybe brush their hand or arm when handing over the money. Sometimes you caught their gaze and they smiled at you, revealing perfect white teeth and, occasionally, a sensuous pink tongue before turning away, laughing, to collect another fare from another kid.

I continued. 'Sometimes we got to stay until it got dark and then the place took on a whole new dimension with twinkling fairy lights, flashing strobes on the waltzers and crackling blue sparks as the dodgem cars careened around their track.' I paused and smiled nervously at my audience. 'Then late one evening, just before heading for home, I decided to have one last shot on the dodgems. Somehow, I managed to get my car stuck in a corner between a couple of parked and empty dodgems. I tried but couldn't get the damn thing to move. As a result, one of the girls had to jump onto the back of my car and help me steer it out into the open again.

'As we moved off, this dark-haired vixen leaned over me to grab the steering wheel and slipped. She ended up in the car beside me, her legs caught between the steering wheel and my body.

'I remember she mumbled some kind of apology but I was struck dumb.' I paused and glanced over to see if my wife and Jane were bored or about to take the piss out of me, but they still seemed interested. 'Yeah, well, my lingering memory is of her scent, an intoxicating mix of perfume, sweat and woman. Her hair was draped across my shoulders and softly tickled my face. Then, as she untangled herself, she had to lean into me in order to right herself and her breasts brushed against my chest and arms. They lingered there, soft and warm, for only the briefest of moments, but it was enough and I was smitten.'

I paused and took on some wine.

Then, laughing at my younger self I said, 'I came sneaking back to the Meadows for the next three days and hung around the dodgems like a love-sick puppy, hoping for a glimpse of her, secretly desperate for a sign that she reciprocated my feelings. Unfortunately, apart from an occasional smile as she took my money from the car after I'd climbed in, she remained aloof and unobtainable.

'I remember being overcome with a wonderful agony which, thankfully, faded with the shortening summer days. The Shows soon moved on again, and the girl with it. I never found out her real name, but as Hannah already knows, I christened her Sabrina after watching the old film of the same name with my dad. It just seemed to suit her, well, in my head anyway. In reality she was probably called Mavis or Senga.' I paused and took in the smiling faces of Hannah and Jane. 'In any event, she was my first teenage crush. I was shy and naïve as a kid and as Hannah probably remembers, I made up a whole fantasy future for me and this mystery girl.

'I devised dozens of devious ways to kill off her parents – car accidents, food poisonings, fires, diseases and murders, with their bodies ending up buried in the woods. The very unlikely end result was always the same: following the demise of her mum and dad, she had to come and live with me and my family. In my head we would become great friends, which eventually would turn into love. Then we would get engaged and have a fairy tale wedding in a Welsh castle.'

I had to pause here as Jane had choked with laughter, and wine was running down her nose. Not an attractive sight.

'Yeah, Jane, I know. I also knew even then that there were more than a few obvious flaws with the fantasy, not least that the girl must have been nearly eighteen and was probably more than capable of looking after herself even if the awful fate I'd wished upon her parents had befallen them. Another major flaw in my selfish fantasy was that she would be very unlikely to fall for a skinny, spotty 14-year-old kid, regardless of his devotion and puppy love fixation.'

Jane had recovered. 'Welsh castle? Where the hell did that come from?'

I laughed and shrugged. 'I have absolutely no idea. I've never even been to Wales but I had it all worked out down to the very last detail. I also knew exactly how many guests we'd have: it would be 123. We'd have chicken and chips in a basket and our honeymoon suite would have a huge door that opened onto the battlements of the castle – where we would stand and wave as all our guests departed into the night.'

Jane shook her head. 'You're a bloody headcase.'

I smiled and couldn't disagree, and ended my tale there.

The remaining parts of the fairy tale were just as unlikely, and even back then I knew it was crazy, but fuelled by teenage lust it was unlikely that I would let the facts get in the way of a good fantasy which sustained me for the remainder of that summer and into the winter beyond. Foolish and wonderful dreams of youth, lost in time and space.

Occasionally Sabrina would pop back into my head in a dream where my subconscious mind still harked back to being a teenager, instead of a thirty-something father with responsibilities and worries. When I woke from these dreams, she lingered in my thoughts for a while before evaporating in the steam of my morning shower. She was a long-lost familiar friend who hadn't visited me in a while. I missed her.

'And you never went back the following year to see if she was there?' asked Hannah.

I nodded. 'Of course I did, but she didn't return and I was over it by then anyway. I'd started going out with Martine so that made things easier.'

The second bottle of wine was opened and it was Jane's turn.

'OK, Jane, your turn. I know all about it, of course, but Scott doesn't,' Hannah said expectantly.

The normally confident and outspoken Jane stared at me for a few seconds. 'Nah, I don't think I can, Hannah.'

'Oh, come on, Jane, Scott's just bared his soul to you. Besides, if you don't, I'll tell the story and I'll make it much worse.'

Jane smiled. 'Not possible, sweetie.' She sighed and rolled her eyes. 'Oh, OK then.' She leaned over, topped up her glass and took a large gulp of wine. 'But not one word of this ever, ever leaves this room, OK?'

I nodded, and reckoned we were all probably equally on the hook in that regard anyway.

'Right, then.' Jane frowned and delved back into her memories. 'It was about three weeks after my sixteenth birthday.'

'Sweet sixteen,' I said unnecessarily.

'Yeah, I was very sweet and very naïve, hard for you to believe now, I know, but I was once. So there I am at this

69

party with a bunch of school friends. In those days I hung about with a gang of girls: there were about ten of us that did everything together, including Hannah, though she wasn't my best friend at that point. Do you remember it took ages to organize anything as we were always waiting for someone, or one of us would wander off and we'd need to round everyone up again? It really was like herding cats.'

'Bitchy cats,' added Hannah.

'Yeah, definitely,' agreed Jane. 'Well, on this particular night, we'd all been drinking some cranberry alcopop things at Helen's house beforehand, and passing around a joint. At that point, I think I'd smoked about ten cigarettes in my whole life so this was a bit of an unknown for me. Anyway, we were all very giggly by the time we arrived at this party. I can't even remember the guy's name who was hosting it, he was in the year above us at school and lived in this huge old house in Duddingston. It was pretty run down and smelled a bit but that might have been down to all the hormonal, sweaty teens running around the place. After a few hours there was only Helen and I left. Everyone else, including you, had paired off with boys and were scattered around the house snogging and maybe doing a bit more, I wasn't sure at the time.'

Hannah giggled. 'God, yeah, I remember that. I ended up with Adam from the year above me. He'd always fancied me and I'd never as much as given him the time of day, I don't think I did after that night, either; weird how drugs affect the brain.'

I peered over at Hannah. She'd smoked some weed in Amsterdam when we'd been there but I couldn't imagine her doing that at sixteen, but I suppose it was way before my time. It was weird to think of my wife before I knew her, and how she'd snogged and shagged people. It was never a comfortable thought. Jane was continuing with her story so I stopped worrying about the past.

'The combination of all the alcopop crap and weed had made everything feel lovely and fuzzy and this guy started chatting to me. I vaguely knew him. He was a sixth-year prefect and damn good-looking to boot. I remember thinking, "I wonder why he's talking to me".

'Then Helen started talking to him. Helen was a wee tart, she was the first one of us to lose her virginity the previous year, and had also shagged her brother's best friend the previous weekend – at least so she claimed. All I knew was that she was after my man, so before she could do anything I pulled this guy down and started sucking on his face.'

'Classy,' I said.

Jane shrugged. 'It worked. Helen buggered off and I was left snogging this big, dark-haired honey. After a while we left the busy living room in search of some privacy. This old house was massive, spread over four floors. It's probably worth over a million quid now. Eventually we found a small attic room with nobody in it and although there was no bed in there, we found a cupboard full of blankets and sheets, so we pulled some of those down onto the floor.

'At this stage I wasn't sure what was happening. I was a virgin and although I didn't want to be one forever I wasn't in any hurry to lose it, but I was high on booze and dope, and before I knew what was happening we were naked. It was weird because I'd never been naked with anyone before and it felt really nice, you know, to have your skin next to someone else's, someone that I liked. Anyway, I would have been perfectly happy with that, but obviously this guy …'

'What was his name again?' asked Hannah with a smile.

Jane shook her head at Hannah. 'You know what I nick-named him – the Wizard of Oz – but his real name was Paul, I think.'

'The Wizard of Oz?' I asked.

Jane smiled. 'I'll get to that. So yeah, here we were, naked and horny in some damp, cold attic and he starts touching me, he knew what he was doing and soon I'm crying out – my first proper orgasm that wasn't self-induced. At this point, he's not put his dick or tongue anywhere near me so I'm thinking, this is amazing.

'Then it's his turn. He pushed himself towards me and initially I just held onto his cock, kind of like how the Jamaican team passed the baton in the four times hundred-metre relay.'

Both Hannah and I burst out laughing, sharing the same image of the Jamaican sprinters holding onto each other's cocks at the Olympics instead of the baton.

Jane smiled and took on board some more wine.

'So there I am holding onto this erection. I've never seen a real-life hard cock before, and it's kind of scary and fascinating all at the same time. As I'm holding onto it, he starts to move his hips and I'm wanking him off by default, I suppose. Then he says to me, "You can either suck me or I can put a condom on and make love to you."' Jane rolled her eyes. '"Make love to me", like it's our wedding night or something. Given that I've never touched a cock before, the thought of putting it in my mouth filled me with bloody terror. He must have seen it on my face so he doesn't say another word and fumbles in his jacket pocket and produces this old crinkled packet. It looked like the damn thing had been in there for years, probably had, and was no doubt way past its sell-by date – I was lucky I didn't get pregnant. So he opened it up and rolled the condom down onto his cock and before I know it, he's on top of me, trying to guide his dick into me. Bearing in mind I'm a virgin, it takes him a while to get it in and I'm giggling like an idiot, a drunk, slightly stoned idiot, I suppose.

'Eventually he gets it in there, and although it's a wee bit sore initially, I'm so wet it doesn't last long, then he's thrusting and grunting away like some dog on heat. By this time, I'm actually laughing so much the tears are running down my face. The whole thing just seems so absurd, so funny. He, of course, doesn't care. He's banging away, trying to ignore me, then suddenly he stops moving, pushes himself up on his elbows and stares at me. I immediately stopped laughing as the look he gave me was quite scary.

'After a moment, he smiled and slowly started moving his hips again. He's still inside me at this point. He keeps his eyes locked on mine and says slowly, "You're a witch".

'Remember, I'm a 16-year-old girl …'

'Sweet sixteen,' I reminded her.

'Well, not quite so sweet now, but to be honest – by that point in my life – I'd been called a lot worse so I just go along with it, smile and nervously say, "OK".

'Then he says, "You're my little witch, my little wicked witch of the west, aren't you?"

'I'm thinking that maybe he's having a little joke, teasing me because I didn't suck his dick or something, so I just said, "If you want".

'Then he replies menacingly, "No, *you* must want. You must want to be my witch, you must want to join my coven and become my witchy slave."

'Strangely, my first thought was that I haven't sat my standard grades yet. I'm not joining anyone's coven until I've done that. So I said to him, "Maybe after my exams have finished." That seemed to satisfy him because he does a few more big thrusts, comes, and kisses me hard on the lips. Then he moves over, takes the condom off and holds it up in the air. He stares at it for a minute or two then says to me, "In this little sheath is the potion of life, the answer to all your problems. One day, when the dark forces grip the earth again, you will need this."

'Now even at sixteen … and three weeks … I know that's a pretty big claim for a small, smelly pouch of semen. He obviously notices that I'm looking sceptical, well, grossed out actually, and he says, "Witch, behold, this is the oracle, this is what you need to sustain you in the long, hard weeks and months to come. Whenever you feel stressed or need guidance, take this out of your secret place and touch it, fondle it and keep it close."

'As he's referring to my "secret place" I'm half-expecting him to grab me and try to shove the condom deep up inside me, but thankfully he didn't. Instead, he stood up and started to get dressed. I self-consciously did the same. Neither of us said anything for ages. I was scared, to be honest, as he'd gone all weird on me. I was kind of wondering if all men did this after they'd had sex. Just as I was about to go downstairs with him, he turns to me, holds up his hand and announces, "No, witch, you must stay here until I'm gone. Some at this party may be jealous if they learn that we have lain together and that you have taken my seed. You must always be mindful of your power over me and don't abuse the source."

'Now I'm thinking, this is fucking weird, he's talking like some sixteenth-century fairy tale character or something.'

'*That's* when you think he's weird, not when he was shagging you and calling you a witch?' I asked incredulously.

'Scott, I was sixteen … what did I know? I sat up in that cold, dark room for about ten minutes before I dared leave. When I did get back downstairs, the party had started winding down and most folks had gone home. Thankfully the Wizard of Oz had left too, so I caught up with some of the girls. I tried to put the whole experience out of my mind initially, it felt almost like a bad dream. A few days later, I bumped into him at school and he completely blanked me, which in a strange kind of way was a relief, and probably meant I didn't need to join his coven. Eventually, I plucked up the courage to tell Lynda, my best friend at the time, and she couldn't believe it either.'

'What about the "potion of life"?' I asked, laughing. 'Do you still have it?'

'Yuck. What a thought. No, I just left it lying on the windowsill in that little room. Might still be there for all I know.'

'Casting its magic spell for all eternity,' added Hannah.

Jane nodded and drained her glass. 'Wouldn't surprise me, especially after the postscript I'm about to tell you. The following year, on Halloween, the Wizard of ... Paul ... got arrested for indecent exposure or something similar.'

'What happened?' I asked.

'He'd chained himself naked to the Scott Monument in Princes Street Gardens.'

'Why?'

Jane smiled. 'The report in the paper said he was "waiting for the dark angels to come and take his seed".'

'Who are the dark angels?' I asked.

Jane sniggered. 'How the hell am I supposed to know? Maybe they're related to the dark forces his cum was supposed to guard against. The guy was a fruitcake with a semen fixation. Shame, he was really good-looking as well.'

Hannah and I both laughed until it hurt.

Jane topped my glass up and poured a little into Hannah's, then said, 'OK, sweetie, your turn.'

'My turn for what?' Hannah asked, examining her pitiful volume of wine.

Jane sat back in her chair. 'Your confession time, how your cherry got popped.'

'You both know so I don't need to tell.'

Jane shook her head. 'Rubbish, I bet Scott's only ever had the sanitized version, not the full, uncut blow-by-blow account. So come on, girl – out with it.'

Hannah groaned. 'I'm tired, maybe another time …'

Jane waved her finger at Hannah. 'If you won't tell it, I will.'

Hannah smiled at her friend. 'OK, OK, give me a minute. I need to pee.'

Chapter Eight

HANNAH RETURNED AND sat down on the couch. One look at our expectant faces told her that we hadn't gone off the idea of her confession, so she swallowed her meagre portion of wine, shook her head and tied her hair back into a ponytail.

'Right, well ... you both know that my first time was with Callum Anderson. He was the son of our neighbour and I'd known him for years.'

'Aww, the boy next door,' teased Jane.

Hannah laughed. 'Yeah, he was, I suppose. We were both the same age. Well, I was a few months older, I think, but there wasn't much in it. Being Catholic, he went to a different school, St Paul's, and caught the bus every day. I suppose over the years we saw less and less of each other. When we were young, we played together nearly every day and used to wander about, holding hands. Then his parents got divorced and they moved away. I think that was when we were around twelve and we lost touch altogether, which was a shame, but at that age there's so much going on that you don't really notice. Then on my seventeenth birthday,

I get this card through the post and it's from Callum. In his message, he said was hoping to go to St Andrew's University next year, exam results permitting, and wondered if I wanted to meet up. He'd written his phone number at the bottom of the card.'

Hannah paused and gazed longingly at our nearly full wine glasses.

'Sorry, hun, don't think you should have any more,' Jane advised.

'That's just so you can have more yourself.'

Jane laughed. 'You've seen straight through me, but no, you've had enough. Don't want the baby waking up with a hangover. Come on, quit stalling.'

Hannah sighed. 'OK, so when we met up a few weeks later, I hardly recognized him. He'd grown up into this real hunk ...'

'Hunk?' I laughed.

Hannah giggled. 'OK, maybe that was a bit American. "Handsome young man" then, if you prefer. Whichever way you looked at him, he was lovely and although I hadn't seen him for years it was like we'd been chatting only yesterday. He was like, really grown up, not like some of the immature idiots in my school who thought that insulting you and throwing stuff at you across the classroom was endearing and would make you fall in love with them ... dicks.'

I squirmed uncomfortably. I remembered being like that at school and thought that this kind of direct approach with girls would actually work. That shows how much I knew at that age. Maybe romance should be taught in schools, it certainly would have been more use to me than the standard grade I got in woodwork.

Whilst I was musing on my potential national curriculum additions, Hannah was still talking. 'So we agreed to meet up again the following week in Pizza Hut.'

'Oh, very tasteful,' I added.

'You love Pizza Hut,' Hannah pointed out. 'You love the free sweets you get at the end. You always eat more than Tessa and Lois put together.'

'Fair point, not sure I'd go there on a date, though.'

'You might if you're seventeen,' argued Jane.

I nodded. 'Maybe.'

Hannah continued smugly, having made her point. 'So we had a nice time in Pizza Hut and then as his mum was away for the weekend, we went back to his flat. We talked about his mum and dad splitting up and how painful it was for him ...'

'Probably angling for a sympathy shag,' I suggested meanly.

'Yeah, I guess he was and it worked – he got one,' Hannah said defensively. 'He was such a sensitive soul, he had taken the divorce badly, and his mum had gone back to work full-time soon afterwards, so he spent a lot of time on his own, listening to sad songs in his bedroom and playing games on the Internet.'

Wanking himself silly at online porn more likely, I thought. I glanced over at Jane and she smiled conspiratorially at me. She obviously wasn't buying the whole Saint Callum thing, either.

'He told me that he'd only seen his dad about six times since his parents split up. He'd moved to London initially, then started a job in the Middle East. Callum reckoned it was important for sons to spend time with their fathers, shows you how mature he was.'

Jane had obviously heard enough. 'Yeah, OK, Hannah, we get how sensitive and grown up he was, let's move on to where your knickers are so sticky you have to peel them off with pliers.'

'*Jane*,' exclaimed Hannah. 'There's no need to be so crude.'

Jane laughed and I allowed myself a smile. Better that came from her than me.

'OK, we started kissing on the couch and then went upstairs to his bedroom. It was a typical teen boy's bedroom with posters of semi-naked women and …'

'Skip the bedroom description, Hannah,' requested Jane. 'I can imagine how his bedroom looked – and smelled, probably.'

Hannah snorted. 'Yeah, actually it was a bit pongy, dried sweat and … I don't know, hormones, I suppose.'

'Smells like teen spirit,' I offered helpfully.

Hannah nodded. 'Yeah, I suppose that's a good description. Now every time I hear that song, that's what I'll think of.'

I wasn't sure that was a good thing or not. I don't suppose it really mattered, but I didn't really want Hannah going all misty-eyed over an old boyfriend every time Nirvana played on the radio. I should have kept my mouth shut.

'Come on, Hannah, keep going,' insisted Jane.

'It was you two who started talking about songs.… Anyway, you know the rest, we had sex on the bed, it was nice and … well, that was it.'

'Hannah,' said Jane firmly.

'What?' Hannah answered defensively.

Jane shook her head. 'That's not the end of the story and you know it. Is that all you ever told Scott about your first time?'

Hannah shrugged and refused to make eye contact with her friend or me.

'C'mon, Hannah, you either tell him the full version or I will.'

'You wouldn't dare.'

'I would, I've had loads of wine, plus he told you everything about Martin and Sabrina.'

'Mar*tine*,' I corrected.

'Yeah, Mar*tine*, so c'mon, out with it.'

Hannah frowned. I could tell she was angry with Jane, but I said nothing and waited with anticipation.

'Oh, all right. Well, it was Callum's first time too, I don't think he'd had a proper girlfriend yet and I was his first, which I suppose made it even more special. I didn't tell him this but I'd had a few boyfriends by then and been to a few parties and done some stuff, but not full sex, so I just intuitively knew. It was sweet, we were both going to be each other's first and we had known each other for ages. So anyway, we'd got naked and he was fumbling around, not really knowing what he was doing, but I guided him and got him to touch me in the right places, if you know what I mean, and I tried to give him a blow job, but to be honest I was crap ...'

'Things haven't changed,' I said jokingly, and ducked as Hannah threw a cushion at me while Jane screeched with laughter.

'Shhh, Jane,' Hannah warned. 'You'll wake the girls. After a few minutes I gave up and helped him put a condom on. Then he's on top of me, thrusting away like the Duracell bunny but he's nowhere near me, so I had to stop him, guide him in and then he lasts like thirty seconds and collapses onto me, all red-faced and sweaty.'

I'd never heard any of this and was glad that Saint Callum wasn't so perfect after all.

'I'm lying there, still really horny, and I'm thinking I'll wait a few minutes, then I'll get him up for another go. So, we are talking about people we used to know and things like that for a while, then I slowly start pumping his cock. The condom has come off and he's really slippy and slimy, which is gross and sexy at the same time, and I noticed that his foreskin wasn't moving much. Now I'm no expert at this stage in my life, I think I'd touched about three cocks by this time, but it just doesn't feel right. But he seems to be enjoying it, he's breathing fast and grunting so I speed up and grip it tighter to stop it slipping so much in my hand, then ...'

I'm watching Hannah's face and she visibly cringes before continuing.

'... there's this, God, I don't know how to describe it, it's like a ripping sensation and suddenly my hand is soaking wet.' Hannah laughs. 'My first thought is that he's gone and come again and now I'll have to wait even longer to get some satisfaction. But I notice his face has changed from a picture of ecstasy to one of pain. I pull back the duvet and my hand is covered in blood, there's blood everywhere. Again I'm not thinking straight, I wonder if my period has come early or something. Then it occurs to me that there's too much blood for it to be from me. I'm still holding his cock and I realize that it is literally pumping blood out all over my hand. It was one of the most horrific things I've ever seen. I remember screaming and jumping out of the bed and backing up across the room to the bedroom door, and all the time I'm staring at this cock pumping blood out all over the bed. I actually thought he was going to die, but instead of helping him or anything, I grab my knickers and jeans and run into the bathroom and vomit down the toilet. While I'm retching, all I can see is his cock pumping out blood, it was truly horrific.

'Eventually, I kind of pull myself together and realize I've only got half my clothes and need to go back into the room to get the rest. Also I'm thinking, what if he dies? Will it be my fault? I've broken his dick – is that manslaughter?'

'Manhood slaughter,' laughed Jane.

Hannah bit her bottom lip. 'Yeah, more than likely, but remember I'm in shock at this point so I go back in and poor Callum's in a right mess. He's gone soft now, not surprisingly, and the blood is only slowly trickling out so I go back into the bathroom and rinse out a facecloth and bring it back and hand it to him. I'm scared to go near him in case I do anything else wrong. I then decide that he really does need some medical attention but I don't know what to do. The hospital's miles away, and we can't exactly go on the bus with him bleeding like that, so I phoned an ambulance.'

I had to laugh. 'What the hell did you say on the phone?'

Hannah smiled. 'Well, I didn't know what had happened really so I just said that my boyfriend had hurt his cock and needed to go to hospital.'

Both Jane and I are rolling about now. It *was* funny, but after the amount of wine we'd drunk, to us it was hilarious.

I recovered and asked, 'What did they say to that?'

'Well they asked me some questions, which I answered the best I could.

"How had the incident occurred?"

"I was pulling on it."

"Why were you doing that?"

"We were in bed having sex."

"I see, what are the symptoms? Is it bent now or bleeding?"

"I don't know, it might be bent. He's gone soft so I can't tell. It is bleeding, though, lots."

"Right, so you don't know if it's bent but it is bleeding?"

"Yeah, it's bleeding loads but not as much as it was."

"OK, what are you doing to stem the bleeding?"

"I'm not doing anything, I'm talking on the phone to you."

"I know that, but have you tried putting pressure on it?"

"I think I've put enough pressure on it for one night."

83

"Well, can you get your boyfriend to put pressure on it?"

"I think he's in shock."

"Well, you need to try to stop the bleeding and I'll get someone with you as soon as I can."

'I gave them the address and went back through to poor Callum. He was just sitting there, staring at his poor penis. I went over to him and said, "I need to put pressure on it to stop the bleeding." The poor guy just looked up in terror and shuffled up the bed on his bum to get as far away from me as he could. About twenty minutes later, a paramedic on a bike turns up and explains that Callum's foreskin has ripped, it had probably been too tight to begin with and my over zealous wanking had been too much for it.' Hannah sighed. 'Not the best end to a date I've ever had.'

Jane and I were beside ourselves with laughter. Eventually Jane asked, 'I think you've told me but I can't remember, did you ever see him again?'

Hannah smiled and sighed. 'Not really, he didn't get into St Andrew's and ended up at Bristol University instead where he studied law, so he moved away a few months later.'

'He probably went to study law to find out how to sue you for his damaged dick,' I said.

Hannah laughed. 'I wouldn't be surprised. I did speak to him on the phone a few times after he went there, but eventually we kind of got on with our lives. He occasionally pops up on Facebook and as far as I can tell, he's married and lives in Essex somewhere. I'm not even sure what he does for a living. One thing's for certain though, we weren't going to go on a second date after that.'

Jane went over and gave my wife a cuddle. 'Never mind, hun, these things happen for a reason.'

Hannah nodded. 'The one regret is that I didn't get an orgasm.'

Chapter Nine

AFTER WE'D PUT Jane into a taxi we went to bed. It was nearly midnight, and we'd both probably regret our late night in the morning as Tessa and Lois would be up at six, demanding attention. Hannah had postponed giving her friend a lecture about children and warning against becoming a single mother until another, more sober time.

Jane's view of children had obviously changed dramatically since the night she had described kids as "little poop machines", but then again, as she wasn't getting any younger, maybe her hormones were bugging her.

A few weeks later, Hannah told me that Jane still seemed determined to press ahead despite her advice to the contrary, but had agreed to think about it over Christmas, which was a very busy and expensive time for us. We couldn't possibly afford all the presents Tessa in particular asked for, but we'd managed to scrape some funds together to buy enough to keep her and her sister happy. Hannah was very organized and everything was wrapped and hidden away long before the festivities began. Christmas Eve arrived in an enchanting flurry of snow and wind.

Despite Edinburgh's northerly latitude it rarely snowed, so this was a rare treat.

Whilst Hannah spent the afternoon shopping for some last-minute essentials (Christmas dinner would be spoiled, allegedly, without cinnamon-coated nuts), I took the girls to the park with their sledge. As usual, the first half-hour was magical until their little hands started to ache with the cold and they started crying for Mummy.

I took them to a nearby café where we all warmed up before returning to build a snowman. I did most of the snow-gathering and after about twenty minutes, I felt like crying for my mum too. Eventually, though, we put the finishing touches to our snowman, whose face – I have to say – appeared to be more than a little malevolent. He had a lopsided, evil-looking grin and silver-grey stones for eyes. I was convinced he was watching me. I was glad when it was time to go home to get away from his steely stare.

Back home, Hannah was busy in the kitchen so I got the girls changed and seated in the living room watching the CBeebies Christmas panto. Then I went to see if I could help/hinder Hannah.

Twenty minutes later, I was banished to the living room to watch the panto too, having eaten too many cinnamon-coated nuts for Hannah's liking.

Although they were excited, the tiring afternoon spent in the snow meant we got the girls to bed early, allowing Hannah and me to snuggle up on the couch to watch an old black and white film version of *Scrooge*. This made it feel more like Christmas. We sipped on Earl Grey tea whilst eating the remainder of the nuts. Outside, the snow was falling even more heavily and the wind made it almost blizzard-like. It was a nice evening to be inside, warm and toasty.

We'd just reached the stage in the movie where the Ghost

of Christmas Present appeared when there was a knock on the front door. At first I ignored it, thinking it had been part of the film, but then it came again, louder this time.

'I wonder who that could be on Christmas Eve,' Hannah said.

'Santa?'

She giggled. 'Well, we don't have a working chimney any more so you never know.'

'I'll find out, shall I?' Hannah was making no attempt to move.

She kissed me. I tasted cinnamon on her lips, a real Christmas-flavoured kiss. I shivered as I left the cosy living room for the draughty hall with the wind whistling through the letter box.

I tried to peer through the spyhole in our solid wooden front door, only to find that it had been obscured by a slightly chewed Skittle. Tessa, I assumed, and as it was a lime-flavoured example, not one of my favourites (nor Tessa's, given the fact it was stuck to the eyeglass), I left it untouched, unlocked the door and opened it cautiously. I peered through the crack and saw what looked to be a slightly stooped-over snowman, holding a scruffy travel bag in one hand and a soiled, snow-covered handbag in the other. It was shaking, either in fear or more likely with the cold given the amount of snow falling off it.

My initial reaction was that she (I perceptively assumed it was a she due to the handbag) was some kind of beggar looking for a Christmas hand-out, though I hadn't known them to go door to door before, but given the freezing weather maybe desperate measures were called for.

'Can I help you?' I enquired.

The scarf-covered face slowly lifted to look at mine and I was stunned. Underneath the snowy exterior, the exotic eyes that locked with mine belonged to no other than

Marilyn, our erstwhile once-in-a-lifetime sexual experiment, deviance, or whatever you wanted to label our experience as.

I was beyond shocked. I couldn't imagine what had happened to transport this shared exotic fantasy of ours thousands of miles from her steamy Thailand peninsula to a frigid Edinburgh December evening, or how she'd got here. Whatever the reason, it wouldn't be anything good.

We stood staring at each other for what seemed like ages, but in reality could probably be numbered in seconds before she shivered violently, sneezed and sent cascades of melting snow crashing onto the grey flagstones like a mini avalanche.

I stepped aside and she moved slowly past me into the hall. I called out, 'Hannah, we've got a visitor – the ghost of summer past is here.'

Chapter Ten

HANNAH STRUGGLED UP from her prone position on the couch and asked, 'What are you talking about, Scott?'

Then her eyes widened and her face visibly paled as she set eyes on Marilyn.

She stared open-mouthed before uttering the under-statement of the year: 'What a surprise.'

Marilyn was dressed in a number of layers. Most appeared to be designed for a cool evening in the sweaty oppressive heat of South East Asia where on a winter's day the temperature could drop to sixty-eight degrees Fahrenheit. The temperature outside must be just above zero because it was still snowing, but the wind-chill factor must have made it feel like minus ten. She'd probably never experienced anything like that in her entire life.

Hannah was first to react and took off the first layer of soaking-wet cloth and sat our guest in front of the gas fire, which she flipped up to maximum. Then she left, went to the kitchen, and returned with a steaming mug of coffee, which she handed to Marilyn. All this time, I was standing stock-still in amazement, still unable to believe she was here.

After Marilyn had thawed out, Hannah began the interrogation.

'Marilyn, what are you doing here?'

She rubbed her abdomen and said, 'Calla pregnant.'

'Who's Calla?' I asked.

Marilyn smiled proudly and said, 'I Calla, Marilyn my work name. I not use it any more.'

I took this to mean she no longer worked as a hooker.

'You have given up being a … prostitute?'

Marilyn/Calla scowled at me. 'I working girl, not prostitute.'

I sighed and Hannah took over. 'Calla, why are you here? How did you find us?'

Calla frowned, leaned over and fished about in her old battered handbag. She pulled out some ticket stubs, a passport and a dog-eared, dirty and tatty luggage tag, which she handed to Hannah. My wife quickly scanned them and then passed them over to me. The ticket stubs showed a direct flight to Gatwick and train tickets from London to Edinburgh. The journeys had been practically consecutive, which meant she must have been travelling for nearly thirty hours straight. The passport showed her full name, Calla Hi Tee, with her non-smiling photograph staring out at me. However, what really grabbed my attention was the luggage tag. It had our home address and phone number written on it. She must have taken it from one of our suitcases whilst she was in our room in Thailand. I was shocked and also slightly impressed at her ingenuity. That explained how she was here; the why I could guess, but I needed to hear it for myself.

Hannah shook her head. 'OK, Calla, I can see how you found us, but why?'

Calla held her tummy and said, 'I bring baby to meet father.' She stared at me and once again held my gaze until

I had to look away.

Hannah was not happy. 'Calla, are you asking us to believe that one broken condom resulted in Scott getting you pregnant? Don't you use other birth control like the pill or something?'

I wasn't sure Calla understood my wife completely; in fact, as time went on we would learn that Calla's ability to speak and understand English seemed to fluctuate, depending upon circumstances. In this case she simply said, 'Calla use condom, condom break.'

Hannah was not about to let her off that easy. 'How do we know Scott is the father? You could have got pregnant from some other man, you hardly even look pregnant.'

She shook her head violently – so hard in fact it made her hair flap around her face. 'No, no, no – condom break, you see condom break, you are baby father.'

I sighed and Hannah smiled at me sympathetically. On some level she was responsible for this whole mess and knew it. I would never have participated in a threesome without her.

Hannah locked eyes with me, and I knew she didn't want me to say anything else until we'd had a chance to talk alone. We made Calla as comfortable as we could on the couch with a pillow and blanket, then Hannah pulled me into our bedroom.

'What the fuck are we going to do with her, Scott?' she whispered urgently.

'I don't think we need to whisper, she can't hear us, and even if she could she probably won't understand much.'

'OK, fair point, but what *are* we going to do?'

'What was it you said to me in Thailand? "Use your imagination."'

'Eh? Oh right, yes, so I did, but we can't do that now.'

'Well, I can't, I'd get accused of maiesiophilia.'

'Yeah, very good, Scott but … actually, why is she here?'

'She might be after some money.'

Hannah laughed sarcastically. 'Well, she's come to the wrong place, then.'

'She won't know that, though, compared to what she had back home we probably look like millionaires.'

Hannah paced, or rather lumbered, around the room before stopping to face me.

'Can't we call social services or something?'

'It's Christmas Eve.'

'They must have an emergency service or something.'

'Yeah, probably for abused children, but not for unexpected visitors. Otherwise, given the time of year, they'd be inundated.'

'So we're stuck with her?'

I shrugged. 'Unless you want to put her out on what is probably the coldest night of the year.'

Hannah sat on the bed and narrowed her eyes as if she was seriously considering that as an option. 'Do you think she really *is* carrying your baby?'

'I don't know, it's a hell of a lot of trouble to go to if she's not and I would imagine it's pretty easy to find out.'

Hannah nodded. 'That's what I was thinking. So we'll get a test done to confirm it as soon as possible and take it from there?'

'Sounds like a plan; it's going to be a few days before we can do that, though. What do we do with her in the meantime?'

Hannah stood up and rubbed her lower back. 'Make her feel welcome, I suppose.'

'It's Christmas Day tomorrow, what should we tell the girls?'

'Oh, we'll think of something. I'll need to try and find something to wrap for Marilyn so she doesn't feel left out.'

'Hang on, Hannah, a minute ago you were willing to throw her out on a freezing-cold night and now you're wrapping Christmas presents for her?'

'Well, it *is* Christmas.'

The last point was hard to argue against. 'But we need to have a story to tell everyone.'

Hannah had her head in the wardrobe so her voice was muffled. 'Let's sleep on it and we'll work it out tomorrow. I've got a pair of slippers here that I've never worn and that hideous purple and pink scarf your mum bought me last Christmas. Do you think Marilyn would like them?'

I inspected both items. 'The slippers are great, I think her feet look about the same size as yours, but I agree with you about the scarf. I can't even see Mr Blobby wearing this, even though it's his colour scheme.'

Hannah snatched it back. 'You're right, I'll give her some chocolates, they're universally loved. Unless she's got a nut allergy. Do you think she's got a nut allergy?'

I managed to say 'Errr' before Hannah interrupted. 'Never mind, you go and see if she needs anything while I wrap these up.'

Back in the living room Marilyn had fallen asleep on the couch. I gazed at her; even in a deep sleep she was incredibly cute; her almond eyes framed with long dark lashes moved in her sleep as she dreamed, and her little cherry lips parted slightly as she sighed. I felt some of the guilt slip back into my gut that had been there when we'd left Thailand. Somehow, deep down, I knew there was going to be a price to pay for our little sexual adventure and now it looked like that price had turned up in person and the bill was due.

I realized with a start that if indeed the baby had been conceived during our honeymoon, then it meant Marilyn would be due to give birth around the same time as

Hannah, and I might be faced with multiple births. I know many parents have to cope with such things since the advent of IVF and the increase in the numbers of twins, but I reckoned that not many had to face multiple births from multiple partners. Well, not in Edinburgh, anyway. Still, I reminded myself we were a long way off from that yet. I placed the blanket that had slipped onto the floor gently over her and left the room, switching the light off.

Hannah was in bed when I got back and I slid in beside her. 'She's asleep.'

'I'm not surprised after that journey. Well, this will be a Christmas to remember, huh?'

I laughed. 'Well, you wanted to shake things up for us in Thailand.'

'I know, but we need to draw a line under that now, I think. Also we need to stop calling her Marilyn, her name's Calla, according to her passport, that's with two Ls. That should help us feel differently towards her.'

Hannah snuggled up next to me and we both drifted off to sleep, wondering what other surprises the Christmas holidays would bring.

The following morning, before we went through to see what Santa had delivered, I had a word with Tessa. I explained, 'We've got a lady visitor sleeping in the living room.'

'Did Santa bring her?'

I laughed. 'No, I don't think so, though I must admit it does feel a bit like that. We met her in the summer. Remember when we were on holiday? She's going to help Mummy and Daddy look after the new baby when it's born. Her name is Calla and she doesn't speak English very well.'

Tessa beamed. 'Lois doesn't speak very well.'

'Yes, I know, but that's because she hasn't learned to

speak yet, she will soon be as good as you are at talking, sweetie.'

Tessa frowned. 'Hasn't Calla learned to speak?'

'Yes, she can speak, but she uses a different language. Do you remember on holiday how you couldn't understand what everyone was saying?'

She wrinkled her nose. I could see the wheels going around in her head. Tessa, like most young children, lived in the present. The past and future had little meaning even though she was nearly six.

'I think so, Daddy, everybody was talking rubbish.'

I laughed. 'Yeah, something like that. Good girl, so you need to speak slowly and clearly to Calla so she can understand you, OK?'

'OK, Daddy,' Tessa agreed brightly. 'Can we open our presents now?'

In a strange kind of way, having Calla in our home at Christmas was just like having another child. She was wide-eyed with wonder at all the decorations and presents. When she opened the two parcels that Hannah had wrapped for her, she said something that sounded like 'wine gum' and her eyes welled up with tears.

At first I thought maybe she didn't like chocolate and wanted wine gums, but then she gave Hannah a hug so I assumed all was well. We learned later that she was actually saying *swyngam*, which was a word she would use a lot. It meant beautiful in Thai.

Introducing the girls to Calla was easy. The Thai woman smiled and they instantly bonded. It was uncanny. Maybe it was her vulnerability that Tessa and Lois identified with, maybe it was more complex than that, who knows, but the girls' acceptance of her into their lives, as we discovered, would be the easiest part of having Calla to stay.

Later in the morning, when we got some time, Hannah

and I sat and Googled lots of sites related to paternity tests.

Hannah pointed to the screen. 'It says here that most doctors won't do a paternity test on an unborn baby.'

'Why?'

'Because it involves inserting a needle into the womb to gather amniotic fluid, which they class as a high-risk procedure.'

'So what do people do, then?'

'It says here that it's really easy to do a non-invasive test once the child is born, so most people just wait.'

'Most people don't have a strange pregnant girl living with them, though.'

Hannah chewed her bottom lip. 'I suppose we could ask her to get a test done, you know, threaten to throw her out unless she gets it.'

'But that would risk harming the baby?'

Hannah nodded.

'Would you be happy with that?'

Hannah sighed. 'No, definitely not. I wouldn't do it to mine so I can't very well ask her to do it to hers.'

'So we're stuffed, then?'

'Looks like it.'

We didn't even mention it to Calla, not that she would have understood anyway.

What we did need to do, though, was develop a proper cover story, as we didn't want to have to tell our nearest and dearest that we'd had a threesome on our honeymoon that had resulted in me impregnating a prostitute, who then decided to journey 6,000 miles to show us her bump.

Hannah sat sipping tea with me in the kitchen whilst the girls (which now included Calla) sat in the living room, watching *You've Been Framed: The Christmas Collection*.

'Why don't we just elaborate on what you told Tessa this morning? You know, say that we met her on holiday and casually mentioned that we were considering hiring an au pair to help look after Tessa and Lois so that I could go back to work full-time. Due to language issues, she took it as an open invitation to travel to the UK and seek us out. However, in the meantime, I found out I was pregnant and any thoughts of going back to work full-time were off the agenda for the time being.'

'That's pretty good, babe, but there are two big holes in that theory, number one being that we wouldn't have the money to pay an au pair even if you were working full-time, but I don't suppose too many people will work that out. The second issue is obvious and likely to become even more obvious by the day. Our so-called au pair is six months pregnant. That means we might need to come up with a cover-cover story, which is likely to get too complicated. Well, it would for me, anyway.'

Hannah nodded. 'Yeah, I know, but it'll have to do for now. Let's go and tell Calla.'

We switched the TV off and tried to explain. 'Calla, we are going to tell everyone that you are here to be our au pair.'

She blinked and switched her gaze between us. Hannah tried again. 'You'll be our babysitter.'

Calla held her abdomen. 'I not sit on baby, baby here in tummy.'

Hannah sighed and sat down on the couch beside Calla. 'Listen, Calla, we need to tell our family that you are here to look after Tessa and Lois, otherwise it's going to get very difficult for us.' Calla blinked at Hannah again and said nothing.

I wasn't sure she'd understood a word Hannah had said. So I gave it a go. 'Calla, you look after our babies.'

That seemed to register. 'I like babies.'

I smiled. 'Good, we like babies too.'

'I have baby soon.'

'Yes, Hannah will have a baby soon as well.'

Calla peered past me at Hannah. 'We look after babies together.'

I nodded, that was probably as good as it was going to get for now. If she just muttered to everyone about babies, we might get away with it for a while.

I turned to Hannah. 'Now that she's here, we need to work out where she's going to sleep.'

'Does she have to live with us?'

'Well, I can't see us getting a hold of anyone from the council until after the New Year. Maybe she could stay in a hotel or something.'

I asked our guest, 'Calla, do you have any money?'

'What is this money?'

'You're joking, right? You know what money is: bahts.'

'Ah, yes.' She opened her purse and handed me a ten-pound note.

'Is that all you've got?'

Calla nodded and showed me her empty purse. I slumped back onto the floor.

'Looks like she's staying for a while.'

'Well, if she is, she can't sit about in my dressing gown all day. Calla, come with me, let's see if any of my clothes will fit you.'

Hannah returned alone a few minutes later. 'I've left her rummaging and trying things on. For the time being she can sleep in here, we can give her the single duvet and put up the camp bed from the hall cupboard. I'm sure that will be comfy enough for a few nights or a week or so if it comes to that. Beyond then, once she gets bigger, I'm not sure that'll work.'

I agreed. 'Yeah, fair point, hopefully by then she'll be in the hands of social services or something.'

'Jane's on her way over,' Hannah announced.

'I take it you invited her and she didn't sense that we might be having a crisis?'

Hannah laughed, lightening our mood. 'No, I phoned her, I want to tell her the truth. I want at least one person I can talk to openly about what's going on.'

'You can talk to me.'

'Yeah, but you're right in the middle of it, so I want someone with an outside perspective.'

I nodded, it made some kind of sense. I just wished it wasn't Jane, she could be so judgemental.

'Maybe I'll tell Dave too.'

Hannah snorted. 'If you have to, he'll just want to shag her.'

'Hannah, he's not that bad.'

'He is so, he wants to shag everyone.'

'Calla's six months pregnant and hardly speaks English.'

'And your point is…?'

I laughed. He *had* told me he'd sworn off women for a while. I believed him, Hannah didn't. The main reason I wanted to tell Dave, though, was despite all the bad things Hannah had to say about him, he had one brilliant trait: he understood women better than anyone I knew. Given my current predicament, that might come in very handy.

I gave Hannah a hug and she leaned into me.

'How do you think Jane will take the news?' I asked.

My wife sighed heavily. 'She'll be annoyed probably.'

'Does it really matter that much what Jane thinks?'

'It does to me.'

Jane arrived within the hour, her red hair pulled back into a severe ponytail. It appeared to be so tight that it must hurt. Maybe that was why she breezed past me when I opened the door with barely a word. Hannah made sure Calla was out of the way, she was seated in the living room with the girls laughing at *You've Been Framed* – the celebrity lookalike special.

In our bedroom with the door closed, Hannah outlined to her friend the problem we had. Jane's face was like thunder when she'd finished.

'What? You had a threesome with a cheap Thai hooker?'

I said thoughtfully, 'Actually, I think they're all cheap. Well, compared to the UK, anyway.'

Jane turned her angry gaze on me. 'Is there a comparison site or something that you used, then, like hooker-supermarket or Compare the Tart dot com?'

I squirmed and tried not to laugh; that was funny. I was sitting beside Hannah, who nudged me with her elbow, trying to stop me laughing out loud. It also occurred to me that although Calla had been cheap at the time, she was turning out to be potentially very expensive in the long run.

For some reason, Jane's real anger was directed at Hannah, probably because she'd not told her about the liaison with Calla. Hannah also hadn't yet explained that it was all her idea. As if reading my thoughts, Jane turned to face me but kept her eyes on Hannah.

'I take it this was Scott's idea? Men always want to do that sort of thing.'

Hannah squeezed my hand and I kept silent.

'Of course it was,' Jane exclaimed triumphantly, my silence vindicating her opinion as she turned her green eyes on me. 'But why? Look at where it's got you, you're gonna be left with a little ...'

I knew what she was about to say and I met her gaze, willing her not to say 'bastard' because then I'd be in the middle of a 1950s melodrama and my life would be over. To her credit, she checked herself and called it a mixed-race kid.

'So what happens now? Do you simply just live with two wives like one of those Morons from the States?'

I think she meant Mormons, but I didn't bother correcting her as I think her mispronunciation was intentional. She suddenly switched her attack to Calla.

'What kind of name is that anyway?'

'I think it's quite common in Thailand,' I suggested.

Jane shook her head and said, 'I'm going to make some tea, does anyone want anything?'

Hannah and I said no, and she left to go and cool down.

Alone with Hannah I asked, 'What did you think of her reaction?'

'She cares about us, that's why she was upset. Remember, she was looking after our kids when we were away doing this so she probably feels put upon as well.'

'No point in asking her to babysit anytime soon then,' I said flippantly, but I knew her reaction would only be a fraction of the reception we could expect if our families ever found out.

Jane came back into the bedroom and perched on the edge of the bed, holding her steaming mug close to her mouth whilst staring out of the window at the gently falling snowflakes. She continued gazing out at the weather and asked, 'How do you know this baby is actually yours?'

Hannah looked to me to answer. 'Well, we don't, the timing seems about right but we won't know for sure until the baby is born.'

'Can't you do some kind of paternity test on the foetus?'

I leaned my head back onto my pillow and answered. 'Yes, but it involves some risk to the unborn child and a lot of doctors won't agree to do it. Besides, we wouldn't want to take the risk of harming a baby for something that can be checked really easily when it's born.'

'I suppose from her point of view, it's a win-win

situation, isn't it?' Jane asked thoughtfully.

'How come?' asked Hannah.

Jane smiled cynically at both Hannah and me. 'God, you two can be so naïve. How did she know where you lived?'

'After the condom broke she nicked one of our suitcase labels.'

Jane nodded thoughtfully and sipped her tea. 'OK, does that not seem a little … premeditated to you?'

Neither Hannah nor I spoke so Jane carried on.

'Look at it this way. If I was in her shoes and found myself pregnant either by you or someone else and I wanted to keep my baby, I've got a problem. My occupation doesn't lend itself well to motherhood and I would imagine the healthcare system in Thailand is pretty crap, so the temptation of heading off to the UK with its free maternity care and great health system must be pretty attractive. Hell, it's one of the reasons why migrants head here in their droves. So let's say I'd just had a little threesome with a Scots couple and my condom … I take it she brought the condom with her?'

I nodded.

'OK, so I have this condom that conveniently breaks and on my way out, I nick the label from their suitcase to get their address …' Jane paused and finished her tea. She was staring out at the snowflakes again. 'Right, so I've got two options, a little paternity blackmail where I write, asking you for money to support the child, which I say is yours…. The flaw with that is that she has no guarantee you will pay her anything. The best option is to save up some cash and get a flight over to the UK to confront you in person. It's very difficult then for you to do anything but take her in.'

Hannah and I looked at each other; we'd not thought any of this through. Hannah might have had it not been for her baby-brain, but I probably would never have got this far. My brain wasn't wired to be devious, otherwise we'd probably have a much better standard of living than we currently enjoyed.

'So you are saying she might have been pregnant before coming to us?' Hannah asked incredulously.

Jane shrugged. 'Possibly, or maybe she got pregnant soon after by her boyfriend, pimp or whoever fits into her life that way, or maybe it really is your kid and she's just an opportunist. Either way, she's not going to volunteer that information so for the next three months or so, so you're stuck.' We all sat in silence for a few minutes before Jane added, 'Do I get to meet this lady of the night, then?'

As if on cue, the bedroom door opened and Calla popped her head round. 'Calla hungry.'

Jane narrowed her eyes and peered at her. 'Does she always talk like that?'

I nodded. 'I don't think her English is all that great.'

'I suppose being a hooker doesn't require great language skills,' Jane observed dryly. 'Does Calla want some cheese?'

Calla stared at Jane for a moment, then nervously flicked her gaze between me and Hannah. 'Who this? What is cheese?'

Jane laughed. 'Oh dear, you don't even know what cheese is?'

Calla ignored Jane and smiled sweetly at Hannah, who said, 'C'mon, let's see what I can find in the fridge.'

Hannah left with Calla, and Jane turned to me and said, 'Doesn't say much, does she?'

'Well, she's out of her comfort zone, we don't even know yet how good her English is. She turned up at our door covered in snow, and shivering. It's probably the coldest place she's ever been. One positive, the kids seem to like her.'

Jane snorted. 'She's barely out of her teens, she's little more than a kid herself, no wonder they get on. I'm just going to my car to get the kids' presents.'

On her return, we all gathered in the living room and Jane watched as our excited offspring tore open the paper on the various toys and dolls Jane had bought.

'You shouldn't have got them so much, Jane. They won't know what to play with first,' Hannah observed, but she was wrong. Tessa got out her crayons and coloured pencils and both she and Lois started drawing and colouring in all the empty boxes.

Hannah shook her head in exasperation. 'Typical, we spend all that money and they'd have been happy with a few boxes and some crayons.'

Calla sat with the girls and helped them draw. We watched for a few minutes and noticed that she had some real talent. Her little animal drawings were exquisite and even more impressive given the limited materials available. She produced some lovely little deer with happy expressions on their faces and even the little wolf she drew was very lifelike.

Jane commented sarcastically, 'Well, it looks like there's no end to her talents.'

Hannah and I exchanged glances but said nothing.

Over the next week and a bit we had to get used to sharing our space with a relative stranger. She put a further strain on our resources and added to the stress of living in a small space.

'Daddy?'

'Yes, Tessa.'

'Why are you standing in the hall?'

'I'm waiting to get into the bathroom.'

'Mummy's in the bath.'

'Is she?'

'Uh huh.'

'Hannah, are you in the bath?'

'Yes.'

'I need to get ready for work.'

'I know, I'm going as fast as I can. If you make me some tea I'll hurry up.'

In the kitchen I made a pot of tea, munched on some toast and waited for Hannah. Eventually she waddled into the room, ate my last bit of toast and laughed at my impatient face.

'What's funny?'

'You'll see.'

'Will I?'

'Yep.'

I pottered down the hall but the bathroom door was locked. 'Tessa, is that you in there?'

'No, Daddy, I'm here,' my daughter yelled from her bedroom.

'Who's in the bathroom?'

'Calla.'

I sighed.

Back in the kitchen, I ate more toast and waited. Hannah emerged from the bedroom, all dressed and ready to go. I was still in my dressing gown.

'Hannah, this is my first day back and I'm going to be late.'

'If you're not fast you're last.'

'Thanks, Hannah, that's helpful. I'll remember that little bit of philosophy tomorrow morning. Thing is, I've got work today. You don't start back until next week and the schools aren't back until then either so I should have got priority this morning.'

Before my smiling wife could make a reply, Calla's head appeared around the kitchen door, her long black hair dripping wet.

'Calla hungry.'

I was annoyed at her too. 'Calla, why do you need to get up at the same time as everyone else? You don't have to go anywhere so you could stay in bed.'

Calla blinked at me and then smiled at Hannah. 'Calla hungry.'

After Hannah made her some toast and buttered it for her, Calla stared at it and announced, 'Calla like honey.'

'I'll add that to the shopping list,' sighed my wife. 'Calla, I'm not sure how much of this you'll get, but can you not leave your dirty clothes on the floor beside your bed? Can you put them in the washing basket?'

Calla chewed on her toast. 'What is this basket?'

Hannah sighed, picked up a dirty tea towel, and took our visitor by the hand and showed her where dirty clothes were to be put.

That evening, Hannah discovered that all the towels, even the clean ones, had been put in the washing basket, but none of her dirty clothes. Hannah had also tried to get her to wear the bathrobe she'd lent her, but every morning she emerged from the bathroom wearing just her underwear.

'Scott, you've got to stop staring at her, she knows you're staring and she likes it.'

'I'd stare at you if you wandered around in your underwear.'

'Dream on.'

'You used to wander around our flat with no clothes on at all.'

'That was before I had Tessa and Lois.'

'What's changed?'

'Everything, and I'm pregnant.'

I couldn't say anything about liking her pregnant shape without bringing down upon myself the whole maiesiophilia thing, but other than that I couldn't understand; it was one of those things I was just supposed to know. The problem was that I didn't.

Hannah continued, 'Anyway, this has got nothing to do with me. If she's going to stay with us for a while, I can't have you staring at her.' She folded her arms and peered at me curiously, her eyebrows knitting together as I processed what she'd said.

'You don't have feelings for her, do you?'

I met Hannah's gaze. 'No, of course not,' I answered honestly, smiling.

'OK, good. But we need to try and make sure she covers up. I'd love to know a bit more about her background, what led her into the kind of life she had. That way I'd get to know her better as a person. At the moment, it's difficult as most conversations I try and have with her just don't work. She maybe understands one word in ten if I'm lucky.'

'Our accents don't help. I don't think there's a huge mystery of why she ended up as a hooker: poverty probably, plus she's pretty so maybe it was an obvious choice.'

'Mmm … I don't know. There are lots of poor, pretty girls in Thailand and they don't all end up as prostitutes in brothels.'

'I don't think they call them that over there.'

'Prostitutes?'

'Brothels.'

'Oh. What do they call them?'

'I don't think they call it anything, the girls just kind of hang around in bars and then have rooms upstairs or go back to the bloke's hotel.'

'Anyway, I'd like to know what drove her into that life.'

'Leave it to the social workers, they'll find out.'

'But they won't tell us. Anything she tells them will be confidential.'

'Good.'

'Don't you want to know?'

'What, why the hooker watching TV in the next room from us slept with a Scottish couple, stole their luggage tag, then hightailed it across thousands of miles of ocean only to turn up at their door during a snowstorm and announce that the man is the father of her unborn child? No.'

'She's not a hooker any more.'

'I still don't really want to know about her background, I only want her to go away.'

'But then you won't get to see her in her underwear.'

'If I can arrange for her to go away, will you start walking around the flat in your underwear again?'

'No.'

'OK, then, she can stay.'

A cushion smacked me full in the face, just as a fully clothed Calla walked into the kitchen.

'Calla hungry.' There was no filling the girl.

She spoke very like Lois, short phrases designed to communicate in as few words as possible.

Hannah made a few suggestions. 'There's food in the fridge, Calla, I think there's some cheese, a bowl of tuna-mayonnaise, though that might be a bit crusty by now as we made it up yesterday morning, and there's some cold pizza.'

'Calla not like.'

Hannah sighed. 'Well, I'm going to the shops later, you come with me and you can pick what you like.'

'Calla hungry.'

'Yeah, we got that message,' said Hannah. She pointed. 'There are some biscuits in the cupboard above the cooker.'

That was news to me. I was dying for a biscuit yesterday and couldn't find any. The cupboard above the cooker only contained glasses as far as I knew, that must be one of

Hannah's secret hiding places. Now that I knew she'd probably change it.

Calla wobbled off to investigate.

I left for work with a pocket full of illicit biscuits.

Chapter Eleven

EARLY JANUARY, APART from being icy cold and dark, brought in all sorts of mechanical problems to the dealership, as old or badly maintained cars pushed to their limits by the cold weather simply gave up the ghost. The first Monday morning back at work after the holidays was an exceptionally hectic one and the service department was besieged by demanding car owners.

I sneaked away to the staffroom at lunchtime and was halfway through reading the *Sunday Post* that had been left on the table (well, if I'm honest I was reading the comic section that contained *The Broons* and *Oor Wullie*) when my phone started ringing. The display told me it was Hannah. She hardly ever phoned me at work.

I answered it anxiously. 'Are the girls OK?'

'The little ones are fine, the big, foreign one not so much. I've had a few problems with her today ... well, actually, I've still got them. Shit, they're heading over here again – listen, I need to go, we can talk later.' Hannah hung up.

I had absolutely no idea what that had been about. I

110

finished my tea and went back to work. The afternoon was quieter and I managed to shut up early and get home by six.

I was greeted at the door by an anxious-looking Hannah. I also noticed that her mother, Carol, was there too.

'What's going on?'

Before Hannah could speak, Tessa said, 'Mummy's on the TV.'

'Mummy's on the TV?'

Hannah nodded. 'It's true. C'mon through, my mum's monitoring the channels.'

'Your mum's monitoring the channels?'

'It would be better if you stopped repeating what everyone is saying, Scott.'

In the living room, our newly extended family were all sitting, intently watching the news. Even Lois, who never watched anything that wasn't either made by CBeebies or had Harry Hill introducing cats falling off tables.

'What's going on…?'

'Shhh,' shushed Carol, 'it's coming on again.'

Hannah had perched on the edge of the armchair and I sat between her feet. She put her hand on my shoulder and I reached up and held it.

'Watch,' she commanded.

The foyer area of the big Asda we frequented suddenly appeared on the screen and speaking into the camera was a woman of Asian descent; she could have passed for Calla's older sister.

Then the camera panned out and focused on Calla herself, who was standing and staring at a huge stack of toilet rolls like it was the most interesting thing in the universe. The reporter moved over and spoke to her; I assumed it was in their native tongue because Calla suddenly became very animated and smiley.

My initial thoughts were that it would have been nice for

Calla as she'd had nobody that she could properly converse with since she'd arrived.

Then the reporter started speaking into the camera. 'Although we originally came here to review what everyday shoppers thought about rising food prices, it appears that we may have uncovered something a little more sinister. This young pregnant girl appears to have arrived from Thailand just over a week ago, and in that time it appears that she's been kept prisoner in an Edinburgh flat, made to look after her captors' children, wear second-hand clothes, and there have been hints that she is expected to provide sexual favours in return for food.'

The reporter paused and the camera panned over towards the toilets where Hannah was emerging with Tessa and Lois.

Now, Hannah squeezed my hand. 'Lois needed to pee and of course Tessa came too, that's why we left Calla alone for a few minutes.'

The reporter rushed over to Hannah, shoved the microphone in front of her face and fired off questions.

'Is it true that you've been keeping this young Thai girl prisoner in your flat and demanding sexual favours from her in exchange for food?'

Hannah opened and closed her mouth several times but before she could form a reply, the reporter demanded, 'Is it also true that you use her for child-minding, dress her in old clothes, and took all her money away?'

It was clear that Hannah was overwhelmed and instead of saying nothing, which probably would have been the best course of action, she blurted out, 'She only had a tenner.'

It made all the other accusations that the reporter had levelled at her seem valid. The reporter, armed with this little nugget, rushed back over to Calla, leaving Hannah standing gobsmacked.

'That was when I tried to call you,' Hannah explained, squeezing my hand again. 'But I didn't really get much time, watch.'

The reporter whizzed back over to Hannah. 'Miss Hi Tee confirms that you did take her money, what do you have to say about that?'

Hannah opened and closed her mouth a few times before uttering, 'Her money's in the biscuit tin.'

Even the hard-faced reporter managed a small smile. 'Does Miss Hi Tee know this?'

Hannah replied, 'I think so.'

The reporter nodded. 'OK, what about her accusations of sexual slavery, is it true that you have demanded sex for food?'

'Of course not, that's why we're in the supermarket to get some food that she likes.'

'What does she like?'

'Well, she said she wanted some honey, actually.'

'And she will not be expected to undertake any kind of sexual act in return for the honey, or whilst using the honey?'

Hannah was completely overwhelmed, but had at least found her voice. 'Of course not, what's all this sexual non-sense about?'

The reporter ignored Hannah's question. 'What about the fact you keep her locked in the flat all day and only let her out if she's accompanying you or your partner somewhere?'

Hannah was getting angry now that the surprise was beginning to wear off. 'Absolute rubbish, she can come and go whenever she wants, but she doesn't know Edinburgh and tends to only go out if we're going out. Look, why would I leave her standing alone in Asda if she was some kind of slave?'

Good point. Hannah was doing a nice job of redeeming the situation until the reporter asked, 'What about her accusation that she is looking after your children for nothing?'

'Well …'

'And can you clarify why Miss Hi Tee came to Edinburgh in the first place? Is it true that you met her in Thailand and invited her back to your home to become your sex slave? Then when she arrived and you discovered she was pregnant, you instead decided to keep her prisoner and use her as an unpaid skivvy…?'

At that point Hannah grabbed the girls, all three of them, and hightailed it out of the doors towards the car park, pursued by the camera crew and the Asian reporter, who kept firing questions at her.

The news item then switched to some talking heads in a studio who discussed the issues surrounding modern slavery in Britain today.

Carol flipped the TV off and we all sat in silence for a moment or two before I broke the silence.

'Crivvens!' I exclaimed.

Hannah's mum stared at me strangely. 'Crivvens?'

I muttered, 'I was reading *Oor Wullie* at lunchtime and Crivvens just seemed like a good response, especially after "skivvy". What happened next, Hannah?'

'I got in the car and came home. I've been afraid to stick my head outside in case there's a bunch of reporters waiting.'

'It's OK, there isn't. Well, at least there wasn't when I arrived home. How would they know where we lived anyway?'

Hannah sighed. 'Good point, but you weren't there, it was horrible.'

I stood up and stretched my back. Carol asked, 'What's

really going on here?'

I answered, 'None of it's true. Calla just came over after a—'

'Misunderstanding, yeah, I know, Scott. That's what Hannah keeps telling me, but I know there's more to it than that. For the time being I'll believe you – thousands wouldn't.'

She then narrowed her eyes and peered at Calla, who wouldn't meet her gaze. 'What have you got to say for yourself?'

Calla smiled and said, 'I look after babies, Calla like babies.'

'What babies?'

Hannah butted in. 'She means Tessa and Lois.'

Carol looked sceptical. 'I take it the bit about the money is true, then? You took her money away?'

'It's in the biscuit tin, it's only a tenner, for God's sake,' protested Hannah.

Her mum winced at Hannah's raised voice, but carried on. 'Is it also true that you don't pay her anything for looking after Tessa and Lois, and that she only gets to leave the flat when one of you takes her out?'

'Of course not, Calla can go out whenever she wants.'

'Do you pay her anything?'

Hannah hesitated and lowered her eyes and said quietly, 'Well, we've yet to work that bit out.'

Carol nodded sagely. 'Well, I suggest you *work that bit out* very quickly.'

I decided to pipe up. 'We don't know what's going to happen, the plan was to contact social services and see if they can get her somewhere to stay.'

In the main, all Calla had done was to regurgitate the story we had told her to tell, so I couldn't really blame her. The sexual bit I couldn't quite work out, but I suppose the fact she had previously been working as a hooker might have led the reporter to jump to that conclusion.

Later, after Carol had gone, I asked Calla, 'Did you tell the reporter … TV lady … you had worked as a pros … that you used to be a working girl?'

Calla nodded. 'I tell lady, she ask me. Nice lady.'

I sighed. 'It's fine, Calla, you've not done anything wrong. Hannah and I have to be more careful, that's all. Plus, we have to sort out some stuff for you, you need to have some money and possibly a place of your own, you know, so you can have some privacy.'

'What is this privacy?'

I sighed. 'Privacy … privacy is you being on your own.'

Her eyes widened in alarm. 'Calla not want to be on own, Calla like being with Tessa and Lois.'

I smiled. Hannah and I could go to hell in a handcart, but Calla liked Tessa and Lois. I couldn't disagree with that; I liked Tessa and Lois too. They were the centre of my universe.

In bed later that evening, Hannah and I had some decisions to make.

'What the hell do we do now?' I asked Hannah.

'I haven't a clue, Scott, everybody we know will have seen the news item now, and they'll all think we're perverts.'

'I really don't fancy trying to get social services to take her now, not after that. Can you imagine the interrogation we'd get?'

'So you're saying she has to stay with us?'

'Not forever. Just until it all dies down.'

'How long's that going to take?'

'I don't know.'

Hannah started crying. 'What a mess.'

I held her until we both fell asleep.

Chapter Twelve

INITIALLY AT LEAST, Calla's presence in our lives was more disruptive for Hannah than me. I worked full-time, so once I was gone for the day, Hannah was responsible for organizing everyone.

We'd decided that Carol shouldn't be left alone with Calla if we could avoid it. There seemed to be a natural ambivalence between them, probably caused by Carol's suspicion surrounding our crap cover story.

During the next week, Hannah was only in the office for two days and managed to work from home on her other work day, so it meant Carol took Lois out, leaving Calla home alone or with Hannah. On the days nobody was with her she must have got bored, as she tidied and cleaned the flat, which just made us feel even more guilty.

'Calla, you don't have to clean up when we're not here, just chill out,' suggested my wife.

'What is this chill out?'

Hannah shook her head. 'It just means relax, don't do anything, put your feet up.'

'I fall over.'

'When did you fall over?'

'I put feet up, I fall over.'

Hannah looked to me. 'I think that's her attempt at a joke,' I said.

'Oh, it's worse than yours, Scott.'

'Thanks, sweetie.'

'Seriously though, Calla, I don't want you cleaning up in here, we need to sort something out for you. We can't carry on like this long-term.'

Tessa shouted, 'Mummy, can you put the TV on?'

Calla said, 'Calla do it,' and left the room.

After the door was closed I suggested, 'Could she stay with Jane?'

'Jane? Don't be daft, Scott. Jane hasn't got the patience to have Calla staying. Besides, she's our problem, not Jane's. I told you about her reaction on the phone after the Asda thing the other night.'

I nodded. Jane had been pretty scathing.

'We can't keep treating her like another child, she's a grown woman who is going to be a mother in a few months,' reasoned Hannah.

'I know, at some point we need to find her somewhere to live. She can't stay here after the baby's born, we don't have the space.'

'So that gives us what, twelve weeks?'

I nodded. 'Yeah, maximum.'

A few days later, matters were taken out of our hands, to a certain extent. It started with a strange phone call from a man who said he worked for the Home Office. The way he said it made it sound like a home office, rather than *Home Office* so I thought he was selling me stationery or something, and I hung up.

A few minutes later he called again.

'Is that Mr Scott McEwan?'

I recognized the voice. 'Yes, now please go away, I don't want any paper ...'

'Sorry?'

'I said I don't want to buy any paper, or printer cartridges, or pens, pencils—'

He interrupted me in mid-flow. 'I'm not calling to sell you anything, Mr McEwan.' In my experience that was a classic sales pitch, so I hung up again.

Half an hour later, my phone rang once more. I recognized the voice and was about to hang up without speaking when he raised his voice; he sounded annoyed. 'Mr McEwan, my name is Donald McDonald and I work for the Home Office – you know, the government department responsible for immigration, amongst other things.'

I realized I had probably pissed off a government official – despite this, I couldn't believe his parents had the balls to call him that and had to stifle a laugh. I tried to work out if pissing off the government was important or not, but decided to be contrite anyway, just in case.

'Oh OK, I'm sorry, I thought you were ...'

'Yes, yes – I know, trying to sell you something. Well, I'm not. It has come to our attention that you are responsible for a ...' the voice paused then said, 'a Miss Calla Hi Tee.'

I wondered who had tipped him off or if the government just monitored all the TV stations as a matter of course in a Big Brother type of way. Either way, it probably wasn't a good thing that we'd come to his attention. I was right.

'Listen, Mr McEwan, given the amount of effort I have wasted trying to speak to you about this matter, I cannot afford to devote any more time to discussing it over the phone. I am due in Edinburgh on Monday morning and I will book a meeting room at the UK Border Agency office in Newington. I assume you know where that is?'

I bit my lip and answered. 'Yes, I think so.'

'Good, I will confirm our appointment by letter. I suggest you get there early.'

'Don't you want my address?'

There was a sarcastic laugh on the other end of the phone. 'I have your address, Mr McEwan. I work for the government, we have everyone's address.' After his sinister pronouncement, he hung up without saying another word.

When Hannah waddled back in from work, I explained my run-in with Donald McDonald.

'Is that really his name?'

I shrugged. 'So he says.'

'And he's English?'

Good point. I tried to think back to our conversation; I didn't remember any trace of a Scottish accent. 'Yeah, I think so.'

'Weird.'

'Well, what do you think?'

Hannah blinked. 'About his parents? They must have had a screw loose.'

'No, not about his parents, about having to go and meet him.'

'Well, it's obviously about Calla and why she's here with us.'

'Duh,' I said annoyingly.

Hannah punched me – hard. 'Don't do that, I might have baby-brain but I don't know what you want me to say. Just go and say we met her on holiday and she's over here staying with us.'

'So I shouldn't mention the baby?'

'What baby?'

'Calla's baby.'

'She hasn't got a baby yet, she's pregnant and as far as we know, that's just a coincidence.'

'Oh OK, so I don't mention that I might be the father or that we had a threesome?'

Hannah shook her head. 'And I thought it was only me that had baby-brain.'

I changed the subject. 'How was work?'

'I've had better days. I had to explain to my boss about the TV interview and reassure him that we don't have a foreign slave living with us. Old Trenchard was there too – I'm sure he was getting off on the whole thing. I'm surprised he didn't ask me to bring Calla to work so that he could letch all over her.'

'Like a bring your pregnant sex slave to work day?'

Hannah laughed. 'Well, I'll maybe stick that in the suggestion box. What about your work?'

'Most people in my place think I'm some kind of hero, having a wife and a sex slave at home,' I said with a laugh.

Hannah shook her head. 'Typical blokes. Still, at least there's been nothing else on the news and nobody's shouted anything at me on the street yet.'

'I don't think we're that famous, Hannah, you were only on the telly for a few minutes.'

We decided not to mention the Home Office referral to Calla when she came back from her walk in the park, just in case it made her insecure. She'd begun to become more confident – both with us and also her environment – and had started going out for walks on her own during the day. If we explained that the authorities were interested in her, it would only undermine her confidence.

Despite my colleagues' reaction to Calla, I'd started to find work stressful. I couldn't concentrate properly; there was too much on my mind and too much going on at home. The impending meeting with Donald McDonald was also weighing heavily on my mind. I didn't deal well with authority figures.

My department had started to build up a backlog and inevitably, Sandra pulled me into her office on the Friday morning.

'Scott, I'm a little worried about you.'

'I'm fine, Sandra, it's just a bit hectic at home just now.'

'Some of the guys have been talking.'

'What about?'

Sandra smiled. 'Thai sex slaves.'

'Oh.'

'I didn't see the news myself, but from what I can gather, you've got some Thai girl living with you.'

'Yeah, it's a bit of a mess.' I trotted out the well-worn story to Sandra, who gave me the same look that Hannah's mum had done.

'I'm not sure I believe you, Scott. I'm sure there's some truth in there somewhere but to be honest, I'm not that bothered. What I do care about is you and the effect it's having on you. You look exhausted, you're not on top of things as you usually are, and the business is suffering as a result, so between us we need to sort things out.'

'What do you suggest?'

'I want you to delegate more. You can ask Paul to take on the service scheduling, there's no reason for you to do that any more.'

'Mm, I'm not sure.'

'Why not?'

'I let him do it during that really cold spell in December and it was a disaster.'

'I didn't know about that, what happened?'

'Well, we got lots of people coming in on spec with stuff going wrong with their cars as always happens when the weather turns crap, and he decided to set up his own triage system based on how pretty the car owner was. It took me ages to sort it out.'

Sandra laughed. 'Well, let's try it again and tell him that if he pulls anything like that this time, he'll find himself in my office for a spanking.'

'He'd probably like that.'

'He might think he would, but he wouldn't. Give it a go, OK?'

I nodded. 'Yep, fine, I'll go and speak to him now.'

As I got up to go Sandra said, 'Scott?'

'Yeah?'

'You need to look after yourself, OK? I'm not sure what's going on in your world but whatever it is, you need to try and relax a bit more. You're wound up so tight something will snap if you're not careful.'

'I'll try, Sandra, I'll try.'

I was hoping for a quieter weekend but in reality I knew that wasn't going to happen. Living with a pregnant wife for most partners was a challenge, I knew, but I had two pregnant women in my life. Early in her pregnancy, Hannah had experienced some minor cravings, but most of these had been easy to satisfy, like ice cream and chocolate chips, fish fingers and chilli sauce, and celery dipped in mango chutney. However, over the last week her cravings had spiked back up and had become … well … weird.

Calla's early cravings were unknown, if indeed she'd had any at all, but her new urge to nibble on chillies and onions was now insatiable. Maybe it was some kind of hormonal osmosis between the two of them but they were running me ragged, trying to keep them supplied with some of the weirdest combination of foods/substances ever.

Saturday morning's requests started as soon as I'd showered and finished my Coco Pops. (They were actually for Lois, who wouldn't eat anything else for breakfast at the moment – do toddlers have cravings too? It certainly felt like it.)

123

I had planned on taking Tessa swimming, but that idea was soon quashed when Hannah called me into the living room where she was lying on the couch, propped up by cushions and watching TV. A large, empty jar of marinated anchovies was lying upended on the floor.

'Scott, I need some anchovies.'

'I just bought you some yesterday.'

'I finished them.'

'A 500-gram jar, already?'

'Yep.'

'But they don't sell them in Morrisons, I'll need to go to the big Asda and we haven't exactly had much luck there recently.'

'I need them, Scott, NOW.'

'OK, OK. I'm going....' I pulled my trainers on and searched around for the car keys. 'Have you seen the car keys?'

'I think Calla's got them.'

'She can't drive.'

'I know, she's just sitting in the car so she can sniff the vanilla air freshener.'

'Why can't she just bring it into the flat and sniff it?'

Hannah shrugged. 'She says it doesn't smell the same as it does when it's in the car.'

I frowned. 'She said that?'

Hannah smiled at me in my harassed state. 'Not exactly, but I worked out that was what she meant. Can you take Tessa with you? I think she's bored.'

'Is Lois OK?'

'I think so, she's out in the car with Calla.'

'Are you all right with her spending time with Calla? We don't really know her that well.'

'I don't think Lois will hurt her.'

'Ha, ha, very funny.'

'Lois likes her, and Calla is very good with her, and with Tessa as well.'

'Lois is two, she likes anybody who talks to her.'

'She doesn't like your dad.'

'That's because he smokes, she doesn't like the way he smells.'

'*I* don't like the way he smells.'

'That's mean, Hannah.'

'Yeah, I know, but it's true. Normally I don't notice, but my sense of smell at the moment is heightened and the stink of cigarette smoke makes me want to vomit. Cigarette smoke, any perfume by Chanel or Calvin Klein, and any kind of aftershave you put on.'

'And yet the scent of pickled anchovies makes you drool.'

'Marinated, not pickled.'

'Yeah, OK, same difference. Maybe I should dab some pick … marinated anchovy juice on my skin and you might want to shag me.'

Hannah looked up at me from the TV for a second, as if she was considering the joke as a serious suggestion.

'Yeah, you can maybe try that later, I am a little horny actually,' she said with a mischievous smile. 'Oh, and can you get some more Pot Noodles too?'

'Curry flavour?'

'Of course. Oh, Scott?'

'Yeah?'

'Probably best to leave Calla in the car if you take her with you, just in case …'

I gave Hannah a quick kiss without breathing, to avoid her marinated-anchovy breath. If we were going to make love later it'd have to be backwards, that breath would wilt a cactus. I went through to the girls' room to find Tessa. She was on the floor, playing with a wooden double-decker bus.

Each seat had a different wooden figure; some were dressed as businessmen on their way to work, some were mothers with children, and an assortment of other characters made up the rest. They were largely unrecognizable now as Tessa had stuck a piece of sticky mango onto each figure.

'Mum said you were bored.'

'I am.'

'So you thought you'd be destructive?'

'What does destructive mean?'

'It means you're ruining your bus.'

Tessa regarded her toy seriously. 'It's not ruined, it's the mango express.'

'Do you want to come to Asda?'

'Is Calla going?'

'Probably, she's in the car already.'

'Is she sniffing the air freshener again?'

'Yeah, she does that a lot.'

'Calla's funny.'

We walked downstairs and out into the street. Our rusty car was parked right outside with Calla in the passenger seat. Lois was holding the steering wheel, pretending to drive. I noticed the keys were already in the ignition so Calla could listen to the radio. I moved Lois into the back, strapped her and Tessa into their seats and jumped in beside our Thai guest.

Calla's cravings were equally as antisocial as my wife's, and the vanilla air freshener could not make a dent in the stench that emanated from her breath when she spoke; it literally made my eyes water.

'Pooh,' said Tessa from behind me.

'Pooh,' echoed Lois.

Calla ignored them. 'Where we go?'

I had to pull my head as far away from her as I could. I pressed the button to open the driver's side window. It was just as well Calla didn't need to shag people for a living any more as she would never get any punters with breath like that.

Maybe cravings were some kind of evolutionary device to keep their mates busy and repulsed during the gestation period, because if so, it was certainly proving effective.

'Where we go?' Calla repeated, sending another wave of toxic breath rolling over me.

'Asda,' I coughed, wiping my watering eyes.

'Ahh, good … I have no chillies and no onions in penalty box.'

My eyes were literally burning. 'Penalty box?'

Calla glanced over at me and frowned. 'Yes, penalty box – penalty box under bed. I get hungry.'

I didn't make any more comments, mainly because I didn't want Calla to talk any more or I might crash the car due to blurred vision, and it was pointless trying to make any sense out of my pregnant women's desires as logic didn't come into it. Mr Spock would have had a nervous breakdown by now.

The phrase 'my pregnant women' even sounded outlandish in my own head, and I could barely make any sense of it all. I found myself smiling and Calla noticed.

'What funny?'

I shook my head. 'Nothing, just thinking, Calla, about how ridiculous this all is.'

'What is this diculous?'

I could feel her eyes burning into the side of my head. Calla got frustrated when we used words she did not understand, and she was frustrated a lot.

When we had first encountered her in Thailand, our initial impression that her English was good was based on her communicating what she wanted us to do in the bedroom, a place she was comfortable and used to.

127

We'd since worked out that most of her English lessons in Thailand had focused on English premiership football teams and for some incongruous reason, old railway steam engines. We could only assume her teacher had been obsessed with both. Had she been able to take the current Manchester United first team out for a day trip on the Flying Scotsman, she would have been in her element.

As a result, her English was much poorer than we'd initially thought and our Scottish accents certainly didn't help. I did, however, harbour a suspicion that she understood a lot more than she let on, and this came across most obviously when she was annoyed, like now.

'What is this diculous?' she repeated again, louder this time.

My eyes were watering under the assault of her chilli breath. I coughed and tried to lean my head out of the window. I opened all the windows in the car.

'Where you go?' Calla asked, concern on her face.

'Asda.'

'No, where you go with head?'

I laughed. 'Calla, your breath stinks. I can't see to drive, my eyes are watering so much.'

'Calla not stink, I had bath.'

'You didn't bath your mouth.'

Calla glared at me. 'People not bath mouth, you say stupid words.'

I couldn't argue with that. Thankfully, we'd arrived at the supermarket and I pulled up near to the entrance. When I turned off the engine and went to get Lois out of her car seat, I discovered an unforeseen circumstance caused by driving with the windows open.

'Lois, where are your shoes and socks?'

Lois stared up at me then gazed forlornly at her feet. 'I no see.'

'No, I don't see them either. Tessa, where are Lois's shoes and socks?'

Tessa was engrossed, colouring some fairies in a book with crayons. 'I haven't got them.'

'I didn't say you *had* them, have you *seen* them?'

'No.'

'Calla, do you know what happened to Lois's shoes and socks?'

Calla leaned back in her seat and motioned with her arm out the window. I was furious. 'She threw her shoes out of the window and you just let her?'

'Letter? What letter? I have no letter.'

I stared at her for a moment; was she taking the piss or what? This was one of those times when her language skills were called into question. She kept a straight face even when I glared at her. I remembered she was a pretty good actress too and I wasn't convinced.

'Right, well, you'll all just have to stay here with Calla while I go and get the shopping.'

Nobody seemed too bothered, in fact, I was beginning to think my daughters would rather spend time with Calla than with me and Hannah. Given my current stress levels, I could understand that, I wasn't exactly Mr Fun at the moment.

Tessa carried on colouring, Calla went back to her magic tree, and Lois played with her bare feet as if she'd never seen them before. I stomped off in a huff.

There were no roving TV interviewers hanging around the foyer today so I was able to shop in peace. I did receive a few strange looks from the checkout girl when all I bought was two huge jars of marinated anchovies, raw chillies, curry flavoured Pot Noodles and a large net of red onions.

Back home, I left the girls munching their disgusting combinations and stinking out the flat, and went to the park with Tessa and Lois.

Hannah and Calla were becoming more and more comfortable in each other's company. Probably because given their antisocial eating habits, no other adults could tolerate being in the same room with them for more than a few minutes.

The following morning, shortly before I was due to head out for more strange supplies, I was handed a reprieve when Dave showed up and volunteered to go in his Mini Cooper.

Dave used to appear fairly regularly for Sunday lunch before Hannah got pregnant, but he had been a stranger lately. I couldn't blame him, given that the flat stunk. The previous weekend had also seen the start of the pregnant farting competition.

Now my wife, like most women, would never own up to breaking wind. In fact, if you believed her, she actually never needed to do this and her bodily waste exhibited no smell whatsoever. I'd shared a bathroom with her for nearly seven years and knew differently. Last Sunday evening, Hannah had been moaning and groaning on the sofa, curled up in pain. I was on the verge of phoning either NHS 24 or the midwife when suddenly she let rip with the most enormous fart I'd ever heard from a woman. The look of bliss on her face at this release was amazing to witness as the build-up of noxious gases, caused by her less than perfect diet, was released from her lower intestine, providing immediate pain relief.

However, the pleasure was very short-lived as the room was suddenly filled with the most disgusting odour that physically assaulted the senses. It was like an army of tiny marines, tunnelling into my nasal passages with smelly little axes.

On the chair opposite Hannah, Calla was equally

appalled until she smiled and quietly released her own toxic mixture into the air from her rear end. I opened the window and left the room until the stench had dissipated.

In my head, there was something not right about two pretty women breaking wind like extras from the bean-eating scene in *Blazing Saddles*.

As I discovered over the coming days, and evenings, mixing the gases that arose from digested anchovies, curry Pot Noodles, raw chillies and onions produced something close to the stench of a decomposing corpse and I soon learned to disappear as soon as the flatulence started. The amazing thing was that the two of them would happily sit amongst their own smells and I started to wonder if it was being used as a tool to get me out of the living room so they could get the remote control to themselves. Calla in particular, that first evening, immediately grabbed the remote and flicked to *You've Been Framed* – the best of the best bits. Tessa and Lois weren't bothered much and thought it hilarious when their mummy let rip.

Dave had yet to witness the evening stink-fest so he was still unaware what was behind the lingering smell in our small home. I suspect one of the reasons why he liked coming to our chaotic home was that it made him more appreciative of his child-free, stress-free life.

Calla seemed to like Dave. On the two or three occasions he'd stopped by, she'd been pleased to see him, but then again, given she was stuck with me and Hannah, she might have been glad to see even Russell Brand if he'd turned up and offered to take her out in his car.

'I go with you to shop?'

Dave looked to me for approval. I said, 'It'll be a tight squeeze.' Dave laughed.

'Minis are much bigger than they used to be.' He helped Calla to her feet and she waddled through to get her coat.

As I walked them to the front door, Calla asked Dave, 'Do you have magic tree?'

He glanced back at me, puzzled. 'Is that some kind of Thai drug?'

I shook my head. 'You'll see.' To Calla I said, 'Yes, Dave's got a magic tree.'

Calla went ahead and Dave whispered, 'What's a magic tree, is it some kind of euphemism for my cock?'

I laughed out loud. 'Dave, I might be wrong but I think the last thing Calla needs at the moment is your cock. Besides, you'll not get anywhere near her; you'll need to open your window when you get in the car.'

'No way, it's raining.'

'Your funeral.'

'What?'

'You'll see.'

'What's the magic tree, Scott?'

'Air freshener.'

'Oh yeah, so it is. I've got one in the Mini.'

I smiled. 'She'll be your friend for life.'

About an hour later, Dave arrived back with Calla, and he looked a little shell-shocked. I wasn't surprised, especially if he'd been driving with the windows closed. Calla sat back down in her chair, and squealed with delight as *You've Been Framed – The Lost Tapes*, came on. She pulled a red onion from her 'penalty box' and started to munch. Hannah dipped into her anchovies. I couldn't watch so I left the room, and left Dave staring at both of them in what I could only describe as appreciative amazement.

Chapter Thirteen

I ARRIVED EARLY next morning (as recommended) at the address where Donald McDonald had asked to meet me. I wasn't particularly happy at having to give up a morning's work to attend, but didn't feel as if I had much choice.

I hadn't been in the Scottish Office building before and was surprised by the high level of security. I even had to walk through a metal detector as if it was some downtown Detroit high school. Eventually, a large, sweaty man with wire-framed glasses led me through to a pleasant office with views of Arthur's Seat from the window. He left me there with assurances that Mr McDonald would be along soon.

The room itself was modest with a large, round meeting table that had a number of chairs tucked away neatly underneath it at regular intervals. When Donald McDonald entered a few minutes later, I was taken aback. For some reason I had been expecting a tall, strapping bloke with an imposing physique. I'm not sure why, maybe because someone with such an odd name should be able to intimidate others who might want to take the piss.

Instead, he was short and thin and bore an uncanny resemblance to Charlie Chaplin, right down to the tiny bushy moustache that clung, defying gravity, onto his upper lip. He even had similar sad eyes that were part of Chaplin's formidable comic toolkit. He didn't sport a hat or cane, but perhaps he kept those in a closet somewhere else in the building. I don't remember how Charlie Chaplin spoke as most of his movies I remember from my childhood were silent. I would imagine that his voice had an American accent so Mr McDonald's Southern Counties drawl didn't fit with the rest of the image.

'Thank you for being so prompt, Mr McEwan, I've got a busy day ahead of me and I want to get this ... err ... business concluded swiftly.'

I decided an apology would be a good start, and might help me to worm my way into his good books. 'I'm sorry about the confusion on the phone, and for mistaking you for a salesman.'

Charlie, as I thought of him, leaned back in his chair and stared at me for a moment before answering. 'As regards to the phone calls, forget about it, a lesson for both of us.'

As he had accepted my apology so gracefully I decided to mention the security. 'I have to ask about getting into this place, are metal detectors *really* necessary?'

His demeanour changed and he stared intently at me; his eyes didn't blink and I had to look away. Having won some kind of civil-servant staring contest he eventually said, 'I can't really comment on the details of government security requirements, but suffice to say, they have been deemed necessary due to the frequent threats we receive in these offices from terrorist groups and ... err, well ... others.'

'Others?'

'Others. Now, turning to the matter in hand. First of all, I need to make you aware that the British Government does not take any accusations or allegations of human slavery lightly. We can't afford to – given our recent high-profile stance on such abuses in other countries – and whilst I realize that much of the media coverage of your situation is probably overstated, we cannot be seen to stand by and do nothing. You must understand that.'

I was annoyed with his attitude. 'Calla is not a slave, she came here on her own, nobody forced her and she's only staying with us until she can find some alternative accommodation. That's it, pure and simple – everything that was said and printed about her and us was nonsense.'

'That's as maybe, but in order to satisfy my department we will need to look closer at your … mmm… what would I call it … your domestic situation. Once our review is complete, we can take things from there.'

'What does "a review of our domestic situation" mean? If you're talking about contacting social services, then that was what we were going to do in order to find Calla somewhere else to live.'

Charlie shook his head, and pulled a sheet of paper from his briefcase. He then fished in his jacket pocket, pulled out and donned a pair of thin wire glasses. 'No, in the circumstances, I feel it appropriate to allocate one of our Edinburgh-based case officers to work with you directly.'

'What does "working with us directly" mean? Both my wife and I work. We have two young children and don't have a lot of time to attend meetings and stuff.'

Charlie sat back in his chair, clasped his hands together and peered at me over the top of his specs.

'Would you say, Mr McEwan, that your life is busy and at times rather hectic?'

'Of course it is. Most couples with young kids would tell you the same.'

He nodded to himself and made some notes. I tried to

read what he was writing but he pulled the paper closer towards himself and covered the notes with his hand, as if I was some naughty schoolboy who wanted to copy his answer.

'Do I get a photocopy of those?'

'My notes?'

'Yes.'

'No.'

'Why not?'

'For confidentiality reasons. Now, would you say your life would be easier if you had access to some domestic help, perhaps a nanny or housekeeper?'

'Probably, but it's a moot question as we don't have the luxury of being able to afford such a thing.'

More nodding and more notes.

'I suppose that if you had access to such help that cost nothing apart from food and board, then this might be attractive to you?'

I shook my head, annoyed at having fallen into his trap, but realized that no matter what I'd said, I would have no doubt ended up in the same place. I decided that as well as bearing an uncanny resemblance to a long-dead silent movie star, Mr McDonald was a manipulative sod.

He smiled, knowing he had me. 'Whilst I don't personally believe you have brought a domestic slave over from Thailand, Mr McEwan, I need to satisfy my department that we have investigated the situation thoroughly and are happy that Miss Hi Tee is here legally and not suffering any kind of coercion or exploitation.'

'You could just ask her.'

'Oh, we will, but we also need to observe for ourselves that she is not subject to any kind of … brainwashing or duplicity.'

Brainwashing! I couldn't believe my ears. Hannah and

I were as incapable of brainwashing as Charlie was of possessing a sense of humour. We probably couldn't do duplicity either, but I couldn't say for certain as I didn't know what that meant. I just sat there stunned while he carried on.

'There is also the question of your wife ...' he paused and consulted his notes, '... Hannah, who admits taking money away from Miss Hi Tee when she arrived in exchange for some biscuits.'

'It was a tenner. That's all she had on her when she arrived.'

'She came all the way from Thailand on a ten-pound note? I find that hard to—'

'No, she didn't come on a tenner ... what kind of person can travel halfway across the globe on a tenner? That's silly.'

'Are you insulting me, Mr McEwan?'

I frowned at him. 'I don't think so,' I answered uncertainly.

'You don't think so?'

I sighed. 'Well, what I meant was I didn't mean to if I did.'

Charlie stared at his notes for a minute. 'So why did your wife take the money away and give her some biscuits?'

'She didn't. She took the money so it wouldn't get lost and put it in the biscuit tin. Calla only had ten pounds left.'

'Did she get some biscuits?'

'I think so.'

Donald seemed happy that Calla had been given biscuits, as he nodded and made some detailed notes that I still couldn't see. 'OK, it also says here that she was dressed in rags and only allowed to eat honey.'

'I think whoever does your research has got their wires crossed. She was given some of my wife's clothes to wear because her own clothes weren't suitable for a Scottish

137

winter, and I don't think my wife would be very happy with you referring to them as rags, to be honest.' I then watched his moustache twitch as he pondered my explanation.

'What about the honey?'

'Oh, this is ridiculous. Honey and biscuits? Surely you have more important things to be doing than asking me about honey and biscuits?'

Charlie stared at me as if honey and biscuits were the most important things in the world. He remained silent until I felt I had to speak.

'Hannah took her to Asda to get some honey because we didn't have any in the flat and Calla wanted some. You know what? I don't think she's even touched it. All she wants to eat now is raw onions and chillies, so we ended up in this mess buying honey that Calla hasn't even touched.'

'You mean she would rather eat onions and chillies than honey?'

I nodded.

'Why?'

I shrugged. 'Because she's pregnant.'

'That's not in my notes.'

'Somehow that doesn't surprise me, Charlie.'

'Charlie?'

'Sorry ... Mr McDonald.'

'Who's Charlie?'

I couldn't believe that nobody had ever told him he bore an uncanny resemblance to Charlie Chaplin, but his puzzled expression seemed to indicate they hadn't. For the first time since we'd met, I'd felt that I'd had him on the back foot with the Calla pregnancy omission and then I had to go and spoil it by calling him Charlie. I really didn't want to tell him who he looked like in case it landed me in even more hot water.

'Err, I just have a tendency to call people Charlie. I don't have a great memory for names ... so I just call everyone Charlie.'

He regarded me strangely; I couldn't blame him for that.

'That must make your life rather complicated.'

I nodded, not wanting to go down this strange conversational road any longer. He sat upright in his chair and shuffled some of his paperwork.

'Right, well ... erm ... as this is an unusual situation for us, I have given it some considerable thought. What I propose is that one of our officers should undertake some close surveillance with your family. In light of this, I have already taken the liberty of appointing the case officer prior to our meeting. Her name is Fiona Montgomery and she will handle the surveillance and interaction with your family both discreetly and sensitively. Given Miss Hi Tee's current condition, she is a ... well, a fortunate choice.'

'A fortunate choice?'

'Yes, you'll understand when you meet her. She has no special dietary requirements and will bring her own toiletries.'

'Toiletries?'

'Well, yes, she wouldn't want to use your toothpaste or your shampoo or other domestic items.'

'Are you saying she's moving in with us?'

'Just temporarily.'

'Our flat is tiny.'

'Mrs Montgomery is very adaptable, I wouldn't worry about it.'

'Not worry about it? How would you feel if a stranger turned up and moved into your home? This is stupid, I refuse to comply with this crap. The whole idea is totally absurd.'

'Well, the alternative is that I pass everything to the social work department and recommend that they treat you as an urgent referral. I would also need to inform the police, who would treat a report from the Home Office very seriously indeed. It is likely they would want to question your family and friends at length, and their investigation is likely to be very intrusive, wide-ranging and disruptive. It would include detailed background checks ...'

'We are honest people who work hard and neither of us has ever been in any kind of trouble.' I was openly hostile now; this was blackmail.

'I am sure you are, but the police would need to satisfy themselves of that and they would appoint an interpreter to ensure that Miss Hi Tee could communicate any thoughts and grievances she had. It would be very disruptive for your family for quite a long time. What I am proposing is the much easier and quicker solution.'

I tried to keep my temper in check; getting angry would not help anything. He was on his own turf and would continue to run rings around me if we continued the conversation. I needed to get out and speak to Hannah. I wished she'd come with me.

'I'll need to speak to my wife.'

I could tell Charlie knew he'd won. He probably always did, but I wasn't going to give him any satisfaction.

'I'll phone you tomorrow, we need this evening to discuss your proposal.'

He nodded. 'OK, here's one of Fiona's cards, just phone her when you've decided what to do and she'll arrange things with you. If you decide against my recommendation, Mrs Montgomery will handle the social work and police referral. I'm sure she won't mind you calling her Charlie as long as you explain why.'

I stared at him, trying to work out if he was taking the piss, but his face remained impassive. I had to have the parting shot.

'I'll remember that, thank you. I just hope she likes honey and biscuits as we seem to have a surplus of them at the moment.'

I left the office with my face burning with anger and indignation. As I stormed back through the reception area, I began to understand why they needed a lot of security. If many people left the building feeling like I did, it certainly was in danger of being blown up.

Having wasted a morning with Donald McDonald, I then had a hectic afternoon trying to catch up at work and as a result, it was nearly eight o'clock when I got home. I'd texted Hannah with a rough description of what had happened and by the time I made it through my front door, I'd more or less come to terms with my fate. Hannah was not as angry as I'd been but then she'd not been subjected to the dismissive arrogance of Mr McDonald. I helped get the girls to bed and then made sure Calla was happily seated in front of the TV, watching *You've Been Framed* – the animal special. I could understand her addiction to the show as the language skills required to watch it were minimal.

I then made some tea, and Hannah and I discussed our options.

'We could refuse to take part in this stupid charade,' I suggested. 'But that would mean we might have social workers and the police all over us.'

'Do you think he would really do all that?'

'Based on my experience today, yeah, I think he would.'

'So we need to let this … what's her name, move in with us for a while?'

'Fiona.'

'Not Charlie?' she asked mischievously.

'Don't you start.'

Hannah got uncertainly to her feet and came and sat on my knee, draped her arm over my shoulder and kissed me firmly on the lips.

'Oh well, one more won't make much difference now. Maybe we should just buy a huge bed and all share it, you know, like at the beginning of *Charlie and the Chocolate Factory*.'

I laughed. 'Mm, maybe not – sharing a bed with a stranger is how we got into this mess in the first place.' I moved Hannah off my knee – she was getting really heavy – and handed her Fiona Montgomery's card. 'Can I leave it to you to phone her and make the arrangements?'

Hannah took the card and put it in her handbag. 'Yeah, fine. You never know, maybe we'll all become great friends.'

I admired her optimism.

Chapter Fourteen

THE FOLLOWING EVENING, I duly arrived home from work to find Mrs Fiona Montgomery sitting at the kitchen table, drinking tea with Hannah like she *was* some old friend around for a chat. Hannah had phoned her first thing and she'd arrived with her suitcase some time after three. She must have been one of the most efficient government workers I'd ever encountered.

'Where are the girls?' I asked, wondering how the two of them had managed to get peace and quiet enough to talk uninterrupted.

'Under our bed.'

'What are they doing?'

'Eating their dinner.'

'Oh.'

I wondered what the social worker/civil servant (whichever she was) thought about that. Her neutral expression gave nothing away. Fiona had light-brown hair and sky-blue eyes. She appeared to be, in my estimation, quite pretty in a willowy way with a small nose and narrow lips. She smiled at me, which was more than I'd got from Donald McDonald, and held out her hand, which I took and shook gently.

'I know this is awkward for both of you and this strategy is not something we usually employ, but occasionally it is the easiest way to bring about a speedy resolution.' Mrs Montgomery's voice was soft and educated, and immediately made me feel inferior given my limited and erratic schooling.

I nodded and remained mute.

'It would be easier if you called me Fifi as Mrs Montgomery is a bit of a mouthful and I don't like Fiona very much. My maiden name was Dunn, so it took a while to get used to my longer, married name. We considered using both our names hyphenated but that would have been even worse.'

I nodded again, and was beginning to feel like one of those dogs you see in the back of cars.

Hannah rescued me. 'It takes Scott a while to wind down when he comes in from work, he'll be much more chatty later.'

Fifi smiled, she had nice teeth. 'I can empathize with that, sometimes when I get home I need a long soak in the bath before I feel like talking about my day to Tom.'

I assumed Tom was her husband, but he could just as easily have been her cat, I supposed.

'Tom works in banking so his days are not usually as stressful as mine.'

Obviously not her cat then, unless Tom was an extremely clever cat.

I found my voice. 'I need a shower, I'm sure Charlie … err, Mr McDonald mentioned that I work in the service department of a car dealership, so it's grime and oil all day for me.'

'No, he didn't, but it's in your file. I'll move and let you sit down, you must be hungry.'

As she struggled to extricate herself from her seat, I was shocked to see what she had been concealing from me under the table. I flicked my gaze to Hannah, who was grinning at me as she'd been waiting for me to notice. Given my recent run of bad luck, it should not have been a surprise to discover that Mrs Fiona Montgomery was heavily pregnant.

I assumed this was what Charlie Chaplin had meant when he'd described her as a 'fortunate choice'. Not very fortunate for me, I decided.

After I'd showered and eaten, we all moved through to the living room where there was a little more room to accommodate three lumbering ladies. Then at 6.30 prompt Dave arrived. I'd forgotten that I'd agreed to go out with him for a beer and was glad to see someone who wasn't carrying a baby, though his growing beer belly made him look like he was going on about five months.

I introduced him to Mrs Montgomery with no explanation of her presence or the fact that our flat had progressed from crowded to claustrophobic. I hadn't in all honesty managed to mentally process everything yet. Hannah was obviously amused. Calla had been introduced earlier and seemed to like Fifi. I suspected it was maybe because she spoke more clearly (and slower) than Hannah and I, which allowed her to understand better.

Fifi behaved as if she invaded strangers' homes every day. She was quite imposing and even without heels she was easily as tall as me. Her ability to either look down or at least meet people's eyelines was, I'm sure, a great help in her occupation.

Dave had a bemused look on his face, and I knew I would be in for a third-degree interrogation as soon as we were alone.

Hannah had made up a temporary bed for Fifi in the

living room. With Calla in there too, it had started to resemble a refugee centre for pregnant women. We had inflated a double, blow-up bed which we occasionally used for guests. This had been pushed against the wall near the TV and covered with a fitted bottom sheet and double duvet that had been in the hall cupboard for six months. The duvet smelt a little musty but given the amount of stale and noxious digestive gases currently inhabiting our small room of an evening, the duvet's delicate scent might not even be noticed.

The distraction of bed-making seemed like a good time to quietly sneak away for a quick drink, and Dave and I disappeared before anybody asked us to do anything pregnancy-related. Calla was visibly disappointed to see Dave leave without speaking to her.

'God, it's nice to get a break from all that,' I said with a sigh as we nipped into the nearest quiet bar.

'So what's new?'

I took a huge glug of beer and stared past Dave and the scrolling news headline on the news channel that was playing on the huge television fitted to the wall. A man had shot someone in south London and armed police had the house under siege. Now that was a good word. That's how I felt, under siege.

'What's new? Well, apart from living under siege in a flat full of lactating flatulent women, Jane's looking for a new man to have babies with and she's got her eye on you,' I teased.

'Bit of a cliché that, isn't it, the bridesmaid and best man from your wedding?'

'She's nice.'

'She's intense. My first wife was intense – intense and insane. So thanks but, no, thanks.'

'I thought your first wife was wishy-washy.'

146

'No, that was Gemma, my second wife, that's why I married her – she was the polar opposite from Lorraine, the intense one.'

'I get them mixed up.'

'Just as well I'm not Mickey Rooney, then.'

'Wayne's dad?'

'What are you talking about?'

'Wayne Rooney.'

'Mickey Rooney was the famous film star who had eight wives and died with only £10k in the bank.'

'Eight wives? I'm surprised he had that much left.'

'Exactly, but Wayne Rooney … what are you like? Not everything revolves around football, you know?' Dave finished his pint in three gulps and ordered another.

'Still, eight wives, you've got a way to go before you equal that, then, Dave.'

'I'm never getting married again.'

'Why?'

'I'm crap at being married. It's bad for my constitution.'

'And your bank balance.'

'Yeah, that too. Listen, why do married men die before their wives?'

'I don't know.'

'Because they're told to.'

We both had a good laugh and that helped me relax a little.

With Fifi's arrival, I suspected that I would be walking on eggshells around the flat for a few days. Her pregnant presence certainly made me feel even more outnumbered and outgunned. I was the only male in a household of five females.

As expected, Dave wanted to know what was going on. 'So how come you've got three pregnant women in your flat, anyway? And another thing, I don't buy into this 'misunderstanding" story, especially not after you were plastered all over the national news.'

'It was local news, I don't think it made it beyond STV.'

'And the local paper.'

'Nobody reads that.'

'I did. So come on, what's going on?'

I smiled. Maybe it was time to come clean. I took a big gulp of beer and blurted out, 'To cut a long story short, Hannah and I had a threesome on honeymoon with Calla.'

Dave choked on his beer and coughed and spluttered for a minute or two. He recovered and said, 'That was horrible, I've got beer coming down my nose.'

'Nice.'

'How the hell did you wangle that?'

'Actually, it was Hannah's idea.'

'Wow, your wife is brilliant.'

'As you can see, it didn't turn out that brilliant.'

Dave laughed and wiped his nose. 'Do you think she's a closet lesbian?'

'Who? Calla?'

'Well … yeah, maybe, but I meant Hannah.'

I laughed out loud. 'No, I don't think so. She said she just wanted to try it.'

'And did she?'

'Oh yeah.'

'Wow! How did that feel?'

'Pretty erotic, but when it was my turn the condom broke.'

'Ooh yuck – you might have caught something nasty.'

'Yeah, that was our first thought, so I got tested for everything but it was fine apart from a thrush-type thing.'

'So what is Calla doing over here, then?'

'She claims that I'm the father of her unborn child.'

'Oh. That's not good. Was she not on anything?'

'What, like drugs?'

'No, the pill or one of those things they shoot up there on a spring thing.'

'A coil.'

'Yeah.'

'Apparently not.'

'So she comes all the way here to confront you, and you take her in?'

'She turned up during a blizzard all wet and shivery, what choice did we have?'

Dave frowned. 'How did she know where you lived?'

'She nicked a label off one of our suitcases.'

'That was clever, and a little devious.'

'That's what Jane said.'

'Surely though, she wouldn't come all this way if you weren't the father. I mean, it must be pretty easy to prove?'

'It's easy to prove *after* the baby is born, not so easy beforehand.'

Dave nodded. 'So you've got to wait until then?'

I nodded.

'OK, but why have you got yet another pregnant woman staying with you? Is she going to take part in a pregnant lesbian threesome?'

I laughed. 'God, I hope not.' I went on to explain the government's intervention into our little predicament.

After I'd finished, Dave thought for a while. 'Mm, obviously the news made it further than just the local papers, then. What if she puts in a report saying you *are* keeping her as some kind of slave?'

'She can't because we're not. She can plainly see that we are victims of circumstance.'

'That sounds like the title to some old historical novel.'

'Yeah, maybe, it certainly feels like I'm living in the middle of some kind of melodrama. She's not managed to have a proper conversation with Calla yet; once she does she'll realize that we are not up to anything dodgy.'

'So this … what's her name again?'

'Fifi, she likes to be called Fifi.'

'This Fifi doesn't know yet that you and Hannah had a threesome with Calla in Thailand?'

'Not yet, no.'

'Nor that Calla has accused you of being the father of her child?'

'No.'

'That's not going to raise her opinion of you and Hannah much.'

'Probably not, no.'

'Shouldn't you tell her first?'

'Why?'

'Well, you said Calla's English isn't great. Just in case something gets lost or mixed up in translation.'

'I hadn't thought of that. You're right, Hannah and I should really tell her first. That'll be our task later on this evening.'

Chapter Fifteen

AFTER AN HOUR and two beers, I returned home alone and a little more relaxed than when I had left. In the kitchen, I made myself a cup of decaf coffee (the full-fat version would give me insomnia for the remainder of the night). Calla was sitting, eating one of Tessa's Peppa Pig yoghurts and putting on nail varnish. She briefly glanced up at me.

'Where Dave?'

'He's gone home, Calla, he told me to say hi.'

She frowned. 'Why he no wife?'

'Erm, he had a wife once, well, twice actually, but not any more.'

I could see her trying to process the information. 'Where wife go?'

'Dave's wife left.'

'Why?'

'Err, because she didn't love him any more.'

'Why?'

This was starting to sound like one of the conversations I often had with Lois. 'I don't know, Calla, it's complicated.'

'What is this complicated?'

I was saved by Fifi coming into the kitchen and sitting opposite Calla, followed by Tessa, Lois and Hannah, which made the room crowded and noisy. Tessa and Lois treated the addition of another mother-to-be to our household with indifference, viewing her as just another adult to torment and play with.

'I know it's not really any of my business,' Fifi said. 'But shouldn't Lois's speech be better than it is? I don't really understand much of what she says. I've written a few things down that I've heard her say. Do you know what they mean?'

I smiled. 'I'll try.'

'OK, earlier she said something about "nit pickers" and got really excited.'

Hannah giggled. 'That's gym nippers, a class she goes to where she gets to run around and do basic gymnastics.'

Fifi nodded seriously. 'Who are "Hairy and Codger"?'

I frowned, then remembered. 'That's Daisy and Connor, kids who go to "nit pickers" with her.'

'For some reason, she also seems to have something of a Yorkshire accent. If things don't improve, you might need to consider some kind of speech therapy for her.'

'What? Because she's got a Yorkshire accent? You're liable to piss off a good chunk of Northern England if you're not careful,' I said with half a smile.

'No, not because of her accent; her word formation isn't where it should be.'

The accent thing was puzzling but I assumed it would fade with time. I wasn't convinced speech therapy was necessary. Lois seemed sharp enough. Yes, her speech wasn't as good as Tessa's had been at the same stage, but we knew kids developed differently.

Fifi then observed, 'Shouldn't Tessa be in bed by now? It's nearly eight o'clock.'

'If we put Tessa to bed before eight, she doesn't sleep.'

Fifi shook her head and sighed in exasperation. 'When my baby is born, we'll have set ground rules, including when they get to eat and sleep, when they start solid food and when they need to be toilet trained.' The way Fifi described this, using a determined voice, made it sound like being a prisoner, not a child in a nursery.

But she had more. 'Thinking further ahead, we've even sourced a lovely little private nursery for when our baby is older that will hopefully give them a little edge when they start school. We also plan to get our children – if we are lucky enough to have more than one – regularly assessed privately, and if they are lacking or falling behind in any areas we'll arrange for some tuition so they can catch up. If things carry on as they are, we should be able to afford private schooling and that would ensure our children have a better chance of getting into somewhere amazing like Oxford or Cambridge, but St Andrew's would be a decent fallback plan. If it's good enough for our future king and queen, it's probably good enough for us.'

Hannah and I were silent after our visitor's little speech; our main concern at the moment was preventing Tessa and Lois from killing each other. Tessa was attending the local primary school, which was OK, but we had not thought too much beyond helping her with her homework. Hiring tutors and 'private everything else' was *way* beyond anything we could reasonably afford. I glanced over at Hannah and knew she was thinking the same as me – were we failing as parents?

I shrugged. We loved our girls and we were trying to raise them the best we could; so what if bedtime slipped a bit now and then? Fifi's middle-class values and dreams were unrealistic, for us anyway, and probably for the majority of parents in these austere times. I addressed Mrs

Montgomery, who had gone all misty-eyed, dreaming of her children's perfect lives.

'What happens if they want to follow a career in hairdressing or become a rock god?'

My comments snapped Fifi out of her reverie. I had rattled her cage, as intended.

'Err, well neither of those options offer ... err, I'm not sure what a rock god is and we'll consult with our child at all stages of their development, and their wishes will be considered, of course.'

I said nothing more. The thought of consulting with either of our two was hilarious. Tessa was a great negotiator, especially when it came to a way of wangling more sweets but consultation around her career aspirations seemed absurd. At the moment she wanted to be a nursery teacher, but that was only because she had adored Gina, one of her teachers. Next week, after a visit to see the pandas, she might want to be a zookeeper.

I also realized that Fifi hadn't had a baby yet and it would be an interesting exercise to revisit our conversation in two or three years' time. It was obvious that she and her partner had a lot more money than us, but that certainly didn't mean they'd be any better parents. I resisted going any further with our conversation as I remembered she was here to make an assessment of us, and antagonizing her would only be counterproductive and likely to increase my own stress level into the bargain. Instead I was conciliatory.

'Well, it sounds like you've got it all planned out; I'm afraid we're not that organized. Now, if you don't mind, we need to get Tessa and Lois ready for bed.'

After the girls were tucked up in bed, I ventured into the kitchen, but only Calla was there, sitting at the kitchen table, drawing. She loved drawing, and although she was brilliant at helping my daughters with their attempts at art, it was when they were in bed that she got to do some of her own stuff. I peered over her shoulder. She was in the middle of sketching a pencil portrait of Tessa. It was very good, the girl had a gift. It was a shame she'd not been able to do something with it in her home country.

'That's very good, Calla, it looks just like her.'

She looked up at me and smiled. She was very cute, but her onion-chilli breath sent me scuttling from the room. I ventured into the living-room-cum-refugee-centre in search of Hannah and Fifi. We'd agreed, following my chat with Dave, that we needed to fill our inquisitor in on the real reason why Calla was with us. We'd agreed that Hannah would do most of the talking.

'So, I expect you're wondering why Calla turned up out of the blue to stay with us?' Hannah asked brightly.

Fifi pulled her file out of her bag. 'It says in here that you claim she misunderstood a casual conversation and took it as an invite to come and work as an au pair.'

Hannah smiled sweetly. 'Well, that certainly *is* one version of what we've been telling everyone.'

Fifi opened her file. 'But there's more to it than that, I assume?'

My wife nodded, lowered her eyes and blurted out, 'Yeah, a little bit. We involved Calla, who was working as a prostitute in Thailand, in a *ménage à trois*.'

Fifi looked up from her file with a surprised expression, then cocked her head to one side, chewed her bottom lip and said, 'OK, I can understand why you might want to keep that secret and it does add a little credence to the notion of her being a sex slave, I suppose. What it doesn't do, though, is quite explain why she travelled halfway around the world to Edinburgh.'

Hannah kept her eyes lowered. 'Well, whilst she was with my husband, the ... err ... condom failed and she

155

claims that he is the father of her baby.'

'I see.' Her tone implied that she disapproved, which didn't surprise me, but I was surprised there was not more of a shocked reaction given my impression of her so far. She retained a thoughtful and businesslike manner. I assumed she was used to dealing with strange and difficult domestic situations, which allowed her to remain impartial. She wrote some more notes in the file. 'And this is why you have accepted Miss Hi Tee's version of events?'

We both nodded.

'How did she find you? I assume you had left the country before her pregnancy was known.'

I chipped in, 'She took a luggage tag from one of our suitcases before she left our hotel.'

Fifi continued, almost thinking out aloud. 'Whilst I can understand her doing that as … mmm, what would you call it? An insurance policy. The decision to travel all the way here in the hope that you would take her in is … well … at best optimistic and at worst foolhardy.'

Fifi closed her file and brushed her hair back from her face with a hand. She looked initially at Hannah, who failed to meet her gaze, then me. 'Have you been able to establish if her claim is valid and that the baby is indeed yours?'

I shook my head. 'No, it's difficult to do a test before the baby is born because it means inserting a needle into the womb, but it's very easy to find out after the birth, so most doctors won't do it.'

'Given the circumstances, you would be within your rights to demand she undertakes the procedure.'

Hannah held her bump defensively. 'I wouldn't do that to my baby so I won't demand she does it to hers and risk harming it.'

'Do you like Miss Hi Tee?'

The question was directed at both of us. Hannah and I

met each other's eyes and Hannah replied, 'She's a sweet girl. We didn't know her in Thailand, obviously, but she's got a lovely nature and is very good with our children. I suppose we feel guilty about what happened out there. When we first met her, she seemed so confident and assertive, but that was her in her comfort zone and she was working. Now that we've got to know her a bit more, she seems like a nice person, though our conversations have been limited by the language problem.'

'So this might be a reason then to suspect that you are taking advantage of her, and treating her like a second-class citizen.'

'But we're not', Hannah objected, 'if anyone's been taken advantage of it's us. We've taken her in, and looked after her.'

'Why did you decide to tell me all of this?'

'We thought it better you find out from us than from Calla,' said Hannah decisively.

'I don't condone or agree with what you did, but I do admire the stance you've taken on the foetal test. One more thing, have you any idea how she cleared immigration so easily? They are usually very reluctant to let foreign nationals through without at least some assurance that they have a sponsor or a work permit. Neither of you have officially notified immigration that you are sponsoring her, have you?'

I shook my head. 'No, how could we? We didn't even know she was coming.'

'OK, fair point. I'll ask Miss Hi Tee about that.'

Fifi struggled to her feet. 'Is it OK if I ask Miss Hi Tee to join us?'

We both nodded.

Calla looked worried when she came back through with Fifi and sat beside Hannah, who put a protective arm around her. The two of them faced Fifi, who visibly winced, I assume under the onslaught of onion/chilli/anchovy breath.

I looked on and wondered at the turn of events that now made us feel protective of Calla from the very authorities we were going to ask for help to get rid of her. Fifi flicked through the limited paperwork that Calla had given her.

'So you currently have a visitor's visa?' asked Fifi, holding up a piece of paper.

Calla nodded. 'I visit Hannah and Scott.'

Fifi paused and reluctantly asked Calla, 'Is it OK if we continue to discuss your current situation with Hannah and Scott in the room?'

I suddenly felt like an intruder in my own home – the feeling was becoming a familiar one, especially since all the flatulence had started. I noted from my watch that the gaseous eruptions were late tonight.

Calla looked puzzled. 'What is this situation?'

Fifi, started to explain, 'Well, the situation is that you are here on a visitor visa and—'

Hannah interrupted, 'No, that's not what she means. When she says things like "what is this situation" she means she doesn't understand what the word "situation" means. Sorry, that's a lot of means.'

'Beanz meanz Heinz,' I said.

Hannah giggled. 'That's not very helpful, Scott.'

I nodded in agreement. 'I know, but it's funny.'

Fifi ignored us and continued with Calla. 'Do you want me to ask Scott and Hannah to leave?'

'No, they stay,' she said very firmly, leaning into Hannah.

Fifi consulted her notes. 'I expected her English to be better than it is, given that she says she attended classes for two years before coming here.'

I smiled. 'It appears that her English teacher had an obsession with football, the English Premiership predominantly, and trains. So she's probably pretty good if you want to talk about that with her.'

'That's not very useful when I want to try and sort out her residency. I do have something that I think will help, though. Could you pass me up that black leather case, please? I can't reach it from here.'

I leaned over and picked up the small briefcase and handed it over. She opened it and took out what looked like a tiny laptop. She fired it up, then took out a small microphone, and set it down on the table in front of her.

She then turned the screen to Calla and held the mic near her own lips and started to speak.

'Since 1983, children born in the UK no longer get automatic citizenship unless one of the parents is a UK resident. Now, obviously you, Calla, are not a UK resident, but as you are claiming that the father of your child is Mr Scott McEwan, and should that prove to be the case, then it is likely that your child will be eligible for British citizenship. Unfortunately, this does not help you become a British citizen as the only way you can become such is to apply for a settlement visa or marry a British resident. I assume, Scott, that you are not about to divorce your wife and marry Calla?'

I glanced over at Hannah, and rubbed my chin as if pondering the question. A cushion glanced off the side of my head.

'No, I'm not,' I confirmed under duress.

I really needed to get rid of all the cushions. Calla laughed out loud at our slapstick display.

Fifi frowned at the three of us. We were obviously not taking the situation seriously enough for her liking. She turned to Calla and asked, 'So, Calla, what do you think is the best course of action in order to secure your citizenship?'

Calla smiled and let slip one of her silent specials. She replied just as the stench of digested chillies and red onions reached us. 'What is this ship?'

We all collectively groaned, mostly from the smell, partly from her answer.

Fifi paused and turned the screen around so Calla could read it. 'This is a new, state of the art translating device, and as I spoke, it should have translated everything I said into Thai.'

On the screen a line of words appeared; I assumed it was in Thai.

Fifi turned the screen back around to Calla so she could read it.

'What does that say, Calla?' Fifi asked expectantly.

Calla peered at the words and said, 'The bus is late.'

Everyone laughed out loud, and eventually even Fifi joined in. 'I need to go into my office tomorrow to deal with some issues concerning another of my cases. Whilst there I will try to source a proper translator.'

Chapter Sixteen

THE NEXT MORNING, after I had been waiting even longer than usual for a turn in the bathroom, the phone rang. I wondered who it could be so early in the day. I picked up the handset and initially thought I had received one of those calls my mum used to call 'funny' as all I could hear was laboured, heavy breathing. This might be fun, I thought, and decided to listen a bit longer to see what happened. My mum once received a spate of 'funny calls' when I was a kid and as a deterrent, used to keep a whistle beside the phone, which she would employ if she suspected her 'stalker' was on the other end of the line.

More than once my dad and various friends and relatives received a deaf ear as my mum reacted prematurely. I didn't have a whistle handy in this case, but it proved unnecessary as eventually the heavy breather started to speak.

'Mrs McEwan?' the raspy voice enquired.

I wasn't about to hand my wife the phone yet, just in case, so I answered, 'Yes,' in my best loud-pitched Monty Python voice.

'This is Lothian Maternity Services, as you are now in

your thirtieth week of pregnancy, you are eligible to attend antenatal classes ...'

'Hold on,' I said in my normal voice, and handed the phone to Hannah.

My curious wife took the receiver from me with a questioning look.

'Midwife, I think,' I explained as I left the room to make some coffee.

Hannah booked in for the free classes, starting that evening. It was short notice but apparently the midwife had left seven messages on our home phone. Lois had a tendency to pull the phone wire out of the wall and we had a tendency not to notice, so that was probably why we'd not got any of the messages.

Fifi was due to attend the class with her husband anyway so she decided to come with us. He was the only winner out of this as I was not excused attendance. The classes were technically not free as advertised as we needed to pay twelve pounds for each session to cover the cost of light refreshments. For twelve quid, I would be expecting gourmet sandwiches and Earl Grey tea at least, but I prepared myself to be disappointed.

The heavy-breathing Mrs Gail Colbeck would be running the classes along with a junior assistant. The upshot of all this was that I was now going to undertake rhythmic breathing and pelvic floor exercises with three very pregnant, and very different, women. I hadn't worked out how or what to tell Mrs Colbeck. I decided to just keep quiet and hope she didn't notice.

Later, after a hastily eaten dinner with my pregnant pals, we rushed out of the door and drove to the local health centre. We all piled into Fifi's nice clean BMW rather than our cramped, untidy rust bucket. On entering the community centre, I searched for a sign that would tell us where to go but all I could see was a badly written notice saying 'Parentcraft' with an arrow pointing straight ahead.

'That's it,' said Fifi, and walked past the sign down a dimly lit corridor.

At the end of the corridor, we joined a line of pregnant people and partners waiting to register. I realized anxiously that I would not be able to avoid speaking to the midwife. As I suspected, the initial paperwork took much longer to complete than it should have done due to the confusion surrounding me, Hannah, Calla, and Fifi.

Gail Colbeck was a large, stressed lady in her fifties with badly dyed black hair, watery grey eyes and, as I had expected, suffering from severe asthma. She took regular extended puffs on her inhaler, which I'm sure wasn't a good thing to be doing. In addition, she was burdened with a nervous manic manner which we were unlikely to lessen given our peculiar circumstances.

'OK, Mr McEwan, are you going to be your wife's birthing partner?' she gasped.

'Yes.'

'OK, now, Miss Hi Tee, what is your relationship with Mr McEwan? It is stated here that he is also to be your birthing partner.'

'He is baby father.'

I could see Gail's brain whirring on this one. She glanced uncertainly back at Hannah. 'Is he your baby's father as well?'

Hannah nodded, embarrassed. 'Yep, 'fraid so.'

The midwife made a note, I couldn't read what it said but I guess this situation was new to her. That made two of us … at least.

She asked Hannah nervously, 'Are you OK with your husband being Miss Hi Tee's birthing partner as well as yours?'

Hannah nodded. 'I don't have much choice really.'

Gail chewed on her pen and checked her paperwork; the NHS obviously hadn't put a tick box for this situation on her blue form and she was flummoxed.

'Err, OK, that seems fine, then,' she lied. Then she noticed with a visible start the third heavily pregnant woman standing by my side. Her mouth hung open for a second before she reluctantly enquired, 'Is Mr McEwan the father of your baby as well?'

Fifi took the opportunity to have some fun with Gail. 'No. I'm just living with them.'

'Is Mr McEwan going to be your birthing partner, then?'

Fifi laughed. 'I hope not, it's possible if I go into early labour, but no. I would expect my husband to be there.'

'Is he living ...' Mrs Colbeck was struggling to get a picture in her head of what was going on; I couldn't blame her. 'Is he staying with ...' she waved her hand across all of us, '... with all of you as well?'

Fifi smiled at Gail's discomfort. 'No, he lives at our house in Haddington with Brooke.'

'Oh, is Brooke your daughter?'

'No, Brooke is my 5-year-old spaniel.'

'Oh.' Gail consulted her form again. There was obviously no tick box for spaniels or multiple households either. She sighed and tossed her paperwork onto the small desk. 'Let's just go to the class and I'll fill all that in later.'

I knew she wouldn't. Life was too short. Before we moved into the main hall, I had a question to ask. 'Gail, what happens if my wife and Calla both go into labour at the same time?'

Gail gazed around, confused. 'Who's Calla? Is she another one ...'

I laughed. 'No, that's Miss Hi Tee's Christian name.'

'Oh.' I could see the relief on the midwife's face. 'Are

they both having their first babies?'

'No, this is my wife's third but Calla's first.'

Mrs Colbeck shook her head firmly, glad to be on some semblance of familiar and professional ground again. 'No, you should be fine, probably a thousand-to-one chance of that happening.'

Given my luck so far, those odds weren't long enough. 'OK, but just suppose it does happen – can they both share a room?'

'No.'

'Why not?'

'Hospital policy.'

'Oh.'

We eventually joined the class and the four of us swelled the numbers to twenty-three. So much for being small and intimate. However, as it was run by the NHS and was free, apart from the twelve quid we'd each handed over, we couldn't really complain.

After a brief introduction Gail asked, 'Is anyone bringing a doula to the birth?'

A couple near us raised their hands. When they spoke they sounded particularly posh.

The midwife acknowledged them and paused for a puff of her inhaler before instructing, 'It would be useful if you could bring them to a session here before your birth.'

Hannah whispered to me, 'What's a doula?'

'I think it's a type of dog.'

'A dog? They wouldn't let a dog into the hospital.'

'They let guide dogs in.'

Hannah glanced over at the posh couple. 'I don't think they're blind.'

'Maybe it's a special kind of dog, one that can smell when you are about to give birth, you know, like those dogs that can smell cancer.'

Hannah shook her head sceptically. 'I wouldn't need a dog to tell me that I'm about to give birth, I can assure you of that.'

As appealing as the idea of a birth-sensing dog was to me, I was disappointed to learn later that a doula was a person, usually a woman, whose purpose was to help the mother through the birth and sometimes beyond.

I considered that maybe Hannah and Calla could be each other's doula, but given that they were due around the same time one would be a lumbering, and possibly still farting, fat doula and I didn't think that hospital policy would allow such a person to go crashing around. We'd be better off with the dog.

The first part of the evening involved Mrs Colbeck gasping through a presentation about the importance of a healthy, balanced diet in pregnancy, so that was a waste of time for my two. Then the junior midwife, Sally Golding, stood up to take over the next session. It soon became apparent that she was not used to speaking in public, and stammered and stumbled over her commentary that accompanied some graphic slides of a presentation entitled 'The Birthing Experience'.

'Now this next slide is a picture of an ... err ... diluted ... no, that's not right, a *dilated* cervix. You can clearly see that during early labour, the cervix has dilu ... dilated to around three centimetres; this is the latent phase during which contractions are usually well spaced out. This slide shows the later stage when the cervix has dilated to nearly ten metres, which is enough to allow the baby's head to pass through.'

Everyone started laughing and poor Sally had no idea why. She smiled nervously and continued, 'The stage prior to the baby drowning ... err, crowning, is where most vaginal tears happen.

'Sometimes it is unavoidable and sometimes the doctor or midwife may need to carry out an episito …. episiotomy … a small cut in your perineum – that's the bit of skin between your vagina and anus. This usually only happens if the baby is in distress and can reduce the likelihood of further tears during a difficult birth.

'Some women and their partners like to massage or rub oil on their perineum before coming into hospital and stretch it by inserting a finger in your vagina or anus … well, you might want to do it yourself actually, I suppose … but it's up to you …'

I leaned over to Hannah. 'Do you want me to put my finger in your bum and stretch your pendulum?'

'What? Right now?'

I glanced round at the sea of faces all staring at Sally's slides. 'If you want. Nobody's watching.'

'I'll think about it.'

Sally concluded her part of the evening by explaining what people did with the afterbirth or placenta.

'Some people take the placenta home with them and eat it. I believe my colleague Gail has a recipe book for a number of placenta recipes, which includes a particularly delicious lasagne if anyone's interested.'

Nobody raised a hand, which didn't surprise me. Sally and Gail appeared to be a little peeved that nobody wanted their recipe book.

'Well, another option is turning your afterbirth into a cuddly teddy for your little one as a lasting reminder of where they came from. A new company has set up in the west of the city who specialize in this and their prices are very reasonable.'

Again, nobody appeared particularly interested in that idea, either, probably because they didn't want their kid spending the formative years of their lives in therapy.

I'm sure they had another thirty or so amazing things you can do with your placenta speech ready to go but thankfully, we were saved by the arrival of refreshments.

I was expecting some frugal fair and I was not disappointed by the semi-stale biscuits, watery coffee and weak tea that was provided in a small alcove at the far end of the large room that we were all sitting in.

Following the break, Sally took the session on exercises for pregnant women that thankfully I got to miss, and she also ran the next bit about how to avoid becoming stressed during labour. Again, this was primarily aimed at the women, but in my opinion there should have been something for us men too – Hannah's previous two labours had been incredibly stressful for me.

The last session was split between Sally and Gail, who used more graphic slides to show what happened during a ventouse birth – where they seemed to attach a sink plunger to the baby's head to pull it out. It looked bizarre and a little amusing, though probably not for the baby. A number of the men present looked particularly uncomfortable and this took me back to when Tessa was born. I was terrified of her.

I didn't want to pick her up in case she broke, I didn't want to hold her in case I dropped her, and on the rare occasion when I got to feed her some of Hannah's expressed milk from a bottle, it was a nightmare as I never got her head position right. I was either keeping her too flat so that she choked or I held her head too far forward so she couldn't swallow properly and choked. She choked a lot in those early days with me.

By the time Lois was born I was competent, having learned from my mistakes with Tessa. I still managed to drop Lois behind the couch one evening, but Hannah didn't know about that, and after I'd brushed the dust and fluff off her face she'd been none the worse for the experience.

By the end of the evening, everyone waddled out of the health centre and headed home. Most of the first-time dads were not saying much, but they didn't know the half of it yet. Men are not adequately equipped for modern fatherhood. In evolutionary terms, we still lived in caves where we only needed to go out once in a while, bang something large, furry and vicious on the head with a club, and drag it back to the cave for the women to skin and turn into meat and clothes.

Women are biologically primed to be mothers. Men are biologically primed to be dickheads when it comes to caring for children. We just don't get it. The problem was that Hannah expected so much more of me. This meant she'd be forever disappointed as she would with any man, except maybe a gay chap who probably would be much better at being organized.

Maybe that would be the answer to the problem. Every woman should dump her husband or straight partner as soon as she's happy with the size of her family and shack up with a homosexual man. Her life would run a lot more smoothly, that's for sure, she would probably also get more than a grunt or a 'yeah, it's fine' when she asked about the top she'd just bought or the new outfit for her daughter.

She would also get to have long, meaningful conversations about the colour of curtains that should go in the living room or what colour went best with her eyes. I still don't understand that – Hannah's eyes are blue, so I said blue. Wrong answer apparently, according to the colour wheel.

So married women should have a homosexual man as a fallback option, especially if they could get by without sex, I suppose, with a Rampant Rabbit. Hannah would manage fine in that department. The only problem might be that you'd get loads of men pretending to be gay so that they could get it on with the yummy mummies. Men are devious that way.

We arrived home to find that Hannah's mum, Carol, had managed to get the two girls to bed and asleep, which was a herculean effort, given their usual reluctance to acquiesce to bedtime. It helped that Hannah and Calla had taken them to soft-play for two hours earlier in the day, but still, I had some real admiration for Carol and told her so.

She smiled, unused to compliments from me. 'They were tired so they went to sleep.'

I knew it wasn't that straightforward, but didn't say anything more. Hannah and Calla passed us in the hall. Carol smiled at her daughter and scowled at Calla. Carol still didn't know the full story of what was going on with Calla, and was one of the few people who still hadn't warmed to her.

Soon after, Carol left for home and my three pregnant ladies settled themselves down for the evening. Fifi's BMW had been subjected to most of the flatulence on the way back from the antenatal classes, so the flat smelled remarkably fresh for once. I waited patiently in line for the bathroom and eventually got to clean my teeth and empty my bladder before heading to bed. I slipped in beside Hannah, who was already snoring loudly. The spike in our lovemaking had now subsided to almost zero. I wasn't completely surprised, given the stage in her pregnancy and our increased stress levels, but the sudden drop-off was a bit like going cold turkey. I had so far resisted the temptation to dab my skin with marinated anchovy juice, a scent unlikely to be endorsed by Calvin Klein, but irresistible to my sleeping spouse. I had a feeling I might need to try it soon.

Chapter Seventeen

THE NEXT DAY at work, I got a call from Hannah asking me to get home early if possible, as Fifi had managed to find a female translator who'd agreed to come to our flat.

'She's not pregnant, is she?'

Hannah laughed down the phone. 'I don't think so but I didn't ask. Fifi says she's married to a restaurant owner in Fife. That's all I know.'

I managed to make it home and wash the day's gunge off me before she arrived. Hannah made sure the girls were happily playing in their bedroom with their dolls' house, and gave them some snacks before settling down in the living room with everyone else.

The translator was called Noon Celic and was older than I expected; I reckoned she was in her early forties. She had greying hair and an expanding figure, but thankfully there was no sign that she was with child. I was tempted to make some joke about the time but managed to resist.

Fifi introduced everyone, and Noon and Calla immediately started nattering away. Calla was particularly animated and waved her hands about expressively.

Fifi interrupted and explained the situation to Noon. 'I know we spoke on the phone earlier, but obviously at that point I couldn't elaborate fully. Miss Hi Tee arrived in Edinburgh shortly before Christmas and has stated that the father of her unborn child is Mr McEwan. This appears to be her main motivation for coming; however, as you may be aware from some press coverage, certain allegations have been made that Miss Hi Tee was being mistreated during her stay here. I've been living with the family for three days now and have not seen any evidence of this but we need to get confirmation from Miss Hi Tee and find out a bit more about her plans.'

Noon nodded. 'Why don't you just ask me what you need to know and I'll put the questions to her.'

Noon then explained to Calla what was going to happen. Calla looked nervous but nodded.

Fifi opened her black book and made a few quick notes.

'First of all, can you ask her why she came to Edinburgh? I just want to ascertain her motivation.'

Noon then had what must have amounted to a two minute conversation with Calla, who became tearful and moved over to sit beside Hannah. Hannah comforted her as best she could, although for some reason two large pregnant women cuddling each other absurdly reminded me of tortoises mating. Once Calla had stopped speaking, she fixed her eyes on me and smiled sadly.

Noon gathered her thoughts. 'OK, it seems that Calla was working as a prostitute in Thailand – which I believe you know already?'

Fifi nodded. 'Yes, Mr and Mrs McEwan made ... err ... use of her services whilst on holiday there.'

Noon continued. 'Yes, she did say that. Well, anyway, it appears that although the main reason for her trip here is because she genuinely believes the baby she's carrying is fathered by Mr McEwan, she also saw it as an opportunity to escape possible and further sexual abuse at the hands of certain men she had become associated with. It appears that she may have borrowed money from one of them which largely paid for her fare over here.'

'Sexual abuse?' questioned Hannah.

'So she says.'

I shook my head. 'But she's a prostitute.'

Fifi sighed with exasperation. '*Was* a prostitute, and prostitutes can be sexually abused; in fact, it happens to many of them and quite frequently – both here and abroad.'

I hadn't considered that but I supposed it was true. I remembered the way she had checked out our hotel room to see where the exits were while she was introducing herself. In a way, I reckoned with someone like Calla who had few opportunities in life, every time someone used her as a prostitute was akin to sexual abuse in a way, as she had few other ways of surviving. Did that mean we were abusers too?

Fifi was probably thinking along similar lines but didn't elaborate. I gazed over at Calla, who tried to get closer to Hannah as tears formed and tumbled down her cheeks. She looked incredibly vulnerable and any last resentment I may have been harbouring towards her for upsetting my life melted away. Hannah slipped her arm around Calla's shoulder and offered her a paper hanky which she used to mop up her tears and blow her nose.

The room was very emotionally charged and when Noon continued, it didn't reduce the tension. 'It appears she was able to obtain the money from this man because he preferred to have … erm … be with her, even when she was quite obviously pregnant.'

'Maiesiophiliacs,' cried Hannah triumphantly. 'They're everywhere.'

'Excuse me?' said Fifi.

I decided to enlighten her. 'It's a long story but Hannah's had a similar experience recently.'

Fifi turned to face Hannah with a shocked expression. 'You've been working as a prostitute?'

Hannah replied sharply, 'Of course not, I've just had someone focus on me ... sexually ... because I am pregnant.'

Fifi glared accusingly at me.

'Not me,' I said defensively, while thinking that chance would be a fine thing, and surely I was entitled to focus on Hannah sexually, being her husband and currently suffering complete deprivation of any carnal relationships. 'Some old bloke in her office; anyway, it's not important.' I noticed Hannah glaring at me now. 'Well, it is important, but not in the context of this conversation.'

Fifi stared at me for a moment, probably deliberating whether she should extend her stay indefinitely to make sure I was not a risk to Calla or Hannah. She then decided, given that she was currently in the later stages of pregnancy and if I was suffering from any kind of sexual pregnancy fixation, she was probably better off out of here.

Fifi made some notes, then turned to Noon. 'Can you ask what would happen if Calla returned home and what family she has that may be able to help support her?'

Another lengthy conversation followed between Noon and Calla. Calla was more animated this time but some tears still spilled from her eyes.

'It seems,' explained Noon, 'her mother remarried recently and Miss Hi Tee does not get along with her stepfather so returning and living there is not an option.'

'What happened to her father?' asked Hannah.

'It seems he was killed in a mining accident some years ago, and this appears to be the reason why she chose the ... err ... career path she did in order to help support her mother. In any event a few things are very clear. The man she took money from is a dangerous character and likely to exact some violent vengeance should she return. She also gave up her apartment and sold what meagre possessions she had to help fund her trip here, which means she would be homeless if she did go back.'

Fifi made a few observations. 'I suppose whatever situation arose in Thailand that drove her to be with you here is largely irrelevant now. What we … I need to work out is if she has a strong enough case to stay, and if so then I'll need to put a good set of arguments together. In her favour is that she's pregnant and cannot fly until after her baby is born, so that gives me a little time.

'Also, the fact that she was having … frequent sexual relations during her pregnancy means I need to arrange for her to have a full medical screening to make sure she's in good health before she enters the latter stages of her gestation. What has her diet been like since she's been staying with you? Is it varied with plenty of fresh fruit and vegetables?'

I laughed out loud. 'You're joking, right? You've sat in this room whilst she's stunk it out, in good company with my wife, I should add.'

I smiled at Calla and held my nose with my fingers, and her eyes brightened and she mimicked my gesture and said, 'Onion and chillies.'

I elaborated, 'Yeah, her diet's mainly consisted of red chillies and raw onions. If they count towards her five a day, then great, if not, then she's also wolfed down loads of crisps, a few sandwiches and the odd chicken dinner here and there.'

Fifi smiled and made a few more notes. 'Well, I'll need to get you checked for vitamin deficiencies, too, I suppose, to make sure you're not lacking something.'

Calla frowned. 'What is this licking?'

Noon stepped in to clarify.

The atmosphere had lightened considerably with the discussions of diet, but Fifi raised the stakes again by saying, 'One more thing, I need to confirm that Miss Hi Tee has not been abused whilst she has been staying with Mr and Mrs McEwan. Can you ask her about her treatment during her stay?'

Noon nodded and I watched anxiously as she put Fifi's question to Calla.

Calla's eyes welled up again and she talked very quickly, being careful not to meet either mine or Hannah's gaze. Towards the end of her explanation, she became very emotional and started sobbing quite openly. It didn't look good for us at this point. Eventually she stopped speaking.

Noon waited until Calla dried her eyes before translating. 'She says when she first arrived it was very difficult for her, she realized she was taking a huge chance coming but felt she had no other option given the mess she'd got herself into. She can understand why you were both very hostile towards her initially and expected it to be much worse than it was. She's spent most of her life running from someone or something. She says her brief stay with you has been the most peaceful and calm time she has had since she was a child, and she wants me to tell you how grateful she is to you both for allowing her to stay.'

Noon paused and Calla smiled as more tears poured from her eyes. Hannah took her in her arms and gave her a big hug.

Noon concluded, 'Calla didn't realize you had children and thinks Tessa and Lois are the most beautiful girls in the world and loves spending time with them. She now almost feels part of the family. She appreciates that you have been very kind to her, even when she landed you in trouble with the TV reporter in Asda; she feels terrible about that and apologizes, but she thinks the reporter twisted her words.'

'She wouldn't be the first reporter to do that,' commented Fifi.

We were all silent for a few moments and all I could hear were Hannah and Calla sobbing in each other's arms.

Fifi broke the silence. 'I've discovered that over Christmas, the immigration staff undertook a twenty-four-hour walk-out strike over pay and pensions, leaving only a skeleton staff at the airports, so that might explain how she evaded any scrutiny on that point.'

Noon stood up. 'I assume that you don't need me any more. It's quite clear to me here that Calla is very happy and has not suffered any kind of unkindness whilst she's been in Edinburgh.'

Fifi nodded. 'Yes, that's fine. Thank you, Mrs Celic, you have been extremely helpful and once I've worked out the best course of action, would I be able to call on you again in case I need to explain some complex information to Miss Hi Tee?'

'Yes, no problem.'

Fifi showed her out and Calla went to sit with Tessa and Lois in their bedroom.

'That was emotional,' I said, stating the obvious.

My red-eyed wife laughed. 'Yeah. God, I feel so sorry for her.'

Before we could speak more, Fifi lumbered back into the living room and plonked herself back down on the couch.

'Right, well, I see no need to stay with you both any longer. I'll gather up my things and head home this evening. I need to try and sort a few things out, but it appears she has a strong case for remaining in the UK for a while at least.' She closed her folder and put her notes onto the coffee table and decided to burst our little emotional bubble.

'One thing I've noticed whilst I've been here is that Calla seems to have no actual money of her own. I'm sure this is partly down to the fact she incurred a lot of costs to get here. As part of her case I will be making an application for benefits, which will also consider her housing needs, but in the meantime it would be a good idea if you could provide her with some funds of her own, so she can make the essential purchases that she will need over the next few weeks. I think around eight hundred pounds would be enough.'

'Eight hundred quid!' I exclaimed. 'Look at us here, Fifi. We have two kids, live in a flat that is far too small for us, and Hannah is about to go on maternity leave. If we had eight hundred pounds just lying around, trust me, it would have been spent on some new clothes for Lois, who is wearing Tessa's old stuff, or we might've got the microwave fixed, or the tumble dryer that went kaput six months ago, a new handle for the fridge door or on swimming lessons for Tessa. Everyone in her class gets to go to swimming on a Wednesday morning except her, because we can't afford the money to send her. How do you think that makes us feel?

'We're barely surviving now – the wedding and honeymoon more than cleaned us out, we actually borrowed money on the flat to pay for all of that and to be honest, we are struggling. In hindsight we shouldn't have done it, but it's too late now. We took Calla in because ...' I actually had to stop and think for a moment: why did we take her in? '... probably because we both felt guilty more than anything. That, and the fact she told us that she was carrying my baby. A fact that has yet to be proved, and in any event, it was clearly the right thing to do. We've made her feel welcome and provided her with somewhere to live. We can't really afford another mouth to feed but we've done it, and now you want us to give her money as well.'

Fifi appeared bemused: in her world eight hundred

pounds was probably a drop in the ocean. In ours it wasn't. She gazed over at Hannah for a moment before saying, 'If you can't afford another mouth to feed, you probably shouldn't have got pregnant again; having a baby is a very expensive business.'

My jaw dropped, literally, and I just stared at her. I couldn't believe she'd just said that. I locked eyes with Hannah; her face was red and her eyes were blazing, but to her eternal credit she remained calm.

'Fifi, I think you should just pack up your stuff and leave our home before one of us says something they'll regret.' Fifi went to speak, but Hannah jumped in. 'Please go now, just leave, and I hope one day you can understand why we are so angry.' Hannah struggled to her feet, and took my hand. 'Come on, Scott, we need to get out of here for a while.' She glanced out of the window. 'It's stopped raining, let's get Calla and the girls, and go to Morrisons for dinner.' She cast a look back over her shoulder to Fifi. 'Kids eat free on week nights.'

Chapter Eighteen

AFTER FIFI DEPARTED, our flat felt much larger. I remembered reading Tessa a story by Julia Donaldson called *A Squash and a Squeeze* where an old woman believed her house was too small so she was advised to take in lots of animals to live with her, then when they were all gone the house felt huge. I suppose I could maybe have done an adult version where instead of animals, I squeezed in lots of pregnant, flatulent ladies.

We did take to heart some of Fifi's words and managed to scrape one hundred and fifty pounds together for Calla, and Hannah took her shopping.

Both of their cravings subsided over the next week and we were left with a cupboard full of marinated anchovies that would never get eaten. I reckoned the stocktakers at Asda would be puzzled too. I'm sure that seeing their jars of Hannah's favourite nibbles vanish from the shelves quicker than half-price Pringles would have led to them ordering in extra quantities, which would now sit untouched for months unless some celebrity chef could be persuaded to include them in one of their recipes.

Another expense that we had to budget for was changing our car. The old Corsa really couldn't fit anyone else in and I doubted it would last through the rest of the winter anyway.

A 10-year-old Vauxhall Zafira had been sitting, looking very sorry for itself in our 'clearance corner' for a week now with no takers.

This corner was where we dumped cars that would go to the auction unless someone bought them – like Chloe and Darren's Saab, they were mechanically sound but usually had a few dents and dings and were effectively 'sold as seen', which meant they had no warranty or comeback if they coughed and died twenty yards down the road.

The Zafira was appealing to me because it had seven seats and a full leather interior, which meant I could carry our currently overcrowded family around in relative comfort with easy-to-clean seats. It was a slightly battered, black, boxy thing. It had aircon and satnav, both of which worked perfectly. Not that we'd probably need either of them any time soon given that it was winter and we never went anywhere. But it was black and Hannah liked black cars. It would do us fine for a while, hopefully a long while, and I explained to Sandra that I needed a few days to get the five hundred pounds together that would let me drive it away.

Sandra then gave me her sceptical stare, the one I'd seen her use countless times on customers she thought were either lying to her or being particularly stupid. I wasn't lying so I deduced that somehow I was being particularly stupid.

'Scott, how long have you been working here?'

Oh dear, I thought, here we go. 'Nearly six years.'

'OK, and how many cars have you bought from yourself?'

I laughed at her terminology. 'Well, not many, cos I get to drive cars home all the time so I don't—'

'How many, Scott?'

'Two, Sandra. An old Merc when I first got the manager's job and my current Corsa, which is held together with Sellotape.'

Sandra nodded. 'OK, and did you pay cash for them both? Bottom book of course.'

'Yeah, cash, both times.'

She stared at me again as if I was stupid. 'Have you not heard of the "staff car scheme"?'

I was vaguely aware of it. 'I thought that was for the sales staff.'

'Nope, it's for everyone. If the price is under two grand, they deduct one twelfth of the cost of the car from your salary each month over a year. If it's more than that, then they arrange different amounts over longer time periods depending on what suits. In any event, it's interest free and means you can drive that home tonight and give it to Hannah. Plus, I can probably knock a hundred off for your Corsa.'

'I don't think we could even send that to auction, Sandra.'

'I agree. But we'll get some scrap money for it.'

That evening, everyone was excited about the new car, or rather, not very new car that we now owned. Hannah was happy because it looked good (well, better than what she was used to) and she could park it outside, and the girls were happy because it was huge inside compared to our old car and they could jump about from seat to seat. They wouldn't do that when it was moving, of course. Well, at least I hoped not. I was excited because everyone else was excited.

'I could even drive this to work,' Hannah announced, beaming.

She wouldn't because only insane people tried to park in the town centre during the week.

Where the car would come into its own immediately was when we needed to ferry Hannah and Calla about as they were becoming less and less mobile as their due dates approached.

I was spared the ordeal of attending the next two ante-natal classes because Carol was unable to babysit. I was delighted, but as Hannah was happy to go with Calla anyway, everyone was a winner. Around two weeks before Hannah and Calla's due dates, we had a visit from Fifi. We were a little nervous, as our parting comments as she left our flat the last time were less than complimentary.

She appeared to have forgotten all about them, however, and now waddling uncomfortably with swollen ankles (she volunteered this information as I wasn't an ankle-gazing type of person), she sat gasping in one of our kitchen chairs, the short flight of stairs having tired her out.

Once she had recovered she explained, 'I've been working on Calla's situation over the last few weeks and it is likely that we will soon be able to allocate her a new home. It probably won't be in the best of areas, but at least she will have her own space. The housing department have agreed to furnish a property for her with the essentials she will need. Beyond that, the benefits she will receive should be enough to allow her to feed and clothe herself and her child. It will take between six to eight weeks before this all happens, so it is likely she will still be with you when her baby is born.'

Fifi paused before confessing, 'It has been a difficult case, especially regarding her residency; the fact she arrived with no visible sponsor has caused me some problems, but for the time being she has been granted a temporary visa extension for a year. Beyond that we will need to see what happens. It would help her cause immensely if she could find gainful employment. You two know her better than anyone, what is she good at?'

I was tempted to say shagging but resisted. 'She's good with children.'

Hannah said in support, 'Yes, she is, she's great with our two and they adore her. I think she's also quite a gifted artist.'

'Does she have any qualifications in art?'

'I doubt it,' I said.

Fifi nodded and made a note in her ever-present black book. 'Anything else?'

We both wracked our brains, before Hannah said, 'She does a mean TV interview.'

Even Fifi managed a smile. 'Yes, I'll stick working with children as her main preference and she could possibly undertake some kind of art-related course later on.' She closed her book and struggled to her feet. 'I'm actually on maternity leave now, but I needed to tie up a few loose ends with this. I'll probably take a year off so it won't be me that sees her case through to conclusion, though given the restraints on the department's budgets, you never know.'

If she was looking for sympathy she'd find none here; Hannah and I could never afford for her to take a year off. Her employer paid her full salary for eight weeks and after that it was the statutory minimum.

After Fifi had left, Hannah and I hugged. It was a relief to know that at some point Calla would be out of our flat. The paternity issue still needed sorting out, but in a way that was less important. Calla was now firmly part of our lives. If the child was mine, as I fully expected it to be, then we would build that into our future plans. It helped that in the short time she'd been with us, she and Hannah had developed a friendship, especially since the night Noon had translated her feelings for us. It was still an uneasy one at present, but once she was independent from us that would improve.

Hannah commenced her maternity leave on the following Friday, and although she could have finished work ages ago, for us it was all about the money, and anyway, she thought she'd get bored at home.

She was supposed to spend the next two to three weeks with her feet up, but she seemed to spend it shopping with her mum and Lois, and occasionally Calla. Hannah was huge, much bigger than she had been with Tessa and Lois, but she told me this was down to her abdominal muscles being much more flexible than they had been with our previous two. She told me this with a straight face and as I loved her, I believed it and decided it had nothing to do with the copious amount of chocolate and crisps she consumed on a daily basis. I was just happy the flatulence and cravings had stopped.

Then, the following Saturday, my morning shower was rudely interrupted by Tessa banging on the door shouting, 'Daddy! Mummy needs you.'

I shut off the water, grabbed my towel and wrapped it clumsily around my waist as I fumbled to open the bathroom door. Tessa's wide-eyed face gazed up at me.

'Mummy's ready.'

'Ready for what?'

Before Tessa could answer, my wife lumbered into view and said, 'A double vodka followed by a quick shag.'

'Eh?'

Hannah sighed. 'You're like the girls, Scott – sarcasm is completely wasted on you. I'm in labour, my contractions have started.'

'OK, I'll just get dressed quickly and …'

'No panic, Scott, we've got ages yet – we're veterans at

this, remember?'

I wasn't sure that having two previous births qualified us as being veterans, but there was no point in arguing with a pregnant woman in the middle of a contraction.

After she recovered she said, 'Actually, maybe you should hurry – MOVE YOUR ARSE!'

My arse and the rest of me moved very quickly.

Chapter Nineteen

CALLA HELPED HANNAH downstairs to the car whilst I got the girls organized. They were going to stay with Hannah's mum while I took her daughter to hospital. Hannah had decided to have Calla along so she could see what UK hospitals were like – just to put her mind at ease. I suspected she wanted Calla with her as she would be an extra bit of support for when I inevitably got stressed out. I feared, however, that Calla might be more of a hindrance than a help, especially if there happened to be any newspaper or TV reporters about.

Hannah's contractions were still a few minutes apart but just as we were nearing Hannah's mum's house, Tessa squealed, 'Yuck! Calla's done pee pees.'

'What's that, Tessa?'

'Calla's done pee pees all over the seat and it's dripping onto the floor.'

I pulled the car to a stop and leaned over into the back seat. Sure enough the seats were soaking, and a pinkish-coloured liquid was dripping from the leather seat onto the floor.

'It's not pee pees, Tessa. Calla's waters have gone.'

'Where water gone?' asked Calla, puzzled.

'It's gone all over the seat,' squealed my eldest daughter.

'What's going on?' Hannah asked, emerging from a contraction.

'Calla's waters have broken,' I explained.

Hannah laughed. 'It's your worst nightmare, Scott. Now you've got two labouring women on your hands.'

'Not necessarily, I'm an old hand at this remember; just because her waters have broken doesn't necessarily mean she'll go into labour right away.' Just then Calla gave a huge moan and gripped her tummy. 'Fuck!' I exclaimed.

'Language,' scolded Hannah.

'I wet,' stated Calla, forlornly staring at her lap a few moments later.

'You are,' agreed Hannah. 'That means you are going to have your baby soon.'

'In car?'

'I bloody well hope not,' I shouted.

'Scott, don't shout,' scolded Hannah. 'You'll scare everyone.'

I nodded, 'OK, just keep calm, everyone, I'm going as fast as I can.'

Hannah put her hand on my arm. 'We're all fine, it's only you that's stressed, sweetie.'

I glanced at Hannah then in my rear-view mirror. She was right, everyone *was* calm. I took a deep breath and kept driving. Hannah got on the phone to her mum. I could only hear one side of the conversation.

'Mum, I'm in labour and we're driving to yours just now to drop off the girls. No, Calla was going to come to the hospital with us anyway as support, but now she's gone into labour too. No, her waters have gone so … She's had one contraction so far … No, I definitely think she's in labour.' Hannah glanced over to me and smiled, 'No, he's fine. A little stressed, but OK considering … No, Mum, I don't think you coming would help, you need to look after Tessa and Lois.… I'm sure Scott would rather stay and look after the girls but he's not getting out of it that easily. OK, see you soon, bye.'

'Did she suggest I stay at home?'

Hannah smiled. 'She did but that's *not* going to happen. You've got responsibilities to both me and Calla. I'm not going to go through agony while you sit and watch daytime TV.'

'I don't like daytime TV.'

'That's all right, then.'

We did a quick handover at Hannah's mum's and then I drove quickly to the hospital.' Calla managed one more contraction before we arrived at the maternity unit. I parked in a space as near to the entrance as I could get.

We collectively waddled over to the maternity building, pausing for Hannah's latest contraction to finish before walking through the doors into the maternity-receiving reception. I wasn't sure what the collective noun for a group of pregnant women was but a 'waddle' would be a great description.

Hannah's contractions remained a few minutes apart but we still waddled as quickly as we could. Hannah and Calla sat down on a hard plastic seat. Hannah was trying her best to comfort Calla, and for me it clearly contrasted the difference in age and experience between them. Calla looked so vulnerable and scared. I stood at the desk, waiting for the admissions secretary to check their bookings on her computer.

'Hannah McEwan isn't due for another three weeks,' she announced in a tone that seemed to imply that we were causing her major inconvenience to her scheduling. Before

189

I could reply, there was a multiple groan and repressed scream behind me as both Hannah and Calla underwent simultaneous contractions.

She waited for them to subside before checking her computer database further. 'What did you say the other name was?'

'Calla Hi Tee.'

'Calla Hatty?'

'No, Calla Hi Tee.' I spelled it out for her.

The secretary peered intently at the screen. I noticed her name badge said Miss Kathleen Dunnit. Kathleen reached into a pocket and produced a pair of reading glasses. My feeling was that she should have done that five minutes ago. She then tapped a few buttons on her keyboard and said accusingly, 'Miss Hi Tee is not due for another three weeks, either.'

She stared at me and narrowed her eyes as if waiting for an explanation. I shrugged.

'Nothing to do with me, I can't help it if the babies decided to come early.'

'The unit is very busy today.'

I wasn't sure what my response to that was supposed to be, maybe, 'OK, never mind, I'll take them both outside and we can have a wee baby-birthing party under a bush', or 'OK, girls, back home. The hospital's too busy to help you so I'll get my kit on and pretend to be a midwife.'''

Instead I said nothing and shrugged again. Kathleen snorted and tutted, and made other noises that indicated that she was annoyed with us but eventually phoned to have Hannah and Calla admitted. Within minutes, a midwife appeared and soon realized that both Hannah and Calla were in labour, but neither were in imminent danger of dropping a baby onto the floor.

She sat beside Hannah whilst a porter fetched a

wheelchair. Ignoring me for the moment she said, 'Hi, Hannah, I'm Gemma, the charge midwife today. Who's your birthing partner?'

Hannah pointed to me and said, 'My husband, Scott.'

'OK, is this your first baby?'

'No, third.'

'All right, as you've been through this before, I'll get you taken through and sorted in the labour suite with your allocated midwife. OK?'

Hannah nodded and was wheeled away by the orderly. Gemma stared at me. 'Aren't you going with your wife?'

'In a minute, once you've sorted Calla out.'

'Is she with you too?'

'Yes, 'fraid so.'

'OK …' Gemma said slowly. 'Why is this happening?'

'I've been asking myself that question for quite a while now.'

'That wasn't exactly what I meant.' She turned to Calla. 'Have you anyone else you could call?'

'I call Mother.'

Gemma said, 'That would be good, does she live nearby?'

'Nonthaburi.'

'Where?'

'Nonthaburi.'

'Is that in Fife?'

'What is this Fife?'

Gemma turned to me. 'Where is Nonthaburi?'

'I don't know, her English isn't very good, but I'm pretty sure it's not in Fife.'

'Do you know her mother?'

'No, never met the woman, she's remarried I think, and Calla doesn't like her new husband. Oh, and she's in Thailand.'

I think this was more information than Gemma needed so she stared at me for a moment, blinked and turned back to Calla. 'If your mother can't get here, who's going to be with you when you give birth?'

Calla pointed at me. 'Baby father.'

'You're the father?'

I sighed. 'Yeah, it's a very long story.'

'And your wife in there is OK with all this?'

'Not exactly, no. But we are where we are.'

'Why didn't you make a plan in case this happened?'

'The community midwife said the odds were thousands to one, especially as this is Calla's first baby.'

Gemma frowned at me sceptically. 'Well, it's happened now. What are you going to do?'

'Well, I'll just have to float between the two rooms.'

Gemma laughed. 'Well, yes, I suppose you'll have to. I'll make sure everyone knows what's happening. I think this is a first for us.'

'Me too.'

Gemma looked strangely at me again. I suppose given the circumstances I would look strangely at me too.

'Your wife has gone into room six. Given that she's on her third, she should give birth first, but there's no guarantees.'

She was right; an hour later, Hannah was pushing and nothing was happening. The midwife who'd been encouraging us with a reassuring smile suddenly became worried. The printout of the baby's heart rate, she called a 'trace', was concerning her.

She called her colleague in and after a quick glance at the readout, she buzzed for the consultant obstetrician. I hadn't been with Hannah the whole time as I'd dodged between the two birthing rooms. Calla was in a room at the end of the corridor, which took me two minutes to reach.

She'd had an epidural and was quite comfortable watching a marathon edition of *You've Been Framed* – the two-hour wedding-clip special.

Hannah's epidural had failed so I had made her my priority. She was my priority anyway, being my wife, but in my own mind the fact she was in constant pain meant I was justified in leaving Calla on her own, at least for the time being.

We tried to find out what was going on with the baby but everyone was too busy and concerned to stop and give us a clear explanation. It took ten minutes for the doctor to arrive and as soon she read the trace and tried to listen in to the foetal heartbeat she announced, 'We need to get this baby out now.' She lowered her voice and tone and spoke to Hannah. 'We need to perform an emergency Caesarean, your baby is in distress and we need to get it out.'

'Ruby.'

The doctor was puzzled. 'Sorry?'

Hannah's voice was soft and faltering. 'It's not an it. She's a girl called Ruby.'

As we rushed along the corridor towards the theatre block, I tried to talk to Hannah, despite her exhausted condition. 'I didn't know we were calling her Ruby, when did you decide that?'

She smiled weakly and whispered, 'When I heard the doctor call her an *it*. She's not an it, she's a little girl … our little girl … and her name is Ruby. I love you, Scott.'

'I love you too, Hannah.'

I dropped back and tried to engage with a midwife, who dismissed me, saying 'We need to hurry, your baby is in distress.'

'What's wrong with it … her? Nobody's telling me anything.'

'We don't know, the baby's heartbeat suddenly became

erratic.'

'What does that mean?'

'Erratic?'

'No, I went to school ... sometimes.... I know what erratic means – what does it mean when the heartbeat becomes erratic, what causes it?'

'It could be lots of things.'

'Tell me some.'

'It could be some issues with the umbilical cord, or any number of other complications, we'll know soon enough,' she said dismissively.

By the time we'd reached the theatre, I was terrified. As Hannah was getting a general anaesthetic and would be completely out of it, they told me there was no point in me going into the theatre and I was left cooling my heels in a small room nearby.

It was almost an hour before anyone came to tell me what was happening. Eventually, the charge midwife, Gemma, who had admitted us earlier, came in and sat down beside me. She was pale and serious.

She then framed the sentence that would echo through the rest of my life.

'There is no easy way for me to tell you this, Mr McEwan. Your baby has died.'

Chapter Twenty

I HAD BRACED myself for some kind of bad news, not for devastation. I was expecting them to say that Ruby was ill and might have to stay in the hospital for a week or two. This was the twenty-first century and I was in one of the most modern hospitals in the world. Babies shouldn't die during birth. I stared numbly at the midwife as she tried to explain what had happened.

'In the end, your wife gave birth vaginally, the head was already showing and the obstetrician used forceps to get your baby out; it was a quicker option than a Caesarean. We took her immediately into the neonatal unit and tried to revive her, but I'm afraid she had died and there was nothing we could do. It made no difference to your baby's outcome.'

Outcome. The word rattled around inside my head. Outcome. Just a process that, unfortunately, didn't quite work out. It was nobody's fault, nobody's responsibility, nobody cared.

I imagined Hannah used the word a lot when she was running through one of her multilayered slide presentations at work. Outcome was such a cold and clinical word. It belonged with other words that sat in that space like objective, solution and situation.

I was totally out of it. I couldn't speak, I couldn't think and I couldn't feel. The room seemed to shrink around me. I felt like I was about to become Alice in Wonderland and shrink to the size of a playing card.

I could hear the midwife's voice from very far away. 'As soon as your wife regains consciousness, we'll take you to her.'

I sat shaking, numb inside my little bubble of shock and pain for almost an hour before a doctor arrived and escorted me through to see Hannah. She was sitting upright in a bed, propped up by pillows. I could tell from her face that she had been given the news. She was pale and exhausted but aware enough to know that we wouldn't be taking our baby daughter home to meet her sisters. We sat and held hands in silence.

Later, a midwife came into the room and sat on a chair near the door. She was young and nervous. I couldn't blame her and didn't envy her job at this point. We both stared blankly at her for a moment or two before she spoke. I noted her badge said Mary Smith.

'Would you like to see your baby before ... well, would you like to see her?'

Tears streamed down Hannah's face. 'Yes, of course I would, she's my daughter.'

Mary vanished and reappeared a few minutes later holding a small bundle. She handed Ruby to my wife and we stared at the peaceful, beautiful face of the most perfect little thing I had ever seen in my life. She looked like she was simply sleeping.

The midwife then spoiled the moment by asking, 'Sometimes it helps to have some keepsakes. We often take a plaster cast of the baby's hands and feet, and maybe some photographs?'

I'm sure many parents do find this a comfort and helpful, but Hannah had definite views.

'Keepsakes?'

'To help you remember your baby.'

Hannah's eyes were sad and sore. 'If I go to Rome on holiday I might want some keepsakes. Why would I want plaster casts of my baby's hands and feet?'

The midwife was now squirming on her seat. 'To take home in a memory box.'

'A memory box to remind me of the most painful, fucked-up day of my whole life? No, thank you.'

I could tell Mary was very taken aback by Hannah's language. Eventually, another midwife came in with a consultant. The new midwife lifted Ruby from Hannah's arms and took her away. Hannah became very quiet.

The consultant, Dr Philip Gregory, asked, 'I know this is a difficult time, and no words we can offer can make you feel any better; however, would you like the hospital to arrange a post-mortem examination? I have to warn you that even after a post-mortem, we sometimes still cannot tell you exactly what the cause of death was.'

I looked pleadingly to Hannah, but she wasn't listening. She was staring at her hands.

'Hannah, what do you think?'

She just blinked at me and tears streamed down her face, she took my hand and squeezed it hard. I nodded to the consultant.

He stood up. 'OK, I need you to sign some forms, but we can do that later. The results may not be back for a few weeks, but we'll let you know.'

I paced the hallways for a few hours while Hannah slept. My thoughts were chaotic and fractured, then I remembered Calla. She'd understandably been pushed to the back of my mind.

I checked on Hannah, who was still asleep, and went off in search of Calla.

I returned to the birthing suite, but she wasn't in her room. A stressed-looking healthcare assistant was cleaning up and pulling bloodstained sheets off the bed.

'Where's Calla gone?'

She looked up from her task. 'Who, love?'

'Calla, the girl ... woman ... who was here.'

'They whisked her off to theatre ages ago.'

'Why did nobody tell me ... us?'

'Why should they?'

'I'm the father.'

'Why weren't you with her, then?'

'I was with my wife down the hall.'

She stared at me as if I had mental health issues. Maybe I did. She said slowly, obviously wanting me to go away, 'They took her away – that's all I know.'

I ran out of the room and down the corridor, back towards Hannah. Nearing the theatre block, I noticed a group of medical staff emerging from a door. I ran up to them.

'Where's Calla?'

'Excuse me?' a sweaty, red-haired man said.

'Calla, she was having a baby in room three.'

'What is your relationship to her?'

'I'm the father ...'

'You weren't there when we transferred her over.'

'What's wrong with her?'

'I don't think I can ...'

Thankfully, a midwife I recognized from earlier stepped in, I think she was called Sheila or Sheena. 'This is the baby's father, he was with Miss Hi Tee earlier. Mr McEwan,

198

Miss Hi Tee had some complications and the baby—'

'Oh no, not again, what happened?'

'If you'll let me finish,' said Sheila or Sheena. 'Miss Hi Tee was having some problems and her blood pressure wasn't looking good, so we took the decision to move her to theatre just in case there were any problems. Thankfully, she managed to deliver her baby about twenty minutes ago. It was a difficult birth but both she and the baby are now doing well. We'll transfer them over to the post-natal ward soon. You can visit her there.'

I sighed with relief and slowly walked back to Hannah. Later, with my wife in a wheelchair, we went to visit Calla. Although Hannah was exhausted, she insisted on going. As we entered the lift Hannah said, 'Don't tell her about Ruby just now, it'll only upset her. We can tell her later.'

In the end we needn't have worried, Calla was out for the count but her gorgeous little baby girl was in a crib beside her bed. As we gazed down, the little cherub opened her eyes and looked at us soundlessly. Tears poured from Hannah's eyes and I had to wheel her away.

The next day, shortly before I took Hannah home, I visited Calla alone and tried to explain what had happened with Ruby. I'm not sure how much of the details she grasped, but my tears told her all she needed to know. She cried with me and I felt grief like I never had before or since. I could let go with Calla in a way I couldn't with Hannah, who needed me to be strong and supportive, or so I believed.

Chapter Twenty-One

I WAS UNABLE to sleep, even though I was exhausted. My mind was in turmoil and just kept replaying the events of the last few weeks. Was there something wrong that I or we should have noticed? Should we have got to the hospital sooner?

Hannah was asleep. The pills the doctor had given her had knocked her for six, and I was tempted to nick a few to see if they would do the same for me, but that would mean nobody would hear Tessa or Lois if they cried out.

Hannah had been home from the hospital for less than a day and in that time we had hardly spoken. I think she was running on empty and I was feeling the same way. Calla was due out tomorrow and she would then come here with her healthy chubby baby. She had nowhere else to go. I'd tried phoning Fifi to tell her what had happened but her phone had sent me straight to voicemail three times. I'd left three messages but so far she'd not got back to me. I wasn't sure what effect all of this would have on Hannah but it was unlikely to do her any good.

I padded down the hall and paused in front of the door

to the nursery-cum-cupboard. I couldn't bear to look in; the room was a representation of something missing, a hole in our lives that wouldn't be filled, a gash in my heart that couldn't be closed.

I sighed with longing and went into the kitchen, opened the fridge and blinked in the light. I searched for something that might make me feel better, but I was disappointed. There was some white wine. Maybe numbness would be better, I thought, and I poured some into a plastic cup, closed the fridge and leaned back against the breakfast bar.

'Daddy?'

I was caught off guard; I jumped out of my skin and spilt some wine. The liquid sloshed onto the worktop. I grabbed some kitchen roll and mopped up the mess.

'Tessa, what are you doing up?'

She was holding her little teddy and slowly walked over and gave me a hug. She only came up to my hip so she really hugged my bum, but the gesture wasn't lost on me. I put the wine down, picked her up and hugged her close. Her scent was familiar and comforting, and I realized with a start that I would never experience this with Ruby. The hits kept coming, the love and space that I'd set aside for her in my heart would never be used.

I knew people would say that we already had two healthy and beautiful children and we should be thankful for that. They were right, of course, but in a way, having children already made it worse, as we knew what Ruby would have become. We knew the journey she would have gone on and the wonderful times we would have enjoyed with her. None of that would come to pass. I stifled a sob and buried my face into Tessa's hair.

'What's wrong, Daddy?'

'Nothing, sweetheart, I'm just tired. Why are you out of

bed? You've got school tomorrow.'

'Daddy, you woke me up, bashing about like a squirrel.'

I smiled, probably for the first time in days. 'I didn't know squirrels bashed about.'

Tessa stared up at me with sleepy eyes. 'They do, Mummy read me a story about a squirrel that bashed up all his friends and ended up alone.'

'I'm not surprised if he hit them all. What happened at the end of the story?'

'That was the end of the story.'

'You mean he didn't mend his ways and get his friends back?'

Tessa crinkled up her nose, which she always did when she was trying to remember something. Eventually she shook her head with certainty. 'No.'

'That wasn't a very happy ending, then.'

'Do all stories have happy endings?'

Good question, Tessa. 'No, sweetheart, not always. Listen, you need to go back to bed, it's very late and you've got a busy day tomorrow.'

'Do I have to go to school?'

'Of course, why wouldn't you?'

'Mummy's sad and might need me to cheer her up.'

'Do you know why Mummy's sad?'

The crinkly nose again. 'Because Ruby's gone to heaven instead of coming home.'

I was secretly glad that Hannah, despite her pain and despair, had taken the time to speak to Tessa. I don't think I could have done it without breaking down.

'That's right, but if you don't go to school, that will make Mummy even sadder.'

'Why?'

'Because then she would be worried about you falling behind in your lessons, and we all need to try not to worry Mummy at the moment. We need to be on our best behaviour.'

'Lois too?'

'Yes, Lois too.'

'And you, Daddy?'

I laughed, Tess had lightened my mood a little. 'Especially me, Tessa. Especially me.'

I escorted my wise-beyond-her-years daughter back to her bed and as usual, she was asleep in minutes. Hannah was like that too. I always found sleep hard to come by, elusive even, and tonight it was nigh on impossible.

I went back to the kitchen and recommenced my drinking. Eventually, I felt drowsy enough to try again. I couldn't face going back into the bedroom with Hannah, so instead I lay down on the living-room couch and slowly drifted off to sleep.

The next thing I knew it was light and Hannah was standing over me.

I rubbed my eyes and went to speak, but before I could get a word out Hannah said, 'I woke up during the night and you weren't there.'

'I couldn't sleep, so I went into the kitchen and drank wine, then I … well, I didn't want to disturb you … so I just slept on the couch.'

'You wanted to be near her, didn't you?'

'Near who?'

'What do you mean, "who"? Calla, of course, who else sleeps in here?'

'Calla's still at the hospital.'

'But all her stuff's still here, the essence of her is here.'

I wasn't awake enough to deal with this or 'essences'. It was all too vague for me and my head was fuzzy with sleep and wine. Over the last few months, Calla had made this her bedroom but she wasn't the only one who had spent a few nights in here.

'Well, Fifi slept here too.'

Hannah's face was like thunder. 'Oh right, I forgot about her, she's another one who doesn't murder her babies. She was right, you know.'

'Right about what?'

'That we shouldn't have had any more children, this is God's way of telling us we can't afford any more babies so we shouldn't have tried to have any.'

Bringing God into it confused me, we'd never been religious, either of us.

'That's crazy, Hannah, it had nothing to do with God or anything else it just ... well, it just ... happened.'

'But she was right, wasn't she? We can't afford any more babies and now ... well, now ... we don't have to worry about that, do we?'

'Hannah, money has nothing to do with it, we would have managed, we would have loved Ruby the same as we love Tessa and Lois. It would all have worked out fine.'

'But it didn't, did it? Our baby is lying cold and dead in the hospital morgue and I wake up needing you and find you in here. What am I supposed to think?'

I shook my head. I didn't know what she was supposed to think, I wasn't thinking anything. I was dead inside but didn't have the words to convey this to Hannah, I didn't have the words to convey it to myself. Also, I didn't have the energy and I didn't have the heart; it was broken. I know that's usually a metaphorical description but I had a physical pain where my heart was, maybe I was having a heart attack, and if it wasn't for Tessa and Lois I would have welcomed such an outcome. But I didn't die. Instead I turned and left the room, I had no wish to fight with Hannah. She was in pain. No, pain was a grossly inadequate description – agony would be better but even that didn't cover it. I was

204

the only one around who could even vaguely feel what she was feeling and she'd turned on me, and I couldn't deal with her pain and my own. I hadn't carried Ruby for nine months. I hadn't built up that intimate mother-daughter bond. I could never feel the way Hannah felt at the loss. Ruby hadn't been part of me physically and men would always lack that insight.

I loved my wife, and her pain made me feel helpless. I had been ready to love Ruby, hold her in my arms (hopefully without dropping her behind the couch) and experience that rush of love and protection I had felt when Tessa and Lois had been born. So no, I couldn't ever feel what Hannah was feeling. She called after me.

'That's right, Scott, you just walk away. Why don't you just keep going until you get to the hospital where you can cuddle your living, breathing daughter?'

I didn't reply. I couldn't, anything I said would just make things worse, if that was possible. Instead I did the emotionally impossible, went into the nursery and closed the door. I then sat on the floor beside what was supposed to be Ruby's cot, and wept.

Chapter Twenty-Two

THE FOLLOWING MORNING Calla was due back from the hospital with her daughter. Hannah had brought in the cavalry in the form of her mother and Jane. For once they were both quiet and subdued.

At about eleven o'clock, a taxi delivered Calla to our flat with her baby. She dropped her bags in the hall and paused. She and Hannah then stood and stared at each other for a moment. It was a tense moment. Given Hannah's mood I wasn't sure what to expect, but then Hannah walked up to Calla and hugged her.

Then our Thai guest, given the circumstances, displayed a huge demonstration of trust and handed her sleeping baby over to my distraught wife. Hannah gazed down at the peaceful face and exclaimed, 'Oh, Calla, she's beautiful,' before tears poured down her face.

This was the cue for everyone else to start, and when I started to feel tears pricking the corners of my eyes I left the room.

Then just to complicate matters my mother arrived. She and my dad had been given the same Calla explanation as everyone else bar Jane and Dave, but were equally as sceptical as Hannah's mum. All of that had now been forgotten, though, as we had to deal with this new crisis.

Hannah and I hadn't spoken since the previous evening and the silence between us continued as Hannah, her mum and Jane took the girls out for the day, leaving me alone with my mum, Calla and her baby.

As Carol and my mum didn't really get on this was probably a good thing.

'How is Hannah?' asked my mum.

'Not good, but what else would you expect?'

'She's just lost a baby. She needs time, time is a great healer.'

The last thing I needed at this point was 'pop psychology' from my mum, who also had an uncanny tendency to state the obvious.

I knew she was there to try and lend a helping hand but given the relationship she had with my mother-in-law, her presence would be more of a hindrance than a help. Thankfully, she vanished around lunchtime and I was left alone with my thoughts.

The next few days passed slowly. Hannah and I managed to talk cordially about Ruby's funeral, which was arranged and paid for by the hospital as she had been registered as an intra-uterine death. None of the financial intricacies made much sense to me and Hannah, nor did we think about it much. All we were concerned about was having a grave to visit. We had to fund the purchase of a burial plot, but the rest of the costs were covered.

It was exactly a week to the day after Ruby was born and died that I found myself seated in the local church, staring at the smallest coffin I'd ever seen. It was white and nestled between two vases of white roses, the same type of flowers Hannah had picked out for our wedding the previous year.

Beside the coffin sat a small brown teddy with a missing eye. It was Tessa's favourite little bear she'd had since she was a baby. She had insisted on giving it to Ruby, saying that her little sister needed something to cuddle when she went to heaven. Lois, not to be outdone, had placed her little plastic Upsy Daisy figure beside the teddy.

Both Tessa and Lois were wearing dark-blue dresses and black coats. Lois was fiddling with a hymn book and kept jumping on and off the pew. Neither of them really understood what was going on, nor did I expect them to, but whenever I stared over at the coffin and noticed the little offerings from the sisters Ruby would never know, it made my heart break that little bit more.

For the ceremony, we'd arranged to use the church we occasionally (very occasionally) attended. Outside in the nearby graveyard was the little plot we'd bought for our little soul, situated near a huge weeping willow tree.

It was a lovely, bright morning with clear blue sky and dazzling sunlight in direct contrast to the dark, sombre mood inside. The service was brief and attended only by our families and close friends. Jane and Dave sat together behind Hannah and my parents, and they both helped us carry the small but surprisingly heavy little coffin outside to the shady corner where Ruby would lie for all eternity.

The box was slowly lowered into the dark earth and after the minister said some final words, we all stood in silence for a few moments. I don't know what anyone else was thinking but I noticed little signs around me that spring was on the way. The branches of the weeping willow tree had little buds forming on them, the roses nearby were emerging from their winter slumber, snowdrops were poking their cheerful little heads through the cold earth, and all around birds were singing and chirping.

Everywhere new life was emerging, except inside the

dark hole that Hannah was staring into. I walked over and touched her arm. She looked up at me and tears spilled down her face. I moved to hug her but she twisted away and ran back into the church. Tessa and Lois ran after her. I had never felt so helpless and useless in my entire life.

Later, Hannah put on a brave face and managed to get through the day. I was glad when she took her sleeping pill and went to bed. Everybody was emotionally drained.

The next morning, I delivered all the paperwork to Lothian Chambers relating to Ruby's brief life. I'd already discovered that stillbirth babies don't get a birth certificate, they get a certificate of stillbirth instead.

It was only a few bits of paper but the process of confirming her existence was of some comfort to me. Maybe it was just because it gave me something to do to get out of the house. I felt lost, completely out of my depth. I didn't know what to do to make anything better. I knew that Hannah was in desperate need of help, but I couldn't get through to her, she'd closed herself completely to me.

A few days later, the hospital phoned and we went in to speak to a consultant obstetrician, Dr Clark, who had the post-mortem results available. She hadn't been present at Ruby's birth. I wasn't sure if this was a deliberate ploy by the NHS to bring some objectivity to the situation or if it was simply down to varying shift patterns. I don't suppose it mattered much.

We sat in stony silence while she tried her best to explain what she thought had happened.

Her tone was sympathetic and quiet. 'Unfortunately, when these things happen, we can never be exactly sure what caused the death of your baby …'

'Ruby,' said Hannah firmly.

The doctor nodded. 'Sorry, what caused Ruby's death.'

'What we have discovered from the examination is that

she had a congenital heart defect. Occasionally these get picked up on routine scans but often they are very hard to detect, and it isn't until children are much older, if ever, depending upon the severity of the defect that the problem is identified. Some people never have it diagnosed.'

'So why did our Ruby die while others didn't?' I asked.

Dr Clark sighed. 'Unfortunately, that's one of the unknowns. What I can tell you is that Ruby appears to have had a ventricular septal defect. In simple terms, it is a hole between the two sides of the heart.'

'And there was no way this could have been picked up?' I noticed that I was asking all the questions. Hannah was silent and very still.

'As I said, it can be very difficult to spot. The severity of the condition varies hugely and is actually very common. Around one in five hundred babies are born in the UK with some kind of heart defect every year. She also appears to have had narrower heart valves than normal, which may have contributed to the problem. You need to realize that being born is incredibly stressful for babies and it might have been that the extra strain of this was just too much for her poor little heart to bear.'

Tears spilled from my eyes and I went mute. Hannah noticed, gave me a sympathetic look, took my hand in hers and decided to speak.

'What caused it? Was it something we did, or didn't do?'

'No, of course not, no one really understands what causes these things. There may be a genetic element, something that goes way back in either of your genetic histories, or any number of other reasons we simply don't have the knowledge to answer yet. One day, when human DNA has been studied more, we might learn why these things happen, but for now it remains something of a mystery.'

'Could we have had a Caesarean right away?' Hannah's

eyes were now filled with tears as well.

Dr Clark had the case notes with her, but I noticed she didn't refer to them. She'd obviously done her homework before meeting with us. I was mildly surprised she didn't have a lawyer looking over her shoulder, given the world was now so litigious.

'As soon as the baby ...' She noticed Hannah's face darken. '... Ruby ... started to display signs of distress, we followed established protocols. Remember, up until that point, everything was fine. You'd previously had two normal and uneventful births and there were no indications this one would be any different. Had Ruby survived we would have probably found the defect quite quickly, given the severity of its nature and maybe then been able to do something. Sadly, we didn't get to that point.'

A few moments of uncomfortable silence followed, broken only by me blowing my nose loudly into a tissue.

Dr Clark opened up our file and withdrew a single sheet of paper.

'I can get you a full copy of the report if you wish, but most parents don't bother.' She handed Hannah the paper. 'This is a leaflet about bereavement charities. There are a few of them on here, and a note of local groups you can go along to. It might not be something you want to do just now, but maybe later it might help. A lot of people feel better talking to others who have had the same experience.'

Hannah nodded, and shoved the leaflet into her handbag. Dr Clark stood up, signalling that her time with us was over.

'If you have any questions, please don't hesitate to phone us, there will always be someone available to speak to you.'

I had a million questions, but suspected nobody, save God, would be able to answer them. We left and drove home in silence, an uncomfortable silence.

The next three days passed very slowly. I was due back at work on the Friday. We simply couldn't afford the luxury of me taking any more time off. Regardless of our pain and state of mind, the bills still had to be paid.

Hannah and I had been avoiding each other as best we could, which was not easy in a tiny flat. I'd taken to going to bed with Hannah, but as soon as she was asleep, I crept through and slept on the floor in the nursery. Somehow being in there made me feel better, I'm not sure why. I don't think Hannah noticed, or if she did, she made no comment.

Calla had been very sensitive about her baby and Hannah. She tried to be out most of the day and only came back when it was nearly evening and we were getting ready for bed. I didn't know where she went, and I didn't ask. It made life marginally easier when she wasn't there.

My conversations with Hannah had all been very limited and usually involved me carrying out her instructions, which I did without question to avoid any kind of confrontation.

'Scott, I've left out Tessa and Lois's clothes. Can you get them dressed and take them out, please? They are driving me mad.'

'Scott, the chicken is in the oven and will be ready in about half an hour. Can you put some veg on and make sure Tessa eats something? She's hardly touched a thing all day.'

'Scott, can you get Tessa out of the bath, please?'

'Scott, can you get Lois in the bath, please?'

'Scott, have you dried the girls' hair yet? They need to get to bed.'

'Scott, can you speak to Calla and tell her to put the baby's dirty nappies in a separate bag before she drops it in the bin?'

'Scott, Calla's been in the bathroom for an hour, can you

get her out? I need a bath and some peace and quiet.'

'Scott, where is the hairbrush I left in the bathroom?'

'Scott, the car won't start.'

'Scott, the boiler needs reset.'

'Scott, can you clean the kitchen floor? It's filthy.'

'Scott, can you ask Calla to go out again tomorrow after Tessa's gone to school and Lois is at my mum's? I need to tidy up in here.'

'Scott, you need to take the girls out, my head is splitting.'

'Scott, you need to help me here, I can't do everything.'

Most of these tasks were usually carried out by Hannah with occasionally my help. If nothing else, it gave me some appreciation of what life was like for Hannah when I was at work.

One evening, I'd managed to get Tessa and Lois to bed early and Calla was with her baby in the living room, also getting ready for bed.

Hannah and I sat down at the kitchen table opposite each other; neither of us spoke. I felt like I barely knew my wife at this point, such was the gulf between us. We were only two feet apart but it felt like two miles. She'd completely shut me out of her life. What a huge contrast to how close we'd been whilst she had been pregnant.

I was vaguely aware that this was likely to be some kind of defence mechanism kicking in but I lacked the insight and maybe the intelligence to fully comprehend it. As it was directed solely at me, I found it very difficult to deal with. Hannah was not the only one hurting.

Hannah's manner was very matter of fact and cold when she spoke. 'Scott, I'm taking the girls and moving into my mum's house for a while.'

'What does that mean?'

Hannah shrugged coldly, her face impassive. 'It means

I'm leaving, I can't cope with everything, and you and Calla just now.'

I was devastated, I knew things were bad, I knew Hannah was suffering, but surely she couldn't be thinking straight. 'Hannah, I love you.'

Her expression didn't change, but she did take my hand into hers and her voice softened. 'Love's got nothing to do with anything any more. I need space to think and sort myself out.'

'We'll get a bigger flat.'

Hannah sighed and rubbed her eyes. 'Scott, I don't need that kind of space, I just need time on my own, I need to grieve, I need to think, I need to plan. I can't really explain and to be honest, I don't want to.'

'You can do all that here. I'll take time off work …'

'How many paternity days have you got left?'

'Err … none.'

'What happens, then, if you don't go back?'

'Well, I dunno … I don't get paid, I suppose.'

'So you would have no money coming in at all then.'

I didn't like the word 'you' in this context. When it came to money we'd always done everything together, it was another example of her detached thought process.

'No,' I answered.

'So you need to go back to work, and I need to move out.'

'Forever?'

'What?'

'Are you leaving forever?'

'Scott, at the moment I can't think beyond tomorrow. In fact, I can't think beyond the next ten minutes, so that's not a fair question.'

'It is a fair question to me. My wife is leaving and she won't tell me why or when, if ever, I'll see her and my kids again.'

'Of course you'll see your kids.'

'That was a three-part question.'

'What is this, *University Challenge*?'

'I never went to university, remember?'

Her voice hardened again. 'Oh I remember all right, maybe you should have. It might have helped you grow up a bit. Will you see me again? Who knows, as for the reason, there's so many, Scott, I don't think I can remember them all.'

'Why don't you try?'

Hannah's face flushed with anger. 'All right, number one, I hate this flat, I hate my life, and I hate the way you try and fix everything.'

'Fix everything?'

Hannah snorted through her nose, which made a little snot fly out and land on the table between us. We both ignored it, a little snot wasn't a big issue right now.

'Yeah, when Ruby died, you were the one who suddenly switched into organization mode, organizing the birth certificate – she didn't even get one, she got a stillbirth certificate, so as far as the world is concerned she never really existed. You agreed to let them do the post-mortem, chatting to the doctors about what should happen to her like she was a piece of meat.'

'Hannah, that's not fair. Someone had to do that, it was necessary, you couldn't do it so I did it. It was really horrible but—'

'Ah, I see it was to spare me the trauma of organizing my little girl's future.'

'Ruby was dead, Hannah.'

'Do you think I don't know that? I'm constantly waiting for the front door to open and my little baby to come crawling in on her hands and knees, fresh earth from her grave clogging up her nostrils like some zombie from a horror movie, with blood dripping from her bloodshot eyes.'

'Hannah, that's terrible.'

'I know it's terrible and believe me, every single minute of every single day, some horrific vision appears in front of my eyes followed by a wave of guilt that leaves me breathless and sobbing.'

'I'm hurting too, Hannah, it wasn't just you that lost a baby, I lost a little girl too.'

Hannah stared at me in silence for a moment as if contemplating my statement. Eventually she shook her head.

'It's not the same, Scott. How can you possibly understand how I'm feeling? My tits are still producing milk for a baby I don't have. My arms ache to hold Ruby – I never knew motherhood could be so painful and unjust. In the hospital when they handed her to me, she was a perfect baby girl that looked like she was sleeping, sleeping forever.' Hannah's gaze drifted away to another time and place before her eyes settled back on me. 'Anyway,' she continued, 'you've got a backup. I don't.'

'That's crazy, we don't even know she's mine and I have no connection with Calla and her baby.'

'She'll be yours, Scott, don't worry about that. We know Calla well enough now; she says the child is yours so it will be. But this isn't about you, Scott. I'm doing this for me, I need to be somewhere where I can cry without feeling guilty, I need someone to hold me and NOT tell me everything will be fine, and I need space to breathe. I'm suffocating in here. I have to get out.'

Hannah paused and tears flowed freely down her face. 'When they lowered her tiny little coffin into her grave, I wanted to jump down on top of her and let them cover me up too. I will never, ever, ever get over that, Scott, never.'

She rubbed her eyes; they were raw and bloodshot. I imagined mine were similar.

'Another thing, Scott, I've been doing a lot of thinking over the last few days and I resent the fact I've sacrificed my career for you and the girls. I should be running a company by now, do you know that? The ability and skills I've got have been wasted where I am and instead of moving on, I've settled for all the crap they dish out just so I can get some flexible hours to manage childcare. Well, I've had enough of living on the edge of poverty, having to make do and mend. Now that I don't have to take my maternity leave, I'm getting a new job as soon as I can find one, some-where that appreciates what I can do and who'll pay me accordingly....' She gazed around our tiny kitchen. 'And I've had enough of this shitty place. I've had enough of you holding me back, stopping me from doing what I want.'

'Hannah, I've never stopped you from doing anything.'

'You've stopped me fulfilling my potential.'

'How have I done that?'

'By making me live here. By lumbering me with two little brats who won't do anything they're told, by making me feel worthless and useless ...'

'Hannah, stop. None of that is true, Tessa and Lois are lovely little girls. They're naughty sometimes but no more than any other children. Look, why don't I move out for a while and then ...'

Hannah put her head in her hands and shouted, 'No, Scott. I need to get out of here. I can't stand it.' She lowered her voice, looked into my eyes and said calmly, 'I can't cope with the fact that in this flat is a room that I can't go into, because if I did, my heart would burst.' She stared at the table as if the salt and pepper pots had suddenly become the most interesting objects in the universe.

Her outburst had shocked me into silence. I didn't know what to say or do. I'd always been a practical sort of guy, I wasn't academic but fixing things was what I was good at, but it was this very trait that seemed to be driving Hannah mad. I knew that anything else I said or offered to do at this point would make things worse so I kept quiet.

The silence seemed to calm Hannah and when she finally looked up, there were tears in her eyes. I resisted the urge to reach out and touch her, though my very soul was crying out, telling me to take her in my arms and hold her.

Eventually she smiled weakly at me and said, 'I'll be gone by the time you get home from work tomorrow, OK?'

I nodded and tried to stop the tears from falling from my eyes and down my cheeks. I failed miserably. Hannah didn't comment, but she stared at my distraught face for a moment. I thought she was going to say something – anything. Instead she hesitated, then shook her head resolutely and left the room.

Chapter Twenty-Three

TRUE TO HER word, when I got home from work the next evening, Hannah was gone, and so were the girls.

I tried calling her mobile but after the twentieth attempt with no answer, I gave up and poured myself a glass of wine from the bottle I'd treated myself to on the way home.

Calla was in the living room nursing her baby and watching TV. I didn't want to disturb her, so I took a seat at the kitchen table and started to read the local paper that was delivered free every Friday.

I drank another glass of wine and attempted the 'very easy' crossword on the back page. I managed to get six clues before I got stuck and gave up. It wasn't 'very easy' for me. I caught sight of Calla tiptoeing to the bathroom. I assumed her baby was now asleep and she'd be going to bed soon. My watch said it was ten o'clock so bedtime for me too as I had to get up early tomorrow as usual for work; it was one of the Saturdays when I had to go in for the morning. Normally I hated working Saturdays but this time I welcomed the distraction.

I waited until Calla had finished in the bathroom and

then emptied my wine-filled bladder, washed my face and cleaned my teeth. The face that stared back at me from the mirror looked pale and worried. This wasn't exactly a shock, as I *was* worried. I could add stressed, confused, scared and any number of about thirty other emotions that I couldn't think of due to my fatigue and wine-fogged mind.

I put my sleepy shirt on that I wore to bed, climbed under the duvet of my now big, lonely bed, and started to sob. I was a little drunk and feeling thoroughly sorry for myself. I fell asleep feeling miserable.

Hours later I woke up and went to the bathroom. When I returned to bed, I couldn't sleep and lay awake thinking about everything. The thoughts of Hannah, my girls and Ruby set me off crying again and I just let the tears flow.

Then the bedroom door opened and Calla poked her head around the door.

'You cry?'

'Yes, sorry, Calla, just feeling sorry for myself, I'll shut up. I hope I didn't wake the baby.'

'Baby sleep – Calla wake and hear you.'

'Yeah, sorry, I'll shut up.'

Instead of leaving like I expected, she came in and closed the door softly behind her. She was wearing an old pair of Hannah's pyjamas; they were baggy and comfortable, the ones Hannah favoured when she had her period. Calla sat down on the bed and stared at my red eyes and snotty nose. I must have looked fabulously sexy – not. I couldn't have cared less.

Calla then pulled the covers back and slipped into the bed behind me. She pulled the duvet up and snuggled into my back. She put her arm around me and held my hand. I continued crying until I fell asleep.

The next thing I knew Calla was digging me in the back.

I opened my eyes and squinted across the room as someone had pulled the curtains open. Hannah was standing staring at us with her hands on her hips.

'Wakey, wakey, lovebirds, rise and shine.'

'Lovebirds?' I said, confused.

Calla started babbling something unintelligible and Hannah held her hand up to silence her.

'I've no idea what you're saying, Calla, and to be honest it doesn't matter. I can see for myself what's been going on.'

'See what?' I asked stupidly before the penny dropped. 'Hannah, nothing happened, she just slept beside me ...'

'Yes, yes, Scott, a likely story.'

'We're fully clothed, she's got her pyjamas on ...'

'My pyjamas actually.'

'Your pyjamas on. Calla just—'

Hannah interrupted. 'Calla, I think your baby needs you more than Scott does, can you go and tend to her, please?'

Calla vanished, leaving me and my furious wife alone.

'So?'

I wasn't in a good position and I knew it. 'Nothing happened, Calla heard me crying and came in to see me, the next thing—'

'You were crying?'

'I was in a state, you weren't talking to me and I was upset and I didn't know what was happening. I still don't. I didn't know if you'd left me for good and I didn't know if I would ever see you again....'

'I was at my mum's, not Timbuktu.'

'It doesn't matter where you were, you had walked out and I didn't know what to do.'

'So you fucked Calla.'

'I didn't fuck anyone, I told you, Calla just came in and held me until I went to sleep.'

I stood up and moved over towards Hannah, then

suddenly I was on the floor. My lip was bleeding and I was in shock. My wife had punched me, really punched me. It wasn't a Mike Tyson knockout kind of punch, but it was hard enough. Nobody had punched me for years, not since school, I think. I was on the ground from shock rather than pain. I didn't know girls could punch; well, I'd seen Hilary Swank throw a few in *Million Dollar Baby* but that wasn't real life.

'Hannah …'

'I'm gone for like five minutes and you are unfaithful.'

'It wasn't five minutes, it was a whole day.' That sounded pathetic, even to me.

'Oh, sorry, so that's how long you need, is it?'

'No, of course not, and I wasn't unfaithful.'

'Oh, excuse me, I must be mistaken. I walk into MY bedroom find you in MY bed with a prostitute and you're not being unfaithful? What exactly were you doing, then?'

'Sleeping, and Calla doesn't do that any more.'

'You know what they say about leopards, Scott. So excuse me if I don't believe you.'

I started to get up. Hannah stepped closer to me; her eyes were blazing. 'I wouldn't get up if I were you, I might just have to knock you down again.'

I remained on the floor. 'I was in my … our bed trying to go to sleep and Calla came into the room, sat on the bed and then just lay beside me and comforted me.'

Hanna shook her head. 'Her baby needs comforting, Scott, not you. You didn't just have a baby that leaves you feeling weak and vulnerable, you didn't just lose a baby that makes you feel … I don't know what I feel actually … numb, I guess. All you lost … what did you lose? Nothing as far as I can see.'

'I lost you and the girls.'

Hannah snorted. 'Well, you have now and it's your own

fault. Don't speak to me any more, Scott, don't phone me, don't phone my mum, not now, not again, NEVER!'

Hannah swivelled, grabbed her keys and marched away, the door slammed and I was alone again. Very alone.

Calla disappeared most of Saturday and Sunday, thankfully. When she did appear she wouldn't meet my gaze and was obviously feeling bad about what had happened, or rather what hadn't happened, but what Hannah had thought had.

After work on the Monday, I arrived home to find a very excited Calla. She was hopping up and down from one foot to the other and laughing. At least someone was happy.

'Have you just won the lottery or something, Calla?'

She stopped hopping for a moment and cocked her head to one side like a spaniel listening for dinner time. 'What is this lottery? No, Calla go to new home, with baby.'

Social services, or maybe Fifi, had obviously done their stuff.

'That's brilliant, Calla, I'm pleased for you.' I went to give her a hug but she suddenly pulled away like I smelled of dog poo or was maybe infected with the Ebola virus.

'Hannah was here, sad.'

Ah, so Hannah had been round. I wasn't surprised she was still sad, leaving me and the flat wouldn't change that. 'What did Hannah want?'

'Clothes.'

'Clothes?'

'Clothes.'

'Oh, clothes for the girls?'

Calla nodded. 'Hannah took case.'

I pottered through to the bedroom and noticed that the drawers had been nearly emptied and the suitcase that lived under our bed had indeed vanished. That wasn't a good sign as Hannah obviously had no intention of coming back any time soon.

Calla watched me with a strange expression on her face. She looked like she was feeling sorry for me. I was obviously now an object of pity.

'Calla?' She'd gone back into the living room where the baby was sleeping. Rather than shout and risk waking the baby, I pottered through and said quietly, 'Calla?'

She ignored me and continued to lean over the crib, staring at her baby.

I joined her. Calla still hadn't given her a name so I just called the baby Baby for the time being.

The dark-eyed, dark-haired little angel was sleeping soundly. Her eyelids fluttered gently as she dreamed. I wonder what 3-week-old babies dreamt about. All she knew about were breasts and vaginas. Actually, come to think about it, I'd probably had a few dreams like that myself over the years.

As I gazed at Baby, she didn't appear to have a single gene from me in her body, not that appearances mattered all that much at such an early stage. It was quite possible that the child would grow up into a carbon copy of her mother, regardless of my input. I hadn't arranged for a paternity test yet, there had been too much going on in my chaotic life for me to even think about it. Now, however, staring down at this gorgeous little creature, I realized that I needed to find out sooner or later. The result would fundamentally affect the relationship I ultimately had with Calla too, assuming she was going to stay in the UK.

'Where are you going?'

'I leave Edinburgh, I move to Little France.'

'Little France?'

'Yes, Little France.'

I laughed out loud. 'You are moving to Little France?'

'Yes, home in Little France.'

Little France is a part of Edinburgh between Craigmillar Castle and the Royal Infirmary and Maternity Hospital, where my life had recently hit the rocks. It was called this due to the huge entourage Mary Queen of Scots brought with her from France when she came and settled there, and lived in the castle after the death of her husband in 1561. For a time, there were more French-speaking people living in that part of Edinburgh than Scots.

It was a great moment and I instinctively looked for Hannah to share it with me, but of course Hannah wasn't there.

Calla showed me the letter that Hannah had brought her. It had Mrs Fiona Montgomery's name at the bottom but wasn't signed by her. I wasn't sure why Hannah had got the letter rather than it being delivered to the flat. I assumed she'd had more success with contacting Fifi or her department than I'd had.

Thursday 17th April

Dear Ms Hi Tee,

Emergency housing allocation
(Social Housing Assessment Amendment number 11, subsection 6)

Following your successful application for social housing for yourself and your newborn child, we can confirm that a flat has been allocated and furnished to standard 4 on the social requirement scale.

The flat is a purpose-built, newly completed property that complies with all local authority regulations (August 2013 version) and will form part of an official tenancy agreement. Copies of the completed agreement are available to view at our local housing office and online at the local authority website.

The property will be available for tenancy on Wednesday 23rd April and keys can be collected from the housing office (address above) any time between 9 a.m. & 4.30 p.m. from this date.

Property address:

Flat 2/1 23 Craigmillar Quadrant
Little France
Edinburgh
EH16 2BT

We hope you enjoy living in your new home.

Yours sincerely

T Black pp

Mrs Fiona Montgomery
Senior IR Adviser

Having read the very dull letter twice, I realized why Fifi or her assistant had arranged for it to be sent to Hannah. Calla wouldn't have understood a word of it. The fact the letter was PPd probably meant Fifi was now enjoying her maternity leave. I wondered how she was coping and how many of her high ideals had crashed and burned since she'd taken home a real live baby.

I spent the next day helping Calla to pack up her stuff. Considering she'd been with us for only four months, and during that time had virtually no money, she'd managed to accumulate quite a lot. We managed to cram it all into three black bin bags with two separate bags and a rucksack for all the baby stuff she would need until Wednesday.

I offered to take some time off on the Wednesday to help Calla, but it seemed that Hannah had arranged everything and I wasn't needed. I found it amazing that she could take the time to help Calla move and yet couldn't find a minute to either phone me or answer my texts. I arrived home that evening to a silent, empty flat.

Chapter Twenty-Four

OVER THE NEXT few weeks, I grew used to the silence that enveloped me like a shroud every time I closed the front door. I'd started to spend even more time at work, closing up later each evening in order to avoid being at home, but the weekends were difficult. I'd become accustomed to my Saturdays and Sundays being packed with kids' stuff, swimming, soft-play, swing parks, museums and general madness.

I missed my children desperately. I missed Hannah too, but not the Hannah who had left me. I didn't know that Hannah.

I supposed that eventually she would want the girls to see me but for the time being I was lost. I had to admit that the silence of the flat was better than the silence of Hannah being here but not speaking to me. There were a few tiny benefits: I now got complete control of the remote and didn't have to watch TV programmes that included custard pies, robots and things that talked that shouldn't – like cars, trains, dogs, cats, dinosaurs and rabbits. Rabbits, I'd noticed, had become particularly prolific in recent months for some reason.

Although I was alone, I had become so Hannah-tized that I still did everything the way she did. I would not even dare start eating my dinner without putting the pans in the sink to soak, I would double and triple check the white wash pile before putting it in the machine to make sure nothing even remotely coloured had crept in while I wasn't looking, and the bed had to be immaculately made before I set off to work in the morning, even though nobody but me would ever see it. The tiled bathroom floor had to be dust-free and the toothbrushes had to be arranged in the rack above the sink in order, mine first, then Hannah's, Tessa's and Lois's. Of course, all the girls' toothbrushes had been removed by Hannah and now mine sat alone on the little rack.

Hannah had been back to the flat a few times over the last week to pick up extra clothes, sheets, pillowcases, bags and other little personal items that, once gone, made the place feel more soulless and empty. It felt like death by a thousand cuts. Each evening I came home to find something else had gone. Tonight I noticed the kitchen clock, a moving-in present from her mother, had gone, leaving a circle of cleaner paint on the wall – a circle of despair. Yesterday it had been the last of the girls' toys that had vanished from their room. I had noticed that one of Tessa's little dolls had been left behind and I'd sat on her bed, hugging it to my heart and sobbing.

Hannah's sneaky activity was having a devastating effect on me. In her head she might have thought it easier to come in when I wasn't here, but it made me feel like a leper.

I was so lost in my misery that when my phone rang and vibrated loudly on the kitchen table, I almost jumped out of my skin. Nobody phoned me any more. I'd got so involved and absorbed in my mad family life and work that

I'd lost contact with most of my friends, except Dave, who never phoned me anyway, he only ever sent texts. I think he had some kind of phone-call phobia. I didn't recognize the number; or rather, the phone's menu didn't recognize the number.

'Hello,' I muttered uncertainly.

'Scott,' the familiar female voice replied.

'Calla, you've got a phone.' Perhaps the most obvious statement I'd ever made in my life.

'Yes, Calla have phone. Can you come?'

With anyone else, the sexual innuendo of that question would have made me smile, but with Calla and our chequered history, my internal alarm bell started jangling loudly inside my head.

'Now?'

'Yes, please.'

'I'm not sure that's such a good idea, Calla, every time I see you I just seem to get deeper in trouble with Hannah.'

'Hannah not here.'

I didn't think she would be.

'Hannah was here.'

Now that was a surprise. 'When?'

'Yesterday.'

'Did she say anything?'

'Hannah say lots, talk very fast.'

'Did she mention me?'

'I not know.'

'You must know if she mentioned me?'

'She not say Scott.'

This was hopeless. Even if I went around to her flat, she wouldn't be able to tell me anything. 'I don't know, Calla, it's awkward.'

'What is this awkward?'

'Never mind, it's just not a good idea.'

'Please?'

She said please with the same pleading tone that Tessa used when she wanted to do something. Calla had probably learned it from her. The thought of my daughter made me catch my breath. How I missed them.

'Please?' she repeated.

I sighed. The mimicry of my eldest daughter had broken through my resolve, which was obviously about as strong as tissue paper. Plus, there was the outside chance that I might be able to coax some information from her about Hannah.

'OK, Calla, I'll see you soon.'

'Goody.'

The line went dead and I finished tidying the kitchen before I left. Hannah hated dirty plates lying around.

It took me fifteen minutes to drive over to Calla's flat. She'd been given a housing association apartment in a newly built block. The area was full of new housing and as it had the new Royal Hospital nearby, the vicinity proved to be especially popular with medical staff.

I parked on the street outside Calla's block, locked the car door and peered at the list of numbers on the intercom. I noticed that she'd already written her name, C Hi Tee, on the little paper tag opposite button number 2/1. She was the only person to have done so and I reckoned it signified a sense of pride. Either that or she was the only person living there.

I then considered that Calla was only twenty-two, and for her to have travelled so far and to now have her own home, albeit one paid for by UK taxpayers, must rank as an enormous achievement for her and probably something she could never have aspired to back in her native country.

I pressed the buzzer and waited. The door lock vibrated and I pushed it open. I walked up the short flight of stairs to the first floor and Calla's cheery face greeted me around the door of her flat.

'Scott!'

I nodded before warily saying, 'Calla, nice flat.'

She was dressed in a tight T-shirt and jeans that accentuated her figure, which appeared to have bounced back into shape instantly after giving birth. Hannah would hate her for that. I brushed past her and caught a whiff of her perfume, which instantly transported me back to the hotel room in Phuket where Hannah and I had first met her. That felt like a lifetime ago now.

Calla closed the door and beckoned me into her living room, which was sparsely furnished with a small, flat-screen TV and a tiny table strewn with magazines and baby toys. The floor had a soft grey carpet covering it, and a two-seater brown leather couch was pushed against the wall opposite the small picture window. At right angles to the couch was a matching leather chair. It was the chair that held the biggest surprise, because sitting in it grinning at me like a cat that had got the cream was Dave.

Hannah was right, he really would shag anything. He obviously read my mind as his opening statement was an apology.

'Sorry, Scott, I meant to phone you, but well, you know how crap I am with the phone so I got Calla to phone you so that I could tell you in person.'

'Tell me what?'

Dave cocked his head to one side like a spaniel with ear mites, a characteristic that was both endearing and exasperating at the same time.

'So that I could tell you that Calla and I are now going out.'

'What do you mean going out?'

'Well, you know, like a couple, friends with benefits, lovers, boyfriend and girlfriend.'

'When did this happen?'

'Well … it happened over the last few weeks, I suppose, but I've liked her for ages. She started to come and see me just after Hannah and you came home from the hospital. I think she felt awkward being in the flat with her baby while you had lost yours. She'd hang around my flat, watching TV mostly until I got home from work, and then I'd run her back to your place. She felt terrible for Hannah, and wanted to do something to help.'

Well, that explained where Calla had been going. 'She told you all this?'

'Yes.'

'She can hardly string a sentence together, Dave.'

'We speak the language of love.'

I couldn't tell if he was serious or not, but I laughed anyway.

'Dave, I'm not sure you really understand the language of love or Calla's view of the world. Six or seven months ago, Calla was lying on her back, opening her legs for strangers. She probably thinks you are just a really keen punter. At some point in the next few weeks, she'll probably present you with a huge bill.'

'We've not had sex.'

That surprised me hugely and I told him so.

'Does it? I'm not a dog on heat. We decided to wait until we were both ready.'

I raised an eyebrow and stared at my friend, and suddenly remembered that Calla's difficult birth meant that she'd needed about twelve stitches inserted into her nether regions. The memory made me wince.

'Is she still too sore?'

Dave smiled. 'Yeah.'

'I thought so. Look, Dave, it's really none of my business …' I had to think about that for a moment. Was it my business? 'Well, I don't think it's any of my business, you're both grown-ups, well, you're an older grown-up than her.'

'I'm only thirty-two.'

'She's only twenty-two.'

'Is she?' He sounded surprised. 'I thought she was older, she acts much older.'

'She's been through a lot and probably had to grow up quickly.'

'Also, there's the baby to think about.'

I agreed. 'Yeah you're right, what about the baby?'

'I thought I could adopt her.'

The thought of Dave being a father was totally alien to me. 'You don't need to do that, I don't think, not yet anyway. Aren't you getting a bit ahead of yourself here? Most of your relationships only last a few months.'

'I've been married twice.'

'As I said, most of your relationships only last a few months.'

'That's not fair. I think I'm in love with Calla.'

'She's a hottie, she's a former hooker, she's vulnerable, you might be in lust with her, so the love thing I doubt very much.'

'I'm old enough to know the difference.'

'You'd think so.'

'Who made you the Love Doctor?'

'Nobody, my track record isn't that great either.'

Dave nodded slowly. 'Yeah, sorry about that. How is Hannah?'

'I don't know, I've not heard from her.'

'Oh yeah – she'll still be annoyed about you sleeping with Calla.'

I stared at my friend. 'How did you know about that?'

'Calla told me.'

I sighed. I couldn't imagine how Calla had managed to

communicate this to Dave and didn't want to.

'You know what, though, I think it was just Calla's way of reaching out to try and comfort me.'

Dave smiled. 'Yeah, she's comforted me a few times, and a bit more.'

I shook my head. Dave was a dog. 'Well, Calla's actions didn't help anyway. Everything lately has been a disaster. I think Hannah blames me for losing the baby.'

'How can she do that? It wasn't anything to do with you.'

'I know but I'm probably the only one she can blame, somehow she thinks it's a punishment on us for being evil people.'

'You're not evil; unlucky maybe, but not evil. Look, Scott, I can't even imagine how it feels to lose a kid. I've spent a lot of time with Calla's baby and she's amazing. The way she looks at you with complete trust. The gurgling sucking noises she makes, the way she grips my finger – I'm completely smitten.'

'That's great, Dave, but the baby might still be mine and I don't know what to do about that.'

'Does it matter?'

'Sorry?'

'Well, I mean, you're not going to come and live with Calla, are you?'

'Well, no … I don't know what I'm going to do about anything.'

'But you don't want to live with Calla?'

'Not really, no. She's lovely and caring, but no, I love Hannah.'

'That's all I needed to know. If the baby does turn out to be yours, then, well, we'll cross that bridge when we come to it. I just needed to know that you had no interest in Calla.'

'Was Hannah here?'

'Yeah, earlier today, she just came to see how Calla was settling in.'

'She knows about you two?'

Dave grinned. 'She does now.'

'What did she say?'

'She seemed pleased for us both, she didn't say much. She looks really sad.'

'Did she mention me?'

After a short pause, Dave said, 'She asked me and Calla to keep an eye on you, make sure you're OK.'

I nodded, unsure of what that meant.

'She told me not to tell you that she asked us to do that, but well, given the circumstances, I thought you should know that she's still thinking about you.'

'She won't speak to me.'

'I don't know what to tell you, Scott.'

'Hannah is the only person I've ever truly loved, I loved her even before I met her.'

'That doesn't make sense.'

'It's love, Dave, sense doesn't come into it.'

There was a moment's silence and Calla came into the living room, sat on the arm of the chair and kissed Dave. She then leaned against his shoulder. Before she could get comfortable, a cry came from somewhere down the hall and Calla jumped up and left.

'She's a great mother,' Dave said, looking longingly at the door Calla had just walked through.

I sighed. 'I miss Hannah and I miss my girls. I can't live without them. It's funny, I used to moan about how we never got any time together, how hard life was with two young kids ruling every minute of your existence and yet now they're gone, it's like someone reached into my ribs and ripped out my heart.'

'Like Indiana Jones?'

'Eh?'

'You know, in the Temple of Doom where that guy had the ability to rip people's hearts out.'

'Not exactly, but not far off, I suppose. I don't know what to do, Dave. I go home and it's so empty, my life is so empty.'

'I've never been where you are, Scott, so not a lot I can say to that. I can tell you something, though, Calla and me have been having some really good conversations, that's partly why I think I'm in love with her.'

'I thought you were sure.'

'I was until I listened to you prattle on, mate. Anyway, the point is we've had some really good chats.'

'How does that work? Her English is best when you talk about trains or football.'

'Ah, that explains a lot.'

'It does?'

'Well, yeah, when she gets excited she tends to babble about footballers. Not heard her mention trains, though.'

'And sex, she's pretty hot on sex.'

'Don't really know about that yet, except the comfort …'

'… thing, yeah, you said that, and she's pretty fluent in sex stuff. No, but listen, how can you have a conversation with her?'

'Thai Chat.'

'What's Thai Chat?'

'It's an app.'

'What's it do?'

'Helps me talk to Calla. Basically, it allows her to speak in Thai which is translated into English and allows me to talk in English which translates into Thai. It's not perfect, but it's pretty good.'

'I wonder why Fifi didn't know about that?'

'Fifi?'

'That woman from the government we had staying with us.'

'Oh yeah, well, maybe she wasn't an Apple fan. It's been out for a while, it's now in the third generation. Anyway, we've had a lot of talks about you, Hannah, the whole threesome thing and what happened.' Dave paused and said, 'Listen, I don't know if this will be of any use to you or not but it seems that you weren't the only one playing away from home.'

'Dave, nothing happened. Calla only slept with me. OK, I know that sounds wrong but that's all she did – sleep. What are you talking about?'

'Hannah.'

'What about Hannah?'

'She was unfaithful to you.'

'For revenge?'

'Well, no, that's just it – it seems she did it first.'

'Did what? And how the fuck would Calla know? Hannah wouldn't tell Calla that she'd been shagging some bloke.'

I felt my fists clenching, my stomach was in knots that made me feel like vomiting. Hannah had been unfaithful to me. She'd been screwing some bloke, probably while I was at work. I couldn't believe it; what had gone wrong, how could such a thing happen and why didn't I know?

Dave couldn't have failed to notice my distress. 'Actually, Scott, it wasn't a bloke. Calla knows because it was Calla that Hannah had sex with. Well, not sex exactly but something.'

'What?' My mind was whirring; how, when ... 'When? And what do you mean something?'

'Err, it seems it was a few days before she moved out.'

'While I was in the flat with her?'

'I don't know, possibly, I think it was at night.'

While I'd been sleeping on the floor in Ruby's room. I didn't know what to say. I was speechless. I was relieved that it hadn't been some strange man, but I wasn't sure what to think of my wife having …

'What do you mean by something?'

Dave sighed. 'That's the problem with the Thai Chat app, it's not that great when it comes to detail. Anyway, from what I can gather, they spent a night together in Hannah's bed, maybe they were just sleeping like you two were.'

I shook my head. If I'd stayed in bed every night with Hannah instead of sleeping in Ruby's room, nothing would have happened.

Dave could see the conflict and confusion on my face. 'Scott, I wasn't sure what to do when Calla told me this. It was only yesterday and I wasn't going to say anything, but it seems like Hannah is punishing you partly for something she's already done, so I thought it only fair you know. Again, I reckon it was Calla's way of comforting Hannah as you weren't going near her.'

'She wouldn't let me near her.'

'Whatever, that's for you to sort out. I've told you so my work here is done.'

'You've told me a lot today. My wife might be a lesbian and you've fallen in love with a Thai prostitute.'

'She no longer does that.'

'OK, an ex-Thai prostitute. Have you any more surprises?'

Before he could say anything, Calla came back into the room carrying her baby. She sat beside Dave and they both beamed at the gurgling little bundle of joy she held in her arms.

Dave took Calla's hand and they both looked sympathetically at me. Dave said, 'One more thing, we talked to Hannah yesterday as you know, and with her blessing we're going to call the baby Hannah.'

Chapter Twenty-Five

I GOT HOME from Calla's flat and didn't know what to do. I felt punch drunk. The fact that Hannah had been in bed with Calla left me reeling. It wasn't anything to do with the fact she'd spent a night with Calla: as Dave said it might have been completely innocent. It was the fact that she'd reacted the way she did to me when she came into the bedroom. I could understand why she was mad, but it was as if she'd done nothing wrong and everything that had ever happened was my fault.

My thoughts were interrupted by my phone that started vibrating across the table again. Two calls in one day. I was popular.

I picked up. It was Hannah's mum.

'Hi, Carol. It's been a while.'

'Well, yes, I know, it's very awkward at the moment as you can imagine, but ultimately my priority is my daughter and I need to try and support her as much as I can. Listen, Hannah asked me to phone you ...'

'Why couldn't she do it herself? Why won't she speak to me?'

'She's struggling at the moment, Scott, you need to give her time to adjust to everything. Ruby's funeral just about finished her off.'

'It wasn't exactly a walk in the park for me either, Carol.'

She sighed into the phone. 'I know, I did try and tell Hannah that ...'

'What did she say?'

'Well, we almost fell out over it, she thought I was taking your side and then, well, she told me about her conversation with you about you holding her back and stifling her ambitions and all that sort of thing.'

'Is that what you think, too?'

'God no, that sounded more like her friend Jane talking than her. Hannah's always been happy with her world ... until now, that is. Anyway, that's not why I'm on the phone. I've to tell you that she's gone back to work.'

'She has?'

'Yeah, she started back yesterday.'

'Bit soon, don't you think?'

'Maybe, but she said it would help take her mind off everything. She's down in London.'

'London?'

'Yeah, she's been sent down by her firm. Something to do with a takeover thing her company's involved in.'

'Why do they need Hannah, do they need someone to rearrange the pot plants or something?' I said unkindly.

Carol managed a small laugh. 'No, she went in last week and told them she was looking for a new job due to being undervalued and handed in her resignation.'

'So they sent her to London as a punishment?'

'Not exactly, no. They refused to accept her resignation and instead asked her to become more involved with the takeover work. It turns out that she knows one of the partners in the London firm. Her boss decided, given that relationship, sending Hannah down to work with him might help smooth the way somewhat.'

'How does Hannah know him?'

'It's Callum Anderson. He used to live next door to us when Hannah was young. They were inseparable for a while, used to wander about holding hands all the time as toddlers. It was sweet. I said to her, "Imagine wee Callum ending up managing a big firm like that."'

'He can't be doing that well if they're selling out,' I said defensively. A bad feeling was beginning to grow in my stomach.

'I think it's to do with his divorce. Very messy by all accounts and he needs to raise a substantial amount of money to settle with his ex-wife.'

The bad feeling suddenly morphed into a feeling of dread. I felt sick. Carol wouldn't know the rest of the history of Hannah and Callum.

'I've tried very hard not to take sides between you and Hannah, Scott, mainly for the sake of Tessa and Lois. I think it's very important, no matter what happens, that you still have a speaking relationship for the sake of your kids. In fact, I was even taking your side most of the time until she told me the real reason that Calla is here, that you are the father of her child and that you admitted to sleeping with her whilst you were on your honeymoon. I couldn't believe you'd do something like that.'

My mouth was hanging open and I was shocked into silence.

'I can't think of any other woman that would have stayed with you after something like that had happened. I can only assume that she felt sorry for you and that you grovelled so much she agreed to stay for the sake of your family. I honestly thought you were much better than that, Scott, I really did. Then she tells me that you did it again

243

with her while Hannah was staying here, which is completely unacceptable in my book and Hannah's, I have to say.

'So you know you've brought all this upon yourself. I've told Hannah to get a good lawyer. She said that Callum trained as a solicitor so maybe he'll be able to help her. In any event, I don't see how you've got much defence, to be honest. As I said, I'm trying not to be too hard as there are your girls to consider, and you have just lost a baby.'

My head was spinning. Hannah had warped the truth so much I wasn't sure what was right any more. I also knew there was no point in trying to tell Carol the real version of what had happened as she would never believe me anyway.

Carol filled the silence by saying, 'I knew there was much more to the story of why she was here, but I could never have imagined the truth. You know what? I wouldn't be surprised if Hannah and Callum hook up again. They are probably both hurting and have a lot in common. Hannah said they did catch up before he went off to university but for some reason they didn't stay in touch ...'

Probably because she broke his cock, I thought.

Carol continued, 'I suppose, given their situations, it might make a kind of sense. She really needs someone she can rely on and trust.'

The last barb really hit home and I was rendered completely speechless. I assumed Carol thought that her telling me she knew everything had shocked me into silence. It was the warped version of the truth that really hurt me. I couldn't believe Hannah could be so nasty. Maybe I really didn't know her after all. We'd been together for more than seven years and I'd never seen this side of her. Why all the lies? But there was more.

'It appears that Callum and his wife had been trying to have children for a number of years, they'd been through three cycles of IVF and everything. In the end, it didn't work and Callum wanted to adopt but she didn't. I think that was the final nail in an already shaky marriage.'

I wondered briefly if the fertility issue had anything to do with Hannah's rough treatment of his willy? I was no expert, but a torn foreskin, painful as it was, probably had little to do with sperm production. Maybe Hannah had done more damage that she'd told either me or Jane.

'I'm not surprised you're not saying much, Scott, but I'm going down to London tomorrow to be with Hannah and the girls ...'

'You never said the girls were with Hannah.'

'Oh, didn't I? Well, they are, and as it's nearly the Easter break it seemed like a good idea for all of us to go. We're staying in one of Callum's empty properties. I can look after the girls while Hannah works and when she's not, we can do some sightseeing. The break will probably do everyone a lot of good.'

I didn't think it would do me any good. I hung up the phone and put it down on the table without saying anything further. I didn't know what I *could* have said to change things. I could have mentioned to Carol that her daughter might be a lesbian, but I don't think that would have endeared me to her or helped my cause any.

My phone bleeped, signifying a text. I immediately picked it up, anxious in case it was from Hannah. It was from Jane.

Hi Scott is Hannah OK? I can't get a hold of her.

I dialled Jane's number and she answered immediately.

'Scott? Hi, is Hannah all right? I've been trying to phone her but she won't answer or reply to texts; has she lost her phone or something?'

'Hi, Jane, no, she's in London.'

'London?'

245

'Yeah, London.' I replayed the conversation I'd had with Carol, leaving nothing out.

'Oh, Scott, that's awful, it doesn't sound like Hannah at all. She must have lost her mind.'

I sighed. 'She's lost something, Jane, but I'm not sure what.'

'It maybe explains why she won't talk to me, though. If she's away in her own wee world of lies and denial, she'll know that I won't play along. I'll try and phone her mum and try and get her to talk some sense into her daughter.'

'Thanks, Jane, any help I can get is appreciated.'

'Don't worry about it, Scott, she'll come to her senses eventually.'

Jane hung up and I wondered if Hannah would come to her senses before or after she'd shagged Callum.

Half an hour later I got a text from Jane.

Carol won't answer her phone and hasn't replied to my texts. I'll keep trying.

I thought about phoning my mum for some sympathy but in order to get any, I'd have to explain the whole story right from the beginning and I couldn't face that. Instead I went to my cold, empty bed at around midnight and wondered where Hannah was sleeping and if she was alone.

Chapter Twenty-Six

FRIDAY'S BUSINESS ENDED prematurely with gloomy heavy rain and a cold blustery wind. I'd managed to shut up the service department early and now sat nursing a cup of hot coffee in Sandra's office. We were the only people left in the whole dealership; neither of us had any reason to rush home.

'Have you heard from Hannah today?' Sandra asked in a concerned tone.

I shook my head and sipped my brew. 'No, nothing. I phoned a few times and sent some texts, but she hasn't replied.'

'That doesn't sound good.'

'Doesn't it?'

Sandra smiled sympathetically. 'No, sweetie, when your wife and two children don't answer when you contact them, it's not a good sign.'

'Well, Tessa and Lois don't have phones.'

'Would you have phoned them if they did?'

I nodded. 'Probably.' I stared into my mug.

The rain suddenly got harder and rattled off the metal

roof. Over the last few days, I'd filled Sandra in on most of what was happening with my life, leaving out only the bit about Calla sleeping with me and Hannah, and the most recent London development.

I felt incredibly lonely. Given that Sandra was sitting watching me wallow in my misery, I probably wasn't the only one.

'What about you, any word from …'

'Sam? No, he's an arse.' She sounded like Jane.

'He must be crazy to dump you.'

Sandra smiled. 'He doesn't want a girlfriend who can think for herself, he wants what all of his teammates have, little Barbie dolls who look nice but don't have a brain and are quite happy to be posing clothes hangers that just ask questions like, "How did you play today, baby?" and "Can I give you a massage?"' The last bit was said in her best Marilyn Monroe voice. 'He also expects me to be someone who won't bat an eyelid when he disappears on a pre-season tour, and screws hookers or anything else in a skirt. That's not me, I'm afraid. Also, I'm a good few years older than he is, which seems to be a big issue for him. I suspect he's looking for a younger model, one with fewer miles on the clock and with less dents and scratches.'

I laughed at the car analogy and the thought of Sandra being a Barbie doll. I intentionally didn't respond to the 'hooker' comment – too close to home for me.

'Anyway,' she continued, 'I'm probably better off without him. I'm an ambitious social climber and he would just have held me back. I'm thirty-six now, and if by some miracle we stayed together, he'd want me to settle down and become a baby machine and I'm not sure that's me, either.'

She met my eyes, expecting me to challenge her on her maternal instincts. I body-swerved that conversation; I was shocked to learn she was that old. I thought she was younger than me, not four years older.

'Sandra, I know you are hugely ambitious and to be honest, I think it is amazing that you run this place, you know …'

'Cos I'm a woman?'

I nodded reluctantly.

'I never took you for a chauvinist, Scott.' Thankfully she was smiling when she said that.

'You know I'm not, but you are so good at this game, and well, you know, I've never quite understood how you ended up here. You are very intelligent, beautiful and driven, you could have done something else.'

'Something more feminine, you mean?'

I sighed, I didn't know what I meant so I asked, 'Why cars?'

Her face became serious and her gaze drifted past me and through the huge windows at the rain and gathering gloom.

'We've spent hours talking, Scott. In fact, I've probably spent more time talking about things with you than any boyfriend in recent years, and yet you've never asked this before.'

'I didn't think it was any of my business, and to be honest, I find you a little intimidating and didn't want to pry.'

'Intimidating?'

I smiled. 'Yeah, intimidating, I reckon a lot of blokes would.'

'Just because I'm good at something – no, I'm better at something than they are – that makes me a ball-breaker?' she asked coldly.

'Probably.'

'Unbelievable. "If you prick us, do we not bleed? If you tickle us, do we not laugh? If you poison us do we not die?"'

I stared at her for a moment. 'Shakespeare, right?'

'Yep, *Merchant of Venice.*'

'That's what I mean. You're way smarter than anyone else here – most of the guys in here probably think Shakespeare is a Brazilian footballer or something.'

Sandra laughed loudly. 'You know what, though, I think there *was* an *American* footballer called Shakespeare.'

'Really?'

'Really.'

'How do you know all this stuff?'

'I spent a lot of my childhood with my head in a book.'

'The Encyclopaedia of Useless Facts?'

'Is there such a book?'

'You mean you don't know?'

'Ha, ha. My upbringing was, well, alternative, I suppose.'

'Your parents were hippies?'

'Something like that. Let's just say I moved around a lot when I was younger and books were my friend.'

'Sounds lonely.'

She shrugged. 'At times. The main problem was schooling, it was difficult fitting in when you turn up as the new girl and then a few months later you're gone again.'

'What did your parents do?'

There was a lengthy pause before she leaned forward and stared directly into my eyes. She was so close I could smell her warm breath, coffee and mints.

'I've never told anyone this before, Scott, well, at least no one in my current world. So you can take it as a huge compliment that I trust you enough and I expect you never to betray that. You must never breathe a word of this to anyone outside this room, OK?'

I nodded, wondering what kind of confession I was about to hear. Was she a convicted criminal, a former drug runner, an international terrorist? In reality, the truth was even more surprising.

'I was a traveller, my mum and dad used to work in a fair, a rough group of folk that had regular pitches around the UK. I really only got to be in school properly during the winter, that's why I read so much and books were …'

I tuned her out, my head was suddenly spinning and my stomach was in knots. I gazed at her in disbelief with my mouth hanging open. Eventually, Sandra stopped talking and noticed that I was staring at her in shock.

She sighed. 'I knew I shouldn't have told you, that kind of reaction is exactly what I would get if I ever put that down on a job application. If anyone ever finds out, my chances of getting promotion will go right down the toilet. In fact, the prejudice is such that I'd probably lose my job here altogether.'

I continued to stare. Sandra got annoyed. 'Scott, shut your mouth, it's not like I murdered my parents and buried them in the woods.'

I shook myself out of it. 'I did, though.'

Sandra was puzzled. 'You did what?'

'Murdered your parents and buried them in the woods.'

'What are you talking about? I spoke to my mum an hour ago, she and my dad now live in a bungalow in Bournemouth.'

'Dodgems.'

'Dodgems?'

'You used to work the dodgems.'

'Yeah, I did, and a little carousel for wee kids. We also had a share in the big wheel but I didn't get to work much on that. How do you know that, anyway?'

My mouth had gone completely dry but I managed to splutter, 'You're not Sandra, you're Sabrina.'

After a few minutes of confusion I managed to pull myself together. I continued to stare at Sandra, not sure what to say. My whole view of her had changed completely. I couldn't believe that I'd never realized who she was, but then it had been, what, eighteen years ago? And she was completely different now, her hair was short and her clothes said class and money, not fairground attraction.

Why would I ever have put two and two together and made three?

Sandra was very patient and waited for me to say something. Eventually her patience ran out.

'OK, who the fuck is Sabrina, and what has she got to do with me?'

I smiled. I don't think I'd ever heard her swear before. I'm sure she did – probably at her underperforming salesmen inside her little glass cube. But I personally hadn't ever heard an expletive leave her lips.

'What's funny, Scott? I'm starting to get pissed off with you now.'

'I was in love with you eighteen years ago,'

'What? I didn't know you eighteen years ago.'

'No, but I knew *you*.'

She leaned forward eagerly. 'OK, enough of the mystery, what on earth are you prattling on about?'

'It's a little embarrassing, actually it's very embarrassing, but as we're in the mood for confessions ...'

I told her about my teen crush and how I'd made up a whole fantasy life for us after her parents had been killed in a variety of ways, including murder. I eventually finished my story and waited for her reaction. I was expecting a tender moment, maybe something like, 'Aww, what a shame, I wish I'd known – maybe we could have spent time together.'

Instead, she leaned back and laughed her head off. She looked up at me with tears of laughter in her eyes, noticed the expression on my face and slipped off her seat onto the floor in a very unladylike fashion and laughed even harder. Not exactly the reaction I was expecting.

Eventually she stopped and said, 'God, that was so funny, I really needed a good laugh. Excuse me, Scott, I need to go to the toilet, I think I might have peed myself a little bit from laughing.'

When she came back, she'd pulled herself together. My expression hadn't changed. She giggled.

'Look, Scott, I'm sorry for laughing. I know it probably wasn't that funny for you, but you've no idea how many young and not so young boys used to try and grope my arse and tits when I worked the rides.'

'I didn't try and touch you. You fell onto me and kind of brushed against me. I wasn't one of the gropers,' I said defensively.

'I'm sorry, I don't remember. You've no idea what my world was like back then. A few days here, a few days there, living in a trailer with my mum and dad ... To be honest, it all kind of merges into one in my memory. I'm flattered that you liked me, but let's face it, you were fourteen and obviously hormonal – I would have been, what, eighteen and trying to decide what to do with my life.'

I was silent for a moment or two, trying to recover from having my biggest 'coming of age' moment completely ruined. Sandra obviously noticed, because she came to sit beside me and gave me a hug. I leaned into her. Her scent was comforting and womanly, just like it had been all those years ago.

'You've not had an easy time of it recently, have you, Scott?'

I didn't think the question needed an answer so I stayed silent, still inside her embrace. The rain continued to rattle off the roof and the wind whistled as it squeezed between the walls of the dealership. Outside was cold and forbidding. Inside I was warm and comforted. I hadn't felt like this in quite a long time.

Sandra decided to tell me a bit more about herself.

'I saved every penny I could from working the fairgrounds cos I wanted to get out of that life, do something different. My dad wanted me to marry Paul O'Neil, the son of one of his friends who owned a few of the rides. I did quite like him, and shagged him a few times, but I had made my mind up very early on that I didn't want to spend the rest of my life travelling around with a trailer full of kids. For a while, I thought motorsport was going to be my way out. I was really into racing and managed to blag myself a job at the Knockhill racing track in Fife. Initially I thought it would be brilliant, learning to drive all kinds of race cars and stuff, but eventually I just ended up running the pace car on track days, and taking corporate entertainment groups round the track before they got a shot of the Formula Three car.' She laughed. 'You know what? It was a bit like being back in the fairground, a lot of the blokes who turned up on track days tried to grope my arse and tits again. So I decided to get a proper job, and here I am. Nobody gropes me any more. I must be losing my touch.' Eventually Sandra sighed and broke the contact. 'I suppose we'd better head home, eh? We can't stay here all night.'

'We could, you know.'

Sandra laughed. 'Yeah, probably, but I can't face the sales team tomorrow in a crushed skirt and jacket. Besides, I really need a shower.' She paused, then suggested, 'Why don't you come home with me and have some dinner? We're a couple of lost souls on a night that demons wouldn't venture out into.'

I agreed, thinking her last line sounded like something out of a Meatloaf song. We quickly locked up and set the alarms. I noticed on the way to her flat that Sandra drove much faster than I did. I also took in the fact that her car was spotless and the leather seats unmarked. They'd obviously never had children anywhere near them.

Her flat in the upmarket district of Trinity was similarly clean and tidy. Not a thing was out of place. No toys littered the floors, no dirty mugs sat on the worktops or in her sink. No clothes were strewn around waiting to be washed, ironed or put away. Her open-plan kitchen-cum-living room was immaculate. The cream leather sofa had two cushions symmetrically placed on each corner, which appeared like they never moved. In my previous hectic existence, they would have been used for pillow fights, stained with mango juice or jam, and left lying under a bed somewhere. The flat-screen TV secured to Sandra's wall at eye level was clean and shiny, with not a single sticky fingerprint anywhere to be seen.

The wooden floor was polished and pristine as was the white sheepskin rug. A small shelving unit sat to one side of the couch and held a small number of porcelain figurines. None were chipped or broken. Sandra's life was incredibly ordered and organized, nothing ruffled the smooth flow of her stream of existence. Even though her flat was like a calm oasis in my life of chaos, I felt incredibly sorry for her.

What a weird emotion.

Sandra lived exactly how she wanted and on her terms, and yet I felt sorry for her.

I was the one currently in need of serious help, maybe even professional help. It looked very much like I had lost my wife, my two daughters, and a third perfect little girl was lost to everyone, and yet here I was feeling sorry for someone who had everything she wanted.

I'd always wanted a family, the whole soft-focus movie-style life with wonderful kids and a loving wife. A big detached house with white window shutters and a large enclosed garden with a swing set sitting under an old oak tree. OK, I knew that life probably wouldn't be so generous to deliver everything just as I imagined it to be, but unlike Sabrina, the reality was much more satisfying than the fantasy. Even with our recent struggles and financial problems, life with Hannah, Tessa and Lois was brilliant, so much better that I ever imagined it could be. Yes, we argued and shouted at times and occasionally we longed for some of the peace and order that Sandra had, but overall I wouldn't have changed a thing. Unfortunately, it looked like fate had changed things for me.

Sandra handed me a glass of chilled white wine, and flipped the TV on for me while she went for a shower.

When she returned, she was wrapped in a white towelling dressing gown and her short damp hair had spiked up a little. What I noticed most, though, was that she had removed all her make-up and looked wonderful and fresh. I caught myself staring and quickly turned back to the TV.

'Is lasagne with a little salad all right? I haven't managed to get to the shops this week.'

'Fine for me,' I confirmed.

Sandra set the microwave in motion and came and sat beside me on the couch.

'So what are you going to do now?' Sandra asked me, whilst muting the TV volume.

'Err, drink your white wine, eat some of your lasagne, and probably continue to feel sorry for myself.'

Sandra laughed and poured herself some Chardonnay. 'No, I meant about Hannah and the girls.'

I sighed. 'I don't know.' I decided to update her on the London trip. 'Hannah's working in London on a merger thing her firm are involved in. Her mum and my girls are there as well.'

'Why has your mother-in-law gone?'

'To look after the girls while she works.'

'Isn't Tessa supposed to be in school?'

'The Easter holidays start today so she's got a couple of weeks off.'

'No disrespect, Scott, but I didn't know Hannah was that important to her firm. Obviously I don't know her but based on what you've told me—'

'She knows the guy who's selling up.'

'I thought it was a merger.'

'More of a takeover; anyway, I don't confess to fully understand all that but the guy is called Callum Anderson and is an old boyfriend of Hannah's.'

'How old?'

'I think he's about the same age.'

'No, I meant "how old" as in how long ago were they lovers?'

'Oh.' I didn't like the word 'lovers'. 'He was her first proper boyfriend.'

'Oh, not good news.'

'It's not?'

'No, not if he was her first love. She probably thinks she's got unfinished business.'

'Why?'

Sandra paused, took a swig of wine and turned to face me. 'OK, let's pretend that I was your first love ...'

'You kind of were.'

'Yeah, OK, then – that should make this easier for you to understand. Let's say you and me spent loads of time together as teenagers. We hung out and snogged at parties or in cars to our favourite songs, held hands on our way to school, all that kinda stuff.'

'Sounds like a Katy Perry song.'

'Yeah, if you like. Let's say we made all kinds of

257

promises to each other and set out all kinds of plans. Like … oh, I don't know … let's say we had decided to secretly get married in the old ruined church at the edge of town, deck it out on a warm summer's evening with ribbons and silk bows, invite only our closest friends and a minister, and then go home to our parents and tell them we were married.'

'I'm not sure it could be much of a secret if you've decorated it with ribbons and bows.'

'Look it's just a story, OK? What else might we have done? If it was me at the time, I would probably have planned how many kids I wanted to have, what jobs we would do and where we would live. I would plan our whole existence for the next twenty years or so until I had it down to the very last detail – a bit like you and your castle wedding nonsense. Then of course, real life gets in the way and people grow up and things change. But, and it's a big but, somewhere deep down, Hannah still hankers after those unfulfilled promises and yearns to be back there when life seemed so simple and everything so full of hope, especially now when everything in her current reality is so shit. I can't imagine what it's like losing a baby, hopefully I never will, but it must be beyond pain. So I can see the attraction in going somewhere where the past is present, if you see what I mean, and she can try and live a different reality for a while.'

'So where does that leave me?'

Sandra smiled. 'It leaves you sitting in my living room where your past is present too in a weird sort of way. You and Hannah are currently different sides of the same coin.'

'That's a bit over my head, I'm afraid, Sandra.'

'I don't believe you. What would your fourteen-year-old self be doing now if he were sitting on a couch with Sabrina?'

I had to think about that for a minute. 'He would probably hang onto your every word, stare at you constantly and then want to take you and show you off to his mates. Then if I had my fantasy exactly as it was back then, you'd come and live with me and become my best friend.'

'What about sex?'

'What about it?'

'C'mon, Scott, you're trying to tell me that you never imagined yourself having sex with me … or rather, Sabrina?'

I'm sure I was blushing. 'Well, yeah, of course, but it wasn't about that, it was this whole … I don't really know how to describe it exactly … it was like an overpowering emotional thing, like you were there to help me grow up and get ready for the rest of my life – a rite of passage – or however you would describe it. I had you on a really high pedestal and in reality, you could never have lived up to the hype.'

'I kind of like the fact that you put me on a pedestal, I don't think I've ever had that in my life before.'

I nodded. 'It's a shame because you're strong, sexy, and smart and really deserve more. You should have someone who worships and cares for you, someone who spends their every waking moment thinking about you, and how they can make you happy.'

'Like you, you mean?' Sandra asked, her voice warm and husky.

Chapter Twenty-Seven

THERE WAS SILENCE and we stared into each other's eyes for what seemed like hours. Then slowly, ever so slowly, our faces drew closer, our noses touched and we kissed. Suddenly I *was* fourteen again and my hormones were on fire.

I pulled Sandra closer and she straddled my lap. She kissed me harder and started to grind herself onto me. I gasped and slipped my hands down to her bottom, trying to pull her more onto my growing erection. I felt like I couldn't get close enough to her. Her robe slipped open and I reached in and caressed one of her breasts, the nipple growing hard under my fingers. I squeezed it gently and she gasped into my mouth, which made me even more aroused.

Suddenly, she pulled back and scanned my face with her gorgeous, deep-brown eyes. Tears slowly formed in the corners and one trickled gently down her cheek.

'What's wrong?' I asked, concerned.

She didn't answer me immediately but continued to sit on my lap and stare at me sadly. 'Who are you kissing,

Scott? Is it me or Sabrina?'

'I'm not absolutely sure, does it matter?'

Sandra lowered her eyes. 'It matters to me. I'm not that hard-hearted bitch you think you know so well that runs a car dealership, not really. It's all an act, a very good act and one which takes everybody in. I'm not convinced you could ever love that person. Scott, you could love Sabrina but I'm not her any more, if I ever was.'

Now I was confused: what was I supposed to say? 'Will the real Sandra please stand up?' Why did women have to be so bloody complicated?

Somewhere inside my head a voice was whispering, so faintly that I could barely hear it, but it was telling me what I already knew. Sandra wasn't for me. She never had been and never would be, no matter what happened between Hannah and me.

It was a desperately sad revelation that made my soul ache, or at least that's what it felt like. It was as if destiny was playing a cruel trick on me and I'm not sure why Sandra knew or thought she knew all this by just kissing me. Maybe it was female intuition, perhaps it was just she had listened to me for years prattling on about Hannah and my wonderful girls.

It would be so easy to make love with Sandra, but I don't think I could ever love her. Not the way she deserved to be loved. What we had at this moment was a fantasy that didn't have enough sustainable substance. I couldn't go back to being a teenager and relive my life with Sabrina. Now, there was a thought … if I did, would I have made different choices?

If I'd been with Sandra and met Hannah, what would I have done, assuming I'd been lucky enough to be able to choose? Meeting Hannah was the best moment of my life. I loved her with every ounce of my being and my soul. I didn't have that history with Sandra.

To her eternal credit, she wiped her tears, tied her dressing gown and got up to tend to our microwave dinner.

She fetched our food and sat beside me on the couch. I could feel her body heat but despite her proximity there was a distance between us now. Whilst we were eating, she steered our conversation onto safer ground for a while, work mainly.

After we'd finished and Sandra had topped up our glasses, she asked with a sad smile, 'So what *were* you thinking when you kissed me?'

Why do women always need to know what you're thinking?

Sandra deserved the truth. Anyway, the truth was easier as I was rubbish at lying and she knew me well enough to tell the difference.

'I was thinking that I'm not fourteen any more and you're not Sabrina, you're Sandra, and I know you really well.'

'But you don't know me really well, do you?'

'No, I suppose not, but I know you better now than I did this morning.'

'You don't think less of me because of my background?'

'God no, the opposite really, you've achieved so much and yet ...'

'Yet what?'

I sighed. 'I don't think you're happy.'

'Is anyone ever truly happy?'

'I'm not really bright enough to answer that kind of question, Sandra.'

'Oh, you're cleverer than you think you are, Scott, but I'll rephrase it – have you ever been truly happy, then?'

I didn't even have to think about that. 'Yes, of course, the day I met Hannah, and after my girls were born everything changed, but life, if it was possible, got even better. I don't think I truly appreciated how great it was as we were always worrying about things like money and stuff, but underneath everything was magic.'

Sandra gazed at me for a moment, then looked away. 'So you are saying I need to be married with kids to be happy?'

'No, of course not, I'm sure there are loads of people who don't get married and have kids and are wonderfully happy, I'm just not one of them.'

'Could you make *me* happy, Scott?'

I shook my head. 'Honestly? I don't know. It's possible, I suppose, but you'd really have to want me and I don't think you do. I'm not as smart as you, I'm not as ambitious as you, and to be honest I don't want to be, it's not my thing, never has been. You need to find your own way.'

'You're right about some of that, I probably can't change now, after all these years, but I could make enough money to support us both, you wouldn't need to work so hard.'

I laughed at the idea of being a kept man. It was tempting for a minute or two.

'Nah, you'd soon get bored with me if that was the case. Look, Sandra, I really like you, you are absolutely gorgeous and so sexy that I want to rip all your clothes off, most men would, but the problem is I'm still deeply in love with my wife. I'm not sure she's still deeply in love with me, right now, but I can't change how *I* feel.'

'So we're not going to have a fuck, then?'

My eyes were wide with shock as I took in her smiling face. I laughed at her mischievous question.

'Well, actually we probably would have, it was *you* who stopped.'

'And how would you have felt afterwards?'

I puffed out my cheeks. 'Guilty as hell.'

'That's why I stopped.'

I couldn't help wondering, and would probably spend the rest of my life wondering, if I had just made a huge mistake by not getting together with Sandra. My wife was currently behaving like the bitch from hell and I didn't deserve that kind of treatment. Then the moment was gone and Sandra moved away from me to the end of the couch and asked, 'So how are you going to get Hannah and your girls back, then?'

'I don't know, I was kind of hoping Hannah would come to me.'

She slowly shook her head. 'Have you learned nothing at all tonight? What were we saying earlier about fantasies?'

'Err, they are very powerful and ... I don't know what else.'

'Sexy.'

'Sexy?'

'Yeah, fantasies are sexy because they don't have to deal with paying the bills, cleaning up after your kids, the general domestic crap that you have to deal with in every-day real life. They are removed from that. At the moment, we are sitting in our own little bubble. Tomorrow I'll be back at work, encouraging, cajoling, whatever else it takes to get my sales team and myself motivated to shift some cars. As it's near the end of the month, I'll probably be in on Sunday as well. See what I mean? Reality isn't fantasy and a lot of the time reality isn't fun.'

I nodded slowly. I could understand that, but Sandra wasn't finished.

'So what is Hannah doing just now? From what you've told me, she might be having dinner with this Callum guy, she's in her little bubble and not worrying about what her kids are doing, what you're up to or anything at all. She's seventeen again, she won't remember she's just lost a baby and is hurting and sad. She'll be all gooey-eyed and lovey dovey and all those other yucky sayings that seem so appropriate when the oxytocin is flowing.'

'Gooey-eyed? Oxytocin?'

Sandra smiled at me. It was a penetrating, deep and sympathetic smile and made me go weak at the knees.

'Gooey-eyed, like this.' She lowered her head and gazed up at me through her lashes. I laughed and so did she. 'And oxytocin is the love hormone – go and Google it later cos I can't be bothered explaining that bit. Probably the more worrying bit, though, is what is this Mr Anderson thinking? Apart from the obvious.'

'The obvious?'

'He's a man, he once found your wife attractive, irresistible even. He probably still does – so he'll want to get into her knickers.'

'Will he get into them?'

Sandra chewed her bottom lip slowly. 'Probably, but not right now – she knows deep down that she's still married and has … what would I call it? … responsibilities. But if they see a lot of each other and really get on, it'll happen sooner or later, and given she's in his territory, probably sooner.'

'Bastard.'

'It could get worse.'

'Worse. How?'

'From what you tell me, part of the reason for his divorce was that his wife couldn't have kids and he wanted them – even to the point of considering adoption.'

'Yeah, so?'

Sandra shook her head at my stupidity. 'Well, Hannah's got a ready-made family, plus she's fertile. Yes, she's just lost a baby and might not want to even think about having any more at the moment, but one day, maybe with someone new. See where I'm going? He could even apply to adopt your girls....'

'Can he do that?'

'I don't know, probably.'

The stakes had just got raised to a whole new level. I should have been able to think this through for myself but hadn't. If for no other reason than this realization, I was glad I'd spent the evening with Sandra.

She could probably see the implications clicking into place inside my head, and came over and gave me another hug. This time I had no desire to rip her dressing gown open. It was a hug between friends, friends who could maybe have become something more, but never would. It was a bitter-sweet moment for me, and possibly for Sandra too.

A few minutes later she yawned.

'If I'm gonna be able to kick some ass in the morning ...' She said this in an East Coast American accent. Maybe she could have an alternative career as a voiceover artist. '... I need to get some sleep. You're welcome to stay, Scott, but I think you'd be better heading home and getting some sleep yourself. You have some planning and thinking to do. I can't drive you cos I've had too much wine, but I can call you a taxi.'

I agreed and picked up my jacket. A few minutes later, her phone beeped, signifying the taxi had turned up.

Sandra accompanied me to the door, and just before she opened it, she stood on her tiptoes and gave me a passionate kiss that left me breathless. Eventually we broke apart and she said, 'That's just so you remember what you're giving up, Mr McEwan.'

She let me out of her apartment. I stepped into the hall and we gazed at each other longingly for a moment, before she lowered her eyes to the floor, sighed and closed the door.

I knew that as she shut the door, more than a few inches of wood were now between us. Never again would I have the opportunity to be with Sabrina or Sandra, or whoever she really was.

Chapter Twenty-Eight

My EVENTFUL EVENING with Sandra had given me the courage of my convictions and whilst eating my breakfast the following morning, I booked a flight online to London City Airport, leaving at nine on Monday morning. The problem remained, however, of finding out exactly *where* Hannah was staying while she was there. I couldn't just wander around like a tourist hoping to bump into her. I had several vague plans in my head. I'd Googled the head office address of Portman, Michaels & Thomson, which was in the East End near Stepney Green.

I could stride purposefully into their offices and demand to speak to Callum Anderson and find out where Hannah was staying. That option was fraught with danger in that he might not tell me, in fact he probably wouldn't, and given he'd sold or was selling his stake he might not even be there any more. I could vary my strategy and maybe follow him around until he met up with Hannah. The flaws with that plan were that I didn't actually know what he looked like, and even if I did manage to identify him, the thought of trying to tail him across London, ducking in and out of doorways like some bumbling Inspector Clouseau, was even less appealing. It also, again, depended on him being at the office in the first place.

As I was trying to come up with a better strategy, I got a text from Dave.

Phone me it's important.

I had to wonder about his inability to use his phone to make a call. What would happen if he ever needed to call for an ambulance?

I called him almost immediately. 'Dave, you really need to start phoning people …'

'Never mind all that. Listen, I forgot to mention to you the other day that I've got Hannah's address in London for you.'

I was amazed. 'How did you manage that?'

'I didn't, Calla did.'

'Calla?'

'Yeah, Hannah took her to register the baby's name last week and—'

'That was the day before Hannah went to London. Shouldn't you have done that?'

'Yeah, well, I would have eventually but I've got a lot on at work just now, and Hannah offered.'

'How did she come to offer exactly?'

'Well, I texted her and asked if was there any chance she could take Calla to Lothian Chambers to register the baby's birth.'

'That was a cheeky text.'

'Pretty cheeky, yeah.'

'And she just happened to tell Calla the London address?'

'Not exactly, no.'

'Well, how did she get it, then?' I asked, my patience wearing thin.

'Well, Hannah had her bags in the car and she nicked the luggage label, thinking it might be useful.'

'She's getting very good at doing that.' There was silence for a moment while I thought. This was a much better option than anything I'd managed to come up with. 'Thank Calla for me, Dave. That's really helpful.'

'She thinks you should go to London and surprise her, you know, you'll be on neutral ground, maybe it'll be a good chance to patch things up.'

'I've already booked the flight. I'm leaving Monday morning.'

'Oh, so you already had her address, then?'

'Not exactly, no.'

'Right, so you were going to phone her when you got there?'

'She's not taking my calls.'

'Right ... so I take it you were going to show up where she's working and confront her there?'

Duuuh. I was so thick at times. It hadn't occurred to me that Hannah would be at the East London head office, doing whatever it was she needed to do for the merger thingy.

'Err ... yeah, that was kind of my vague plan,' I lied. 'I'm not sure about patching things up but I need to do something. What would really help is a time machine that'd allow me to go back to Thailand and undo everything that happened.'

'Can't help you there, mate. I'll text over the address, after that it's up to you.'

My next job was to phone work and let them know I wouldn't be in for a few days. I knew that wouldn't go down well with the management, but I had to chance it.

Hannah had been in London with the girls for a few days now. If Sandra's theory was correct, she'd have been out with Callum either last night or would be going out tonight. The thought made my blood boil but I tried to keep my cool as there was nothing I could do about it. I'd heard nothing more from Jane so I assumed that Carol was still blanking her as well.

I went to pack a bag. I also needed to book some cheap accommodation, if there was such a thing in London.

Later, I busied myself online, trying to find a hotel, and ended up with a B&B in Peckham. I wasn't sure what Peckham was like, the only image in my head visualized the high rise where Del Boy and Rodney used to live in *Only Fools and Horses*, but that had been a long time ago. Anyway, it was ideal as it wasn't too far from the address where Hannah was staying: 23 Lordship Close, East Dulwich.

According to Google, East Dulwich appeared to be a pocket of incredibly expensive South London housing beloved of BBC types, and obviously a prime location for sleazy property-developer types such as Callum, too.

From London City, I worked out the best route via the DLR, underground and overground trains. It looked nice and easy on the map, but given I had the sense of direction of a short-sighted lemming, I would no doubt end up on the Isle of Wight instead.

I got ready for bed that evening, feeling calmer than I had for a while. I was still tortured by the thought of what Hannah was doing with Callum, no doubt egged on by her deluded mother, but I couldn't do anything until Monday.

When the day arrived, I woke stupidly early and made my way to the airport via buses and trams and was checked in and sitting in the departure lounge, nursing a coffee, a full two hours before my flight was due to leave.

Nearly everybody else seemed to be in suits and carrying leather cases and laptop bags. I was in scruffy jeans and carrying my battered old black sports bag that had seen better days. The plane landed on time and soon I was standing on the platform station, waiting for the train to take me into central London. I boarded the first train that came and was surprised to find it almost empty. A few minutes later, I realized why. I was going the wrong way so I jumped off at the next station and caught one going the right way. Not a great start: the Isle of Wight was beckoning.

Eventually, I bungled my way across London and arrived at Stepney Green tube station. The address of Callum's office, according to my map, would be found two streets away. I arrived nervously at the door and was confronted by a dozen brass plates with assorted company names. Inside, a smart, uniformed concierge pointed me to the lift and told me PMT's offices were on the tenth floor. I stepped in and the elevator fired me skywards.

The pleasant, female automated voice counted out the floors for me and when she reached ten, I took a deep breath and waited for the doors to open. I'm not sure what I was expecting to see when the lift opened; a pleasant, smiling receptionist perhaps. What I wasn't expecting was lots of noise and total chaos. As the doors opened, I walked into a pile of boxes. People were rushing about everywhere, carrying files, boxes, chairs and other assorted office detritus. A few people paused, stared at me for a second, then carried on with their tasks. This must be what corporate takeovers looked like on the ground. I eventually managed to stop a harassed-looking older lady, dressed in faded jeans and pink top.

'Do you know where I can find Callum Anderson or Hannah McEwan?'

'Never heard of Hannah … whoever … but Mr Anderson hasn't been in this week and if he's got any sense, he probably won't ever show his face here again.'

I smiled. 'Well liked, was he?'

The woman picked some dust from her hair. 'Well, he used to be, but he's sold us all down the river. Most of us are losing our jobs thanks to him. So he's not exactly flavour of the month.'

She picked up her boxes and vanished back into the clamour.

As I returned to street level, I was very thankful that Calla had snaffled Hannah's luggage tag for me. I now had to negotiate my way to East Dulwich.

I got off at Oval tube station and stared at the nearby bus stop. Buses in Edinburgh bewildered me, but in London I was hopelessly lost. I didn't even know which side of the road I needed to be on. In the end, I took the easy option and jumped in a taxi.

Fifteen minutes later, the driver stopped outside a large detached house. I paid him and stepped out onto the pavement. The wind had picked up and the initially sunny day was now overcast, dull and cool. It accurately reflected both my mood and the reception I was probably about to receive from my wife, assuming she was here and not in town shopping.

I approached the front door and realized what at first appeared to be one house was a series of flats. The front door was conveniently open so I walked in and looked about. I was standing in a large hallway; off to my right was a flight of stairs leading up to what I presumed were the other flats, and to my left was a door with the number one etched into the wood in gold lettering.

I decided to start there and tentatively knocked on the door. After a moment, receiving no answer, I started to move away when the lock was disengaged and a familiar face peered around the door frame.

Chapter Twenty-Nine

'HANNAH!' I EXCLAIMED.

'Scott, what are you doing here, you shouldn't ...'

I pushed the door open and marched into an opulent living space. The room was huge with a large bay window overlooking the street. Near the window was a massive dining table strewn with paperwork. It had ten chairs arranged around it with room for more if required. Further across the room was a fluffy red rug and a seating area encompassing a brown leather L-shaped corner sofa, at least I think that's what you'd call it (although it wasn't anywhere near a corner), a huge wall-mounted TV, and a small coffee table covered with paperback books. The room opened out into a huge kitchen with large patio doors onto a long landscaped garden. There was no sign of the girls, I assumed they were with Hannah's mum, who had probably taken them out to allow Hannah and Casanova some alone time.

The contrast of this light and airy space compared to our cramped, dark Leith flat was not lost on me. Neither was the fact that my shocked wife was trying to straighten her clothes and hair without attracting my attention. Sitting on the couch looking angry was who I assumed to be the infamous Callum Anderson. He was taller than I'd imagined him to be and, I had to begrudgingly admit, good-looking to boot with tousled blond hair, deep-blue eyes and a 'Good Ole American Boy' type of square jaw. He and Hannah would have beautiful babies together, given the chance.

At first, I had been reluctant to barge into the flat, but on reflection it had been the right thing to do. The sight of Callum Anderson slowly tucking his shirt back into his jeans was the last straw in a catalogue of lies and hurt that I'd been harbouring, and in a blind rage I snarled and flew across the room.

I grabbed the smooth-talking, self-assured wife-stealer by his arm and tried to pull him onto the floor. He was stronger than I expected and easily resisted my attempt, brushing me off, so I ended up on my arse instead. I immediately jumped up and lunged at him and landed a punch on the side of his head. This enraged him sufficiently to make him stand up and we started grappling like a couple of demented hermit crabs on the fluffy red rug. We both fell over and he landed on me, momentarily knocking the wind out of me. He took advantage by grabbing me around the neck with his meaty arm. For a moment, I was immobilized and couldn't move and Callum staggered to his feet, dragging me with him. He started to march me towards the still open apartment door, and I was facing the humiliation of being thrown outside like some useless drunk from a down-at-heel nightclub. I struggled madly and I could feel my ear burning where it was being squashed. I suddenly got my arm free enough to throw a punch and to my huge surprise it landed right on his nose. I was rewarded by a scream and a shower of blood.

Callum yelled, the first time he'd actually said anything

since my arrival. 'My ducking nose, you've dusted my ducking nose.'

The pain made him put both hands up to his face and allowed me to escape his vice-like grip. I took the opportunity to try and press home my advantage, and in an unmanly manoeuvre aimed a kick at his shins, which brought another roar of rage. Instead of making him give up, however, it seemed to spur him on and despite the shouts of 'Stop it' from my wife, he rushed me and we ended up on the floor, grappling again.

As we rolled around ineffectively on the floor, it occurred to me that I wasn't much good at this. I think my last proper fight had been as a 12-year-old schoolboy when I'd had a set to with Andrew Ross, who'd nicked my lunch money from my schoolbag. Even my wife had floored me recently with a single right hook. The fact that I'd landed a punch (albeit a lucky one) on Callum's nose and a good thump on his shin probably meant I'd had the edge up until then. But then I'd also had the element of surprise, which I'd now lost and given that he was much stronger than me, the longer this went on reduced the chances of it ending well for me.

Eventually, Hannah managed to pull us apart and we stood still, panting and glaring at each other. Blood was now dripping down onto my shirt and I realized that my nose had taken a hit too and was bleeding. I hadn't felt a thing: amazing stuff, adrenaline.

Hannah shouted at me, 'Scott! What the hell do you think you're doing, coming in here and fighting with Callum?'

She was angry but she was speaking to me, well, shouting at me, which was the only communication we'd had in ages, so I took it as a sign of progress.

'I came looking for you, Hannah, you won't speak to me,

you don't answer my texts, what the hell am I supposed to do?'

'Wait for me to contact *you*, I needed some space from you ...'

'No, Hannah, you needed space so you can come down here and fuck Mr Fancy Pants Property Developer Man here.' It was a really, really crap retort but I couldn't think of anything smart to say.

'What are you talking about, Scott? I'm here to work and look over all the plans that Callum has put together for—'

'The only plan he has is getting into your knickers, Hannah. I might not be as bright as you, or as clever as you'd like me to be, but don't insult what intelligence I have by spinning me that crap.'

That was a much better line.

'Scott, none of that is true, we were—'

'I know what you were doing, or just about to do. I'm not well versed in takeover or merger strategy meetings but I *do* know it doesn't involve you taking your clothes off, and when I came in you were trying to sort yourself out and he was tucking his shirt in, so don't give me that shit.'

Her silence spoke volumes and for the first time in my life, that saying made sense. Callum, however, having found his voice at last, asked, 'So you're Hannah's husband, then?'

I shook my head at his amazing powers of deduction. Then wondered who the hell he thought I was. Perhaps he regularly had strangers suddenly barging into his apartment and attacking him without provocation or warning.

I couldn't come up with a smart answer so just nodded, and wiped my bloody nose on the sleeve of my jacket. Callum nodded back, and wiped some blood onto his hand before flicking it onto the floor. Nice. I should've done that, much more manly.

I turned back to Hannah. 'So how many times have you done it, then?'

'Done what?'

'Made fucking cupcakes – what do you think I'm talking about?'

'I have no idea.'

I sighed. 'Yeah, like hell you don't, Hannah. How many times have you fucked him, made love, lain together, rubbed your bits, screwed, sucked his cock, ridden him senseless ... do you understand what I mean now?'

Hannah shook her head and stared at the floor. 'That's none of your business, Scott, you ...'

'It is *so* my fucking business, you're my wife and he has no right to be anywhere near you ...'

'You don't own me, Scott. I'm not your possession, you can't tell me what to do. I'm a grown woman.'

'You haven't been acting like one.'

'How would you know how grown-ups behave? You're a juvenile prick.'

'Oh, that's nice to know, and how did you come to that conclusion?'

'Who else would come barging into a stranger's flat and start fighting with someone they've never met?'

'I don't need to have met him, Hannah, he was your first love so you're bound to have a soft spot for him, unfinished business and all that.'

'Unfinished business?'

'Yeah.'

It was a shame Sandra wasn't there as she could have explained it so much better than me, but her presence would probably have complicated things even more.

'That's silly, Scott.'

'Is it?' I sensed a softening of her tone, but I wasn't letting her off that easy. 'So you haven't shagged him, then?'

I could see the two of them lock eyes. 'No.'

I didn't know whether to believe her or not. I wanted to. The silence that followed was prolonged, broken only by my and Callum's heavy breathing.

Callum was first to speak. His Scottish accent had almost disappeared with his years of living in the capital but it was still discernible. 'You can't blame her for wanting to be with me, you've done nothing but hurt Hannah over the last few weeks.'

My eyes were blazing as I turned to him. He obviously noticed and took a step back.

'What the fuck do you know? Have you just lost a baby? Have you been trying to hold onto your sanity while everyone you know tiptoes around you, trying not to upset you, trying not to mention the fact that you went to the hospital to have a child and then suddenly come home empty-handed? Nobody wants to speak about it, everybody just wants the whole sordid business to go away so everything can go back to normal, but things can *never* be the way they were, I've got a huge quarry-sized hole right here.'

I thumped my fist to my chest vaguely where I thought my heart was. In reality, I was probably about twenty centimetres too far to the right, but in any event it stopped me speaking for a moment as I had thumped myself so hard it made me cough.

'The pain never leaves, it just goes on and on and on, and the only person I can speak to about it … well … won't speak to me.'

I sat down on the couch and watched my nose slowly drip blood onto the pristine leather.

I could feel Hannah staring at me, but it was Callum who spoke again. There was no stopping this chatterbox once you got him going.

'What about the Gala woman?'

Here we go. I wondered what Hannah had told him. She tried to intervene. 'Callum, just drop it, OK, I don't think ...'

I looked up at the two of them, noticed the concern in Hannah's eyes and said, 'No, no, Hannah, it's OK. What about her, Callum? She's called Calla, by the way, not Gala.'

Callum blinked. 'Calla, Gala, whatever her name is – you fucked her on your honeymoon, for God's sake, and Hannah, for some reason I'll never understand, decided to forgive you. Then even after Calla shows up at your door pregnant, she still doesn't throw you out. Then later when she's in pain, both physically and mentally after the baby's born, you go and do it again. You have absolutely no right coming here and asking if she's had sex with anyone. And to answer your question, no, we haven't had sex, we might have done had you not turned up when you did, but we *will* have sex later when you're gone, don't you worry about that. I can make Hannah feel special and loved again. I would never do what you did to her.'

I was furious, I was disappointed and I was suddenly very tired. I didn't understand exactly why Hannah was lying like she was. It might be her way of trying to distance herself from all that had happened over the last eleven months, but I'd need to talk to her about that on our own without her self-appointed minder present. I wasn't about to leave them to it, however, as Callum would more than likely have her knickers off before I closed the door. I turned my back on Callum to face Hannah, maybe a dangerous move given we were intent on trying to kill each other less than five minutes ago.

'Hannah, I don't know why you're telling everyone so many lies about everything, I know that you spent the night in bed with Calla in the flat after Ruby was born, long before I did.'

The shock of the fact I knew this registered itself on

Hannah's face. Then a sudden revelation came to me, one that would have been useful if it had turned up a week or so earlier.

'As you know, Calla and Dave are now an item. The thing is, they've not had sex yet because Calla's too sore, she had a load of stitches inserted into her, as well you know.' I winced again. 'It means that when she spent the night with me, there is no way we could have had sex even if I'd wanted to, which I didn't. All we did was sleep.'

I watched this knowledge sink in and register on Hannah's face.

'I know you've told your mum a huge pack of lies too, and she took great pleasure in torturing me with the knowledge that you might get together with Callum again.' I turned to bring Callum back into the conversation. 'She also told me that one of the reasons he …' I nodded to the great lump to my left '… was getting divorced was because he and his missus couldn't have kids. Which is why he wants to get together with fertile Hannah and have beautiful babies.'

Callum piped up, 'How did she know that?'

I laughed at him. 'Hannah told her mum, of course, girls tell their mums just about everything, don't you know that?'

I could see the light going on in his eyes. Ah well, I thought, he's learned something from today.

I was silent for a moment, then thought I might as well impart all of Sandra's insights. 'Of course, I don't know if it's his wife's issue or his problem, low sperm count and all that, but getting together with you makes sense in his head as you've got a ready-made family anyway. He could simply pull the wool over your eyes and in a year or two's time, apply to adopt my girls and have himself a nice little family.'

I could see that Hannah was thinking, and she said sceptically, 'And you put all this together yourself?'

I shrugged. 'I've had a lot of time to think recently, a lot of time.'

Callum decided to make a contribution. 'There's nothing wrong with my sperm count.'

I smiled at him. 'So out of all I just said, all you heard was "low sperm count"?'

'No, I heard everything you said and none of it is true. I like Hannah, she's a beautiful woman that you've just taken for granted and not lavished her with the luxuries she deserves.'

'I can't argue with you there, Callum, I haven't. But the thing is you see, we are broke, we have no money for such indulgences, but what I do have for Hannah, which you will never have, is a deep love, respect and trust gained by sharing a space with her for years.'

'Trust? You call fucking a Thai prostitute on your honeymoon trust?'

I shook my head in exasperation.

'Look, Callum, you don't know the full story and to be honest, it's none of your fucking business.'

Callum went all dewy-eyed and announced, 'I loved Hannah before she even met you, I should have been her husband, not you.'

And there it was. Sandra was spot on. I laughed and shook my head again. He was either a great actor or had some genuine emotion for Hannah. It didn't matter either way.

'You had your chance, Callum, a long, long time ago and you blew it – or maybe Hannah blew it …' I paused and glanced at Hannah; she knew what I was going to say next and was cringing, but she made no attempt to stop me: maybe it was like watching a car crash and she just couldn't take any action to prevent it. '... or broke it.'

Callum frowned at me. I was starting to get the impression that he wasn't as bright as he thought he was, or maybe not as clever as I had given him credit for. So I said it really slowly and really graphically for him.

'Hannah broke your cock, Callum, didn't she? Maybe that's why your sperm doesn't work.'

Callum was furious and he leapt at me. I was expecting some kind of reaction, given the tension in the room, but I wasn't prepared for absolute fury. He was on top of me in seconds and pounding his fists into my face. I tried to push him away but it was like he was possessed. I took a few big hits to my nose and cheeks and I heard something crack. The noise was loud and reverberated around the huge room like a firecracker going off. Hannah started screaming, Callum kept on punching, and for me, somewhere in between, everything went black.

Chapter Thirty

I woke up in bed, which was strange as I had no memory of brushing my teeth. Then I felt a searing pain that seemed to start in my head and rush along both sides of my face and down into my chest. I gasped and suddenly I was asleep again.

Later, when I came around properly, I realized I was in a quiet hospital room. Weak sunshine was creeping through a gap in the blinds covering a small window. Beside the bed were a couple of machines that beeped and flashed intermittently, and some wires trailed from them under the sheets. I noticed they were attached to me and I had a painful left wrist where someone had inserted a large needle. A drip was attached to the needle and something was seeping into my body. I had no idea what.

My head was still aching and I could only see out of one eye, my left one. The right eye was swollen shut. I lifted my right hand and tried to prise open the lid. I managed to create a small slit and I could make out some blurry images. I was relieved that I wasn't blind and let it fall closed again.

I tried to rotate my jaw but it was too painful. My face

felt huge, like someone had pumped it up with a bicycle pump. As I ran my fingers across the beach ball that had taken the place of my head, I could detect a line of stitches had been inserted down the left side of my cheek.

I felt like I'd been hit by a bus; maybe I had. But the rest of my body felt OK so if it had been a bus, would the rest of it not have been bashed up as well?

Then the memory came flooding back. Callum Anderson had done this to me. I sighed. I had not expected my visit to South London to end well, but in all my imagined endings, finishing up in a hospital bed with a drip in my arm had not been one of them.

My first emotion was sadness, not anger. Sadness because whilst I had been obviously carted off to hospital in an ambulance, this had left Hannah and Callum alone again and they might have taken up where they left off, and shagged on the couch or in the huge bed that probably existed somewhere in the apartment, or on the huge dining-room table, or on the red fluffy rug, or maybe on them all.

Could Hannah be so cold-hearted? And horny? Given her recent behaviour towards me maybe she could. In which case, if she had chosen to stay with Callum it told me all I needed to know and a divorce would be inevitable, and I wouldn't contest it. I would, however, fight tooth and nail for my daughters; no way was he getting anywhere near them. Not after the level of violence he'd shown towards me. It told me more about him than I cared to know. I know I'd made some disparaging remarks about his cock, which would probably have made most men mad, but not to the extent that you beat someone to a pulp over it, especially as every word was true.

My musings were interrupted by the arrival of a nurse, who came bustling into the room. 'Oh, we're awake, are we?'

I didn't say anything. Her inference was that I'd over-slept, but considering I'd recently had my head panned in by a disgruntled property developer, I felt I had some enti-tlement to an extended slumber.

A name badge told me she was Nurse Rose Scanlon. She looked to be in her mid-fifties, had dyed blonde hair, and sharp features. She took my silence to be a reaction to my symptoms and proceeded to fuss around me for a few minutes and checked the bleeping machines. Her meddling caused the one on the right to emit a loud con-tinuous screech which I assumed in normal circumstances was there to tell someone that my heart had given up the ghost. I was disappointed that no team of physicians came rushing into the room, pushing a cart like they did on TV.

Nurse Scanlon couldn't get it to stop so she bent down and pulled the plug out of the wall.

I hoped she didn't do that all the time or she'd end up on one of these programmes about healthcare professionals who neglect or kill their patients.

She made sure my drip was still dripping, then sat on the edge of the bed and stared at me.

She sat still for so long that I began to feel uncomfortable and decided to speak.

'Ib abythik wrobk.'

She peered at me more closely as if she didn't understand me. I couldn't blame her, I barely understood me either.

It sounded and felt like I had a mouth full of cotton wool. I ran my tongue around my mouth. My tongue felt like an alien invader, like it didn't belong or fit in my mouth properly. Had I had a tongue transplant? Could they even do that? This was obviously the culprit that was making me speak like an imbecile.

'I cab peak ploply,' I explained.

The nurse nodded. 'It's all right, you're pretty banged

up. Your cheekbone was badly broken and when you came in, you needed surgery to fix it. Five hours it took. That was three days ago.'

Three days. I'd been out cold for three days. How did that happen? The broken cheekbone explained the stitches and the loud cracking noise in Callum's apartment, but three days? Hannah and Callum might be married by now.

Nurse Scanlon obviously noted the look of alarm on my face.

'Don't worry about it. Your body just needed rest, that's all, and the painkillers we've been feeding you make you sleepy, too. We thought you'd be out longer than this. The doctors will be around to see you soon and then we'll see about how we're going to feed you. It'll be a while before you can eat anything normally.' She pointed to a sign beside my bed that stated in large letters 'Nil By Mouth'. I hope you like your new room, it's so much more private in here, don't you think?'

Given I had absolutely no memory of the last three days, my bed could have been previously situated on the centre spot at Wembley Stadium during the cup final, and I would have been none the wiser.

She was about to leave when I waved my unencumbered hand to stop her. I wanted to know if Hannah had been in to see me.

'Hab I hab any vibibers?'

She peered at me. 'No, sorry, didn't catch that.'

'Vibibers.'

'Videos? No, we've not got any videos, there's a TV over there though with all the Freeview channels, I'll put that on if you like.'

I shook my head vigorously, which hurt and made me feel dizzy. 'No – nob bibeos – vibibers.'

'Knob videos? We definitely don't have any of those.'

I shook my head again, slower this time. 'Wheb do vibib-ers comb?'

'I don't think you'll need a comb for a while, sweetie, you had your head shaved before surgery.'

I felt my head; I was bald, well, almost bald, I could feel stubble growing back in on my scalp. 'My heb.'

The nurse nodded sympathetically. She understood that, probably because I was touching my scalp. I wondered if I could mime the word 'visitors'. I was useless at charades and I think the word 'visitors' would have stumped many better than me. I tried one last time.

'Hab any bum bib bo bee me?'

'Your bum's bound to be a bit sore, love, you've been lying on it unmoving for a few days. We'll try and sort that out for you later, OK?'

I gave up and laid my head back on the pillow.

Just before she left, Nurse Scanlon did something very surprising. She pulled back the sheets and slipped her hand under my genitals. My eyes were wide open with shock. Rose – I felt justified in calling her by her first name now that we'd become so intimately acquainted – was definitely heading for a slot on Jeremy Kyle at least at this rate.

I felt a sharp pain as she removed the catheter that was collecting my pee in a bag by the bed. Amazingly, I had been completely unaware of it, the painkillers must have been really strong. Now that it was out, I could feel a mild discomfort but added to my overall pain levels, it barely registered. She wound the plastic tubing around her arm, removed the urine bag from the bed and left the room. The thought occurred to me that she was literally taking the piss out of me. I tried to laugh at my own joke, but it hurt too much so I settled back down on my pillow.

I must have drifted off back to sleep because the next time I awoke, I was surrounded by people wearing white coats. The sun had disappeared and all the lights were on. I was startled by all the faces staring at me. The closest and oldest white coat bearer spoke to me. His name badge said Mr Conroy, he had serious eyes and thick grey eyebrows that matched his receding grey hair.

'Awake, then?'

This attempt at patient sarcasm must be the first thing that all medical professionals get taught in their extensive training. Maybe it was to try and shame incumbents like myself into leaving as soon as possible to free up another urgently needed bed. I nodded, though my confirmation was obviously unnecessary.

Mr Conroy gestured at the other serious faces regarding me around the bed. There were nine altogether, excluding Mr Conroy, all of them very young.

'This is a selection of first-year students from our medical school. I brought them all to see you, Mr McEwan, what do you think of that?'

I was underwhelmed. I was accustomed to waking up with maybe Lois or Tessa, or occasionally both, staring at me, but ten faces, all of whom looked at me as if I had just been read my last rites, was disconcerting to say the least. I tried a feeble smile, but it hurt so my face remained passive.

The doctor carried on as if I was the most interactive patient he'd ever seen. 'You had a complex zygomatic arch impaction, which was accompanied by a facial subcutaneous emphysema, which is why we needed to operate soon after you presented.'

The last time I had felt so completely baffled was when I'd tried to decipher a Greek menu with Hannah at one of her friend's birthday parties five years ago. I'd really only understood the word menu, and here I really only understood the word 'presented', but given that I was out cold when they'd brought me in, I didn't remember presenting anything. I'm glad Rose had told me I'd had a busted face, otherwise I would have thought he was suggesting I'd had an alien growing inside me that they'd had to remove and destroy with a flame-thrower.

The puzzled faces around the room told me that most of them knew as much about subcutaneous thingy-ma-jigs as I did.

'Anyway,' the good doctor continued, 'it's good to see you up and about.' I assumed his optimistic diagnosis of my improving condition was for the benefit of his student groupies and not for me. I was probably as far away from 'being up and about' as I'd ever been.

He concluded his summary of me for his groupies with another tirade of complex medical definitions, some of which I'm sure he just made up to impress his entourage, and he finished by asking if there was anything I needed.

I was thinking about Hannah and wondering where she was. Did anybody know I was even here?

'Dub abybobby bo I'm beer?'

The doctor shook his head. 'No, can't get you a beer, I'm afraid, it'll be a while before you can have any alcohol.'

He quickly ushered his clan away before the obviously craving alcoholic became aggressive.

Someone had left the TV remote control by my bedside, so I aimed it at the TV mounted on the wall opposite my bed and flipped it on. Immediately, I was regaled with a very familiar theme tune and the flashing title of *You've Been Framed* – the very best of the greatest moments ever.

I couldn't help smiling, even though it hurt. It reminded me of Calla and I knew at that very moment she would be in her flat, probably with Dave, watching this. Given my lack of ability to make myself understood in the hospital, I had a slightly better insight into how difficult things must be for her in everyday life. I would need to remember that when I got to go home. I heard some raised voices in the corridor. As I drifted off to sleep, I thought that people shouldn't shout in hospitals as there are lots of sick people trying to rest.

The next time I opened my eyes, I thought I must still have been dreaming because sitting at my bedside was Hannah. I closed my eyes and sighed. Then I opened them again, and she was still there.

'Hi, Scott,' she said quietly.

I tried to smile but it hurt, so I nodded enthusiastically. That hurt as well but not as much. I uttered the immortal words, 'Bib you geb mabbied bo Cabbum?'

Hannah was no better at interpreting my mumbles than any of the medical staff. Unlike them, though, she did try and explain why. 'Your tongue is all swollen, Scott, that's why you can't speak properly. Hang on.'

She bent down and fished in her handbag. I was half-expecting her to produce some divorce paperwork. That would have been harsh perhaps, but maybe easier to serve now than when I was fully lucid. Instead, she beamed me the first smile I'd had in ages from her, and handed me a pad and pen. What a brilliant idea.

I took the pen and couldn't think of what to write at first. Then I wrote, *Where have you been?*

She read it as I was writing and sighed. 'I'm sorry, Scott, when they first brought you in, you were out cold and they operated on you for hours. I couldn't get to see you, then the police came and arrested me.'

I raised my eyebrows.

'Yeah, they thought I'd done this to you. See, I was the only one there when the ambulance came and I couldn't speak I was so upset. So I spent the first night in a police station miles away being questioned, not that you would have noticed anyway, you were out of it. Then when I did get away, you were in a general ward and they wouldn't let me stay with you as it would have upset all the other patients. I sat in the corridor for hours but eventually my mum came and got me. The girls needed to see me so I left for a while. The doctors said you would be out cold for days, but I kept coming back every few hours, except yesterday when my mum woke up feeling sick and I couldn't leave the girls on their own. Of course, that was when they moved you into here. They didn't tell me that you'd woken up until this evening and I was furious.'

I wrote, *Was that you shouting earlier*?

'Yeah, I was taking it out on some poor nurse who knew nothing about what was going on.'

All of that information wasn't important to me, but I knew what was. I wrote, *Did you shag Callum?*

The remark caused a remarkable reaction as Hannah immediately broke down and started bawling. I took that to mean yes, and laid my head back on the pillow. I felt tears pricking the corners of my eyes. I let them flow.

Chapter Thirty-One

EVENTUALLY HANNAH RECOVERED, looked up, and noticed my tears. She took my hand, stared into my watery eyes and leaned over my bloated, disfigured face and gently kissed me.

'No, I didn't sleep with him. Neither before you arrived, nor afterwards – especially not afterwards – how could you think I would ever go near that animal again after what I watched him do to you? I had no idea he was like that or had that side to him.'

I blinked, and quickly scribbled on my pad, *What happened?*

Hannah blew her nose into a tissue and managed a sad smile. 'Well, I couldn't get him to stop hitting you, then there was that horrible cracking noise, which I will never, ever forget, and I grabbed him and tried to haul him off you, but he was really strong and he'd totally lost it. In the end, I managed to wrench his arms away from you. He glared at me and just for a moment I thought he was going to turn on me but instead, he stood up and kicked you a few times in the ribs ...'

That explained my sore side.

'… then he stormed out of the room and a few minutes later, I heard the front door slam. By this time I'd phoned for an ambulance. I'm surprised they understood me, I was hysterical. I was so scared because I couldn't get you to wake up, I thought you were dead.'

Hannah paused and stared at me. I think she was looking for some kind of reaction from me. My brain was still too foggy to really work out what kind of reaction she wanted so I scribbled, *Then what?*

'Well, the paramedics arrived and did some stuff to you whilst trying to get me to tell them what had happened. I obviously didn't do a very good job as the police later arrested me.'

Scribble, scribble. *What happened to Callum?*

Hannah started crying again. 'I don't know. Nobody knows.' She kicked off her shoes and clambered up onto my bed and snuggled in beside me, which muffled her crying. It was lovely to have my wife cuddling me, but as most people know, hospital beds aren't really designed for two people to share. After a few minutes, her sobbing subsided and she began to slip off the edge of the bed. She tried to haul herself up and in so doing, accidentally bashed my face with her elbow, which led to me screaming out as a searing pain shot through my head.

'Oh sorry, Scott, are you OK?'

'Ib's okay,' I mumbled as the pain subsided.

She lay with her head on my shoulder.

'Wab aboub my bob?'

Hannah took my hand. 'I'm sure your knob's fine, sweetie, I don't think you got hit there.'

'Nob my nob, my bob.'

'Use your pad, Scott.'

I picked up my pad and pen and wrote, *What about my*

job?

Hannah laughed. It was an attractive sound. 'Ah, not your knob, your job. It's fine. I phoned the dealership and spoke to a few people who were not much use, and then guess who I got a hold of?'

I shrugged. Even that hurt.

'Your bit on the side – Sandra.'

I took a deep breath and wrote, *Not my bit of anything.*

Hannah smiled. 'Only teasing, anyway she was really helpful and sympathetic and said she would let everyone know and arrange some temporary cover. You still won't get paid but at least you won't get fired. She sounds like a nice person, despite all that you've said about her.'

If only Hannah knew. Hopefully she never would. I kept a straight face throughout which wasn't very hard as it hurt to even raise an eyebrow now. I wrote, *Lot of pain – get nurse.*

Hannah slipped off the bed and went to find some help.

A few minutes later, I was hooked back up to an IV line with painkillers seeping into my system. I then needed to pee and the effort of dragging my bruised body and IV line to the toilet exhausted me. I slipped into sleep with the smiling face of my wife beside me.

It took another week to get well enough to leave the hospital and make the long train journey home. I was warned not to fly for at least six months to give all my facial tubing a chance to heal properly.

I hadn't seen my gorgeous daughters for what felt like an age as Hannah had to take them back home for Tessa's schooling, and it was easier to have Lois there too for her mum to watch. Hannah had brought them in to see me the day after I woke up and both of them started crying immediately when they saw me. I must have been a right sight.

Hannah managed to flit between London and Edinburgh for work while the merger with the missing

Callum Anderson's firm continued. Hannah had only remained in the apartment for one more evening with the girls as she was afraid that Callum might return. He never did. Nobody had heard a peep from him since the day he'd walked out of his apartment. It was common knowledge amongst his employees that he had a villa in Spain, which he was about to lose to his ex-wife in the divorce, and an apartment in St Lucia, which he'd managed to keep.

Hannah said everyone assumed he'd gone to the Caribbean hideaway to lick his wounds and would resurface eventually. I'd decided, against Hannah's advice, not to bother pressing any charges against him. I'd had a chat with the police and the thought of traipsing down to London over the next year or two for interviews and court appearances filled me with dread. I just wanted to return home and get on with living.

Hannah and I needed to have a big heart to heart. She'd visited me in hospital every day she was in London, but we'd only nibbled around the edges of the big issues that stood between us. I found it difficult to forgive her for the way she had treated me despite the fact she was obviously not thinking straight.

My swollen tongue eventually returned to normal after three days, and I was glad to be able to ditch the pad and paper.

It was late morning on a Thursday when I finally walked hand-in-hand with Hannah out of the hospital and across the car park to the bus stop carrying my bag of belongings. I was impressed she knew which side of the road to stand on to get the correct bus. The warm May sunshine felt great on my pale skin. I was still in some pain and needed strong painkillers, but nowhere near the amount that was being pumped into my system a week ago.

My facial swelling had reduced to a point where I now

looked relatively normal and would no longer scare small children. My hair was growing back nicely and I now had enough to resemble an American GI. One positive aspect of my recent worrying and hospital stay was that I'd lost nearly a stone in weight. It was a drastic measure to lose weight and not one I would recommend. As a result my clothes didn't fit properly, but I had to admit I quite liked the new svelte me.

We had a few hours before our train was due so we headed into central London and had lunch in a quiet pub. Hannah ordered a bottle of Pinot Grigio. The waitress brought us our club sandwiches and we sipped the wine whilst making small talk. As the wine seeped into our systems, Hannah stepped into the danger zone.

'I spoke to my mum at the weekend, Scott, and told her what really happened with Calla.'

'That must have been difficult, did you tell her everything?'

'Well, I left out the sordid details but pretty much yeah, she knows it was mainly my idea and she wasn't best pleased with me. Especially when she remembered how she'd spent half an hour after you'd been taken into hospital trying to defend Callum's violence.'

'Did she?'

Hannah looked sheepish. 'Yeah, I couldn't cope with telling her the truth at that point and the police had arrested me so there was too much going on. She tried to convince me that you had it coming for treating me so badly and Callum had been merely defending my honour.'

'Why all the lies in the first place, Hannah? I find it really hard to understand and forgive what you've put me through.'

'To be brutally honest, Scott, I'm not really sure. I just couldn't face the truth and I felt I couldn't tell my mum what had really happened. She kept taking your side in everything and I couldn't stand that, even though I now know she was right. When I first left the flat, I was only intending to be away for a few days to get some breathing space. I still loved you but I just couldn't talk to you, then the whole thing with you and Calla just pushed me over the edge. It just became easier to make you out to be at fault for everything that had taken place. I think I came to believe it myself. I suppose I needed someone to blame, and you were the easiest target.'

'That wasn't fair.'

'I know, but it was too late to stop and I started to believe that everything would be better if I just got away from you, permanently. In my head, what I was saying to you made perfect sense. I had given up my career, Jane used to say that loads, and my boss in the office told me something similar when he suggested I go to London and work on the merger stuff.'

'Your mum said you sounded like Jane when you were talking about work.'

'I know, but suddenly I had the chance to go and do something that made a difference, and it took the focus off all the bad stuff.'

'And Callum was the knight in shining armour?'

Hannah smiled. 'He certainly seemed that way at the time.'

'He's a psycho.'

'No argument from me there.'

'And your mum couldn't see that he was a nut job after what he did to me?'

'She never got to see how badly injured you were, remember? She probably thought I was exaggerating. It did give me time to rethink everything. The dull hours I spent sitting at your bedside, and in the hospital corridor trying to work out what had happened helped me see things differently, and gave me some perspective on what was really important. I kept going back to the moment in the apartment when I thought you were dead. I would have been responsible for killing two people inside a month.'

Hannah's eyes filled up, and she paused and drained her glass, then refilled it. I was taking it easy drinking wine, though on top of all my painkillers, it was reckless.

'Anyway, my mum now feels terrible at the way she treated you, and sends her apologies.'

I smiled. 'If it wasn't for her, I'd never have had the impetus to come to London and find you. Then we probably wouldn't be sitting here now, so sometimes you have to fight for what you love.'

'Literally?'

'Yeah, literally, though I didn't expect to get so beaten up.'

'He was much bigger than you.'

'He was.'

I paused for a moment, and stared into Hannah's eyes. 'Would you really have slept with him?'

She broke the contact and peered into her wine glass as if looking for answers. 'Honestly, Scott, I don't know, I was in a mess. I suppose, given the feelings I had towards you at the time, I would have.'

I nodded and appreciated her honesty. 'And that would have been us finished.'

She sighed. 'Yeah, probably, but I wasn't thinking clearly, it was just a nice place to be, away from all the mess. We might still be finished. I wouldn't blame you for walking away from me after all that. My mum said the same.'

I sipped some more wine. 'I'm not sure what I'm feeling at the moment, Hannah, so much has happened. There's something else I need to know. What about your night with Calla? I was afraid, no, I am afraid, that you might be turning into a lesbian. Dave might like that idea but I'm not terribly keen.'

'Oh, Scott, no, I'm not a lesbian. Everything at that point was warped, including me probably. I couldn't stand being near anyone that was close to me, it was like everything I touched turned to pain, but Calla, well, in a way she wasn't close to me. She came in and it was just nice to have someone to hold me without any judgement, it was like she was free of consequences.'

Hannah stared off into the distance.

'Obviously, she knew what was happening and that I was hurting, but she just comforted me and to be honest, not much happened, it was just nice to be held. I'm not sure why she even wanted to be with me, maybe it was gratitude for helping her, we'd become friends despite everything that had happened. Maybe it was just her way of trying to help and she was the only one not trying to tell me everything would be all right.'

'Well, she couldn't, could she?'

'No, I suppose not. Sometimes words are a hindrance. In any event, afterwards I felt a little better and I will always think she helped me. I genuinely believe that, at that point, I was on the brink of a nervous breakdown, maybe I'd already had one, I don't know. Later, when she asked me if she could call her baby Hannah, I knew she was doing it to try and make me feel better, though it's a nice name. I've always liked my name.'

'Why were you so harsh on me, then?'

'You'd been unfaithful.'

'I hadn't.'

'Yeah, I know that now. The thing is I'd only come around that morning to tell you about Calla's letter, that she'd been given her own place, then I found you in bed with her, and well … it just sent me spiralling down again. I was angry at the world, angry at everything and everyone, especially you. Nothing made any sense.'

'I was hurting too, Hannah.'

Hannah took my hand. 'I know you were, sweetie, but I could do nothing to help you. I was a lost soul.'

'So what do we do now?'

Hannah shook her head. 'I don't know, Scott. It's really up to you. My life … well, my emotional life … is in your hands. I have no right to make any demands of you. I love you. I've never loved anyone the way I love you, but I've been so awful to you recently so I'd completely understand if you want out.' Silent tears slipped from her eyes and spilled down her face but she never broke eye contact.

I took her in my arms and held her as she sobbed. No words were necessary. She was the other half of my whole, I couldn't leave her any more than I could leave myself. Despite all she'd done to me, I still loved her as much as the day I'd met her, more probably.

After a while her tears subsided and she asked, 'How do I … we get over something like this?'

I knew she was referring to Ruby, not us. I'd thought about little else lying in my bed for the last few weeks.

'We don't, Hannah, we just learn to deal with it. For whatever reason, Ruby wasn't meant to be. We'll never forget our beautiful baby, but however you feel about it, life is for the living and we have two gorgeous, funny, naughty and needy daughters that love us. We should make sure we visit Ruby's grave whenever we want to, and remember how lucky we are to have what we have. She will always remind me of that, and how important love is and how I nearly lost everything that matters to me in this world.'

Hannah's eyes overflowed with tears, and I pulled her close again. My own tears tumbled down my bruised face.

The waitress appeared, asking if everything was all right with our food that we'd hardly touched, took one look at the tangled emotional mess we'd become and wisely vanished.

Chapter Thirty-Two

BACK HOME IN Edinburgh later that evening, my reunion with Tessa and Lois was tearful and joyful, with both of them jumping all over me for about ten minutes before Hannah calmed them down. I noticed the nursery had been stripped bare, and the only sign that it had ever been earmarked for a baby girl was the pink wallpaper.

I didn't know when Hannah had done this, and I didn't ask.

I spent the weekend with the girls and Hannah, trying to adjust to family life again. Tessa and Lois carried on like nothing had happened, but Hannah and I were a little more guarded. It would take time for us to get back to normal, I knew. We made love on the Saturday night and that helped restore some balance to our relationship, but I wasn't sure I would ever fully trust Hannah again, and I didn't know what effect that might eventually have on our relationship.

One thing I did know, it *was* lovely to be back sharing a bed and to fall asleep every night with her snuggled in beside me.

Hannah tried to invite Jane around on the Saturday evening to apologize, but she refused to come over, which put a bit of a downer on the weekend, at least for Hannah.

On the Sunday afternoon, it was warm and sunny so we visited Ruby's grave and put some fresh flowers in the little vase beside her headstone. The shady corner where she lay was pleasantly cool on such a warm afternoon and Tessa left a note for Ruby in a sealed envelope. She'd written this the day before and although she thought nobody knew, Hannah had read it quickly before she closed the flap.

Dear Ruby,
We all love you and hope you are having fun in heaven.
xxxx

Her handwriting was still messy and she still got some letters around the wrong way but we understood the sentiment.

We sat for a while near the grave and ate the snacks we'd brought with us. It felt comforting to be near her, even though we both knew she was not there really. In my darker moments, I reckoned she'd never really been with us, but as I say, it felt good to be beside the grave. It brought us all together as a family and if for nothing else, that was valuable. It was strange that an event that had torn us apart had the power to bring us back together. There's a lesson in there somewhere, but I was not bright enough to be able to fully grasp it.

We went home via the park and watched the girls playing on the swings and chute. I was with all my girls, and that was all I really needed.

I was due back to work on the Tuesday, having taken an extra day off to sort out one more important aspect of our lives, the question of whether 'little' Hannah, as we now needed to call her, was actually mine or not.

Hannah and Calla had dropped off swabs from both me and the baby the previous week at a private clinic on the south side of the city. The results would now be back from the lab.

We travelled over in convoy. Hannah and I were there, along with Hannah's mum, Carol, Dave, Calla, and of course, little Hannah. I'd texted Jane to ask her to come along, but she hadn't replied.

Sitting all together in a little anteroom, Dave and Calla looked anxious. Dave was keen to assume the role of 'father' to Calla's baby and I wasn't sure how that would all sit if I was the biological parent.

The attractive female clinical assistant came into the room carrying an A4 piece of paper.

Her name badge indicated she was called F. Hopkins. She stopped and was obviously surprised at the relatively large number of people gathered in her small room.

'We don't usually have this amount of interest in our test results.' She smiled at all our expectant faces. 'Who's Hannah's mother?'

'I am,' said Carol.

The puzzled F. Hopkins peered at the ageing face of my mother-in-law.

Hannah dug her mother in the ribs. 'Not you, Mum, it's little Hannah we're talking about.'

'Oh yeah, sorry.'

'Little Hannah's mum is here,' Dave said, putting his arm around Calla's shoulders.

'And you're Scott McEwan, the other participant?'

Dave shook his head. 'No, Scott's over there.' He nodded towards me.

'Right,' she said hesitatingly, looking at me sitting holding big Hannah's hand (though my wife probably wouldn't like me calling her that). Ms Hopkins must have thought she'd stumbled into a recording of the Jeremy Kyle show. 'I'm a little confused,' she said. 'I was really only expecting Miss Hi Tee and Mr McEwan to be here. I have to ask Mr McEwan and Miss Hi Tee, are you both comfortable with so many people knowing your personal details? We pride ourselves here on our confidentiality and sensitivity and I'm not sure—'

'It's fine,' I interrupted. 'Everyone here has a vested interest in the outcome so don't worry. It's very complicated … as you can probably tell, so if you could tell us the results we'll get out of your hair.'

'Miss Hi Tee, are you also happy for me to continue?' Ms Hopkins asked, turning to address Calla. Dave whispered into her ear and she nodded.

'Right, well, I have the results of the samples submitted by Mr McEwan and Miss Hannah Hi Tee.'

There was a pause while she re-checked her sheet of information and I decided that maybe calling Calla's baby Hannah wasn't such a great idea. Hannah Hi Tee sounded a bit like someone shouting out before executing a karate chop. I suppose if Calla became Dave's third wife, the baby would become Hannah Hughes. There were definitely too many aitches in my life.

I gazed around the room at all the expectant faces, all eager to know the truth. Hannah was gripping my hand tightly, Carol was playing with her bottom lip, Dave was holding onto Calla with a serious expression on his face whilst she was staring down at her daughter, who was in her pram making a cooing noise similar to the sound pigeons make when they're wandering about your feet, trying to shag each other. I was a little tense but after what we'd been through over the last few months, the outcome of the test was maybe less of a big deal than it otherwise would have been.

Ms Hopkins raised her eyes to address the room.

'Well, err, I'm not sure what you want the results to be, but I can tell you that Scott McEwan is ...' She paused to check her sheet again, lengthening the tension like they do on *X Factor* and other programmes when reading out the public vote, except I don't think she did it deliberately, she was obviously worried by the reaction she might get. '... Scott McEwan is definitely *not* the father of Miss Hi Tee's baby.'

The initial reaction was stunned silence. I think every single person in the room, even Calla by the expression on her face, was expecting the opposite outcome. Hannah started crying, I'm not sure why but she would probably have cried in any event. She cried a lot these days. Carol looked dumbfounded and Dave looked pleased and punched the air with his fist.

My reaction was one of surprise, a little relief, and humour. I started laughing. All the things we'd been through because Calla thought I was the father of her baby. I'm not sure why I found it funny, but I did. Eventually everybody joined in, including Hannah (big Hannah) and little Hannah kept on with the horny pigeon noises. Ms Hopkins looked pleased because nobody was angry, and soon disappeared to carry on doing whatever it was she did.

We convoyed our way back home. Hannah was quiet on the way back in the car, but mainly because her mother wouldn't shut up about all the trouble we'd been caused by the imposter from Thailand. I found it hard to be mad at Calla: she'd wormed her way into our hearts and both Hannah and I knew she was a genuinely nice person, which, given what she'd been through in her life, was amazing. It was likely that she really had thought I was the father. Dave was the real winner out of all this. He now had a beautiful girlfriend, and a beautiful baby with unknown parentage that he could adopt if he wished with no complications.

The next morning, I was due back at work and Hannah was due in her office too, so it was back to reality for both of us. As it was my first day back, I wasn't rushing so I agreed to drop Tessa off at school on the way in. Hannah was working in the city so she was going to get the bus, or at least that was the plan.

Carol appeared and took Lois away, and then Hannah got herself ready and kissed me and Tessa goodbye. We watched from the window as she came out of the building at street level. She waved and walked down the road. I was just about to turn away when a bright red Porsche caught my eye as it rumbled along the road at low speed. It was a 911 Cabrio with the top down. Inside was a stunning-looking brunette wearing a short green sundress with matching shoes. She pulled up beside Hannah, said something, and Hannah jumped in beside her and they both drove off.

Suddenly my stomach was in turmoil as I tried to work out what possible motive Sandra had for picking Hannah up and whisking her away like that.

I hoped that she wasn't going to tell Hannah all about Sabrina and our near night of nookie. I got Tessa ready, dropped her at school and rushed to work. When I arrived, it was very busy and after everyone had welcomed me back, I was right in the thick of it again as if I'd never been away.

I managed to get a break at eleven and grabbed a mug of coffee before going in search of Sandra. I found her in her pod, going over a load of spreadsheets, and grumbling. She was an absolute knockout; her make-up and hair were done to perfection and her dress showed all her curves. The sales team would be drooling all day.

She smiled when she saw me and pushed the paperwork to one side.

'Welcome back. You've had a rough time of it by all accounts. I hope you think she was worth it.'

The slightly catty comment worried me. 'Why did you pick Hannah up?'

'I was just passing by on my way to work and there she was.'

'Bullshit, Sandra, my street's not on the way to anywhere, least of all work.'

Sandra laughed. 'Yeah, OK then, it wasn't an accident. I just wanted to meet Hannah in the flesh. I was intrigued after speaking to her on the phone a few weeks back. All the years you've worked here and I've never met her, I was curious.'

'There's a photo of her and the girls on my desk.'

'Not real life, though.'

'Sandra, what's this really about?'

Sandra bit her bottom lip and stared at me for a moment. 'OK, I just wanted to know if she was worth all the trouble and pain you've put yourself through, plus I wanted to make sure she knew that there would be somewhere for you to go if she ever let you down again.'

I was alarmed. 'What did you say to her? Nothing about that night in your flat, I hope?'

She laughed at my panicked face. 'No, don't be silly, I just kind of said enough to let her know that I would be interested if she wasn't. Women can do that, you know, without being obvious.'

My mouth hung open for a moment. 'What did she say?'

'She never said anything, she didn't need to, the message was received loud and clear.

Anyway, it's just my parting present to you.'

'Parting present? What do you mean?'

She smiled sadly. 'I'm leaving at the end of the week. I'm taking over a huge multi-franchise operation in north London. It seems they're not making the money they should be and I'm going in to fix it. Should be challenging and if I can sort it, it would be very rewarding. Financially, anyway.'

I was floored. No more Sandra, no more Sabrina. I hadn't really had time to get all my thoughts about Sandra straight in my head yet. I knew things would never be what they were but the thought of not seeing her again made me hugely sad.

'I hope this has got nothing to do with me.'

'Don't flatter yourself, Scott, this has been brewing for a while, long before all your drama played out, but I won't lie to you, the thought of seeing you every day after what nearly happened between us doesn't have me jumping for joy. So it's probably for the best. Anyway, I've been here long enough, time for a change of scenery.'

'I'll miss you.'

Sandra laughed. 'You mean you'll miss staring at my tits like all the other guys in here.'

'That's not fair, Sandra,' I said, deliberately lowering my eyes to stare at her cleavage.

'Go on, get out of here, I'll see you later.'

I turned and opened the door and just as I was about to leave she said, 'Scott?'

'Yeah?'

'I didn't tell your wife I'm leaving, so if she makes a fuss you can tell her that I'm away and I was just messing with her.'

I nodded and went to close her door, and heard her say, 'I'll miss you, too.'

I didn't look back. I didn't want her to see the tears in my eyes.

Later that evening, after Tessa and Lois were asleep, Hannah and I were sitting on the couch watching TV. Hannah muted the sound and turned to look at me.

'Are you sure nothing has ever happened between you and Sandra?'

I smiled, I had been expecting this. 'I'm not in her league.'

Hannah shook her head. 'Not the impression I got.'

'Oh yeah, she gave you a lift this morning, didn't she?'

'I don't think her passing was a coincidence.'

'No, I don't think it was.'

Hannah looked away, then said, 'She cares about you. I think she has feelings for you.'

'Hannah, we've known each other a long time, she was worried about me, that's about the extent of it. Sandra has a whole different view of the world to me.'

'She's very attractive.'

'She is,' I agreed. 'You know who she reminds me of at times?'

Hannah thought for a minute. 'Jane?'

'Yeah, Jane, always chasing after the next big thing.'

'There's nothing wrong with ambition, Scott.'

'I never said there was, but neither of them are happy. I think Jane has realized that and that's why she wants a baby, she wants something different. I'm not sure she's going about it the right way but that's up to her.'

Hannah thought about my last sentence for a minute. I could almost hear the wheels turning. 'Are we happy?'

'We should be. We've got a lot to be thankful for. I know the last few months have been hellish, probably the worst we'll ever have, but, as they say, "What doesn't kill you makes you stronger". I should know, Callum nearly killed me, but the injuries you inflicted on me were much worse. Especially when I thought I might lose my girls.' I gazed at my wife's pretty face. The face I'd grown used to seeing and kissing. 'Are you happy?'

Hannah shook her head. 'Not right now, no, the scars are still fresh. I'm better than I was, I was in a horrible dark place, but I've crawled out of there and I don't want to go back. I still have nightmares about what happened to Ruby, what nearly happened to you; how I treated you and the fact that I went completely off the rails worries me no end. I will get better but you'll need to bear with me. I keep crying all the time. I couldn't get the lid off the marmalade this morning and I burst into tears, who else would do that?'

'Paddington Bear, maybe?'

Hannah laughed. 'Yeah, possibly. The point is I'm not back to being myself and can't help it. I do know that the one thing I do need … want … is you beside me.'

I kissed her and we snuggled up and watched the mute TV for a while, lost in our own thoughts, then out of the blue Hannah announced, 'I want to sell the flat and move.'

'Where did that come from?'

'I just think it would be nice to get out of here and start somewhere new, it's too small anyway.'

'Problem is we can't afford anything bigger.'

'Well, we could actually. If we moved out of town, not too far but for what we'd get for this place, we could afford a wee house with a garden.'

'Really?'

'Yeah, my mum made a few enquiries about new-builds out near Dalkeith while I was up and down to London; the property market's really picked up. The developer would take our flat in part-exchange and offer us around £175,000.'

'That's a lot.'

'It is.'

'How much would a "wee house" cost?'

'About £10,000 more, but now that I've got a decent pay increase we could afford it.

There'd be minimal fees and stuff to pay as the developer picks up most of the costs.'

I thought for a minute. 'What about Tessa's school and commuting and stuff?'

'Tessa would cope, she's only in her first year at primary school and the commute wouldn't kill us, especially if we got a bit more room to breathe.' Then she smiled and made the statement that she knew would sell the deal to me. 'It's got two bathrooms.'

'Two?'

'Yeah, *two*.'

'So what happens next?'

'We need to go and see the houses and make sure you're cool with it.'

'And if I'm not?'

'Then I would just stay here with you. That's where I want to be.' She kissed me and we continued staring at the mute TV.

We visited the building site the next evening, and sure enough there were a number of small houses newly released for sale. The final finishes had yet to be applied so we, or rather Hannah, could specify what type of kitchen units and appliances she wanted to have. She disappeared with the saleswoman to talk specifics so I wandered around the house with Tessa and Lois, mesmerized.

The house was semi-detached with three bedrooms and, as promised, two bathrooms. There was a small back garden, which at the moment was little more than a muddy swamp, but we'd been assured that by the time we moved in – around August – everything would be landscaped and clean.

A few weeks later, all the paperwork was completed and we had become owners of a new-build house.

Three months after that, on a lovely, warm, late-summer morning, we gathered together in our tiny flat for the last time. Jane, Dave and Calla had come over to give us moral support. Our flat was nearly as busy as it had been just after Christmas when I'd had the pregnant trio staying.

Little Hannah, by this time, was sitting up and giggling and making raspberry noises constantly. She found this so much fun, in fact, for hours she would make her face and anything within three feet of her splash zone slick with saliva. Calla found it hilarious, but then her favourite TV programme was the various incarnations of *You've Been Framed* and she frequently fell off the couch in laughter at grown men on skateboards, bashing their bollocks on bollards.

Dave was besotted with Calla and had moved in with her. He'd let out his bachelor pad to two female students. I could understand why Dave found Calla so irresistible; she was fun, young and still unable to believe her luck at having landed so lucky. She was also a great mother and seemed to 'get' Dave, which was more than his other attempts at romance had achieved.

Her English was improving all the time now that she was getting proper lessons, but they still had to resort to Thai Chat for more serious discussions. She had enrolled at a local college for an art course which had crèche facilities and spent four mornings a week there. Her teachers said 'she showed promise', whatever that meant.

Dave, now he had no paternity issues to worry about, was besotted with little Hannah and was quite happy to get coated with her raspberry-blown saliva and didn't complain when she vomited all over him, which happened frequently. Perhaps he really had turned over a new leaf.

I reckoned Miss Calla Hi Tee would one day soon become Mrs Calla Hughes. They made a nice couple and Calla deserved to be happy.

Calla took Dave and Hannah through to our bathroom to clean vomit from them both, and my Hannah went to the kitchen to make some tea before packing the kettle away.

Tessa and Lois lingered in their bedroom, excited by the prospect of a new house and garden to explore, but probably half-aware that in a way this was the end of an era – a fresh start for their weary parents.

I was left alone with Jane. Despite Hannah's grovelling, she still hadn't completely forgiven her friend for her behaviour, or for completely snubbing her during the period after Ruby was born. It might take Jane longer to forgive Hannah than I had, but she would come around eventually … I hoped.

I took the opportunity to ask her, 'Have you found a new man yet?'

'No chance, all men are arses, present company excepted.'

'Why do I get that honour?'

'You fought for your woman.' She said this in a deep voice, trying to impersonate a caveman.

I laughed. 'I lost badly.'

'Doesn't matter, you fought, I haven't found a man that would fight for me yet.'

'You should try the hospital wards, they're probably full of idiots like me recovering from such foolishness.'

Jane nodded her head seriously. 'I'll maybe try that, but in the meantime I'm still considering not bothering with men and going it alone, I've been for a few consultations with the egg people.' The image of Humpty Dumpty popped into my head. 'One of the main problems is that because sperm donors are no longer granted anonymity, there's not a lot to choose from, so my new plan is to extract some of yours, if you are up for it, Mr McEwan?'

She smiled at me, flashed her eyes and moved close to me with her hand aiming at my crotch. I backed up in mock terror until I was against the wall. She grabbed my balls and squeezed them gently. I could smell her perfume and feel her hot breath on my face as she leaned into me. Just then Hannah returned to the room and stood gazing at us.

'What are you doing, Jane?'

'I'm squeezing your husband's balls.'

'I don't think he likes that.'

I nodded, but Jane said, 'He *does* like it really, what man wouldn't want me squeezing his bollocks? Anyway, I need some sperm to make me pregnant.'

Hannah put down the tray of steaming mugs and came over to stand beside her friend, who still had a tight grip on my nether regions. Hannah bent down and studied Jane's hand.

'I don't think you'll get any that way.'

'Really, how do I get some, then?'

'You have to take his cock out and rub it for a while, that tends to work.'

'You'd know.'

'You're right, I would.'

'So can I have some, then?'

'Not right now, I've just made everyone tea and there are chocolate biscuits.'

'After tea and biscuits, then?'

Hannah laughed. 'We'll see. I'll have to supervise, of course.'

'Of course, I think you've done this sort of thing before, haven't you, Hannah?'

'I have, and the last time it caused me all sorts of problems, so this time it would have to be under strictly controlled conditions.'

They both laughed at my worried face, as I wasn't sure if they were joking or not. I hoped they were.